TALES OF THE UNANTICIPATED

The Antholo-Zine of TOTU Ink   Number 27

NOVELETTES

| 8 | **Sarah Monette** • Katabasis: Seraphic Trains |
| 54 | **Patricia S. Bowne** • Raising the Dead |

SHORT STORIES

22	**Martha A. Hood** • Missing Piece
32	**Ellen Kuhfeld** • Dances with Werewolves
39	**Mark Rich** • Beer Can Medusa
46	**William Mingin** • The Lady of the Lounge
68	**Laurel Winter** • Flo & Eb
72	**Douglas J. Lane** • Mister Eddie
82	**Brandon Sigrist** • Tips on Moving to Earth
85	**Bryan Thao Worra** • The Dog At The Camp
88	**Judy Klass** • Nosmo Girl
92	**Stephen Dedman** • The Facts of Dr. Van Helsing's Case
100	**T. Bilgen** • Turning
104	**Patricia Russo** • The Ogre's Wife
108	**Robert P. Switzer** • With Your Blood I Wash My Hands
114	**Jason D. Wittman** • The Tale of Roderick Rabbit

POETRY

20	**Laurel Winter** • Love as an unstable isotope and other theories
38	**durenda** • neptune can't save you either
44	**Brian Thao Worra** • Homunculus
45	**John Calvin Rezmerski** • You Can't Judge a Squid By Its Cover
53	**Deborah P. Kolodji** • Angerboda's Child
70	**Cornelius A. Fortune** • Song the City Sang Off-Key
80	**Laurel Winter** • The Memory of Vermouth
84	**Ann K. Schwader** • We Gave Them to the Aliens
87	**Bruce Boston** • The Monster Unreason
99	**Brian Thao Worra** • Soap
107	**Ann K. Schwader** • Palimpsest Fugue
113	**John Calvin Rezmerski** • Hydrotaxic Personals: Between the Lines
115	**Brian Thao Worra** • An Archaeology of Snow Forts

DEPARTMENTS

2	Editoriels by **Eric M. Heideman**, **Rebecca Marjesdatter**
3	Mathoms
4	Contributors
6	Mail orders
7	Contributors' Guidelines
116	Anticipations

Cover Paintings: "Mama Roux" (front) and "Shunned House" (back) by Augie Wiedemann.
Interior Illustrations: Rodger Gerberding—9, 23, 47, 55; Laramie Sasseville—33, 69, 101; Margaret Ballif Simon—41, 73, 86, 89, 93, 97, 114; Stephanie Rodriguez—83, 105, 109.
Cartoon: Bruce Boston and Margaret Ballif Simon—116.

Editor in Chief	**Eric M. Heideman**
Associate Editor/Business Manager	**Mark Willcox**
Associate Editor/Design	**Amanda Elg**
Poetry Editor	**Rebecca Marjesdatter**
Art Editor	**Rodger Gerberding**
Senior Associate Editor	**Andrew Loges**
Associate Editors	**Greg L. Johnson**, **P.M.F. Johnson**, **Sandra Rector**
Proofreader	**Ruth Berman**
Typesetting & Design	**Mark Willcox**
Printing	**Bookmobile**, St Paul MN (printed in the USA)
Attorney	**Lynn Klicker Uthe**, 952-544-4925
Board of Directors	**Eric M. Heideman**, President; **Mark Willcox**, Treasurer; **Andrew Loges**, Secretary

Editorials:
Twenty Years After

Twenty-and-one-half years ago, when the Minnesota Science Fiction Society Board offered me the chance to develop a small press speculative fiction magazine, I did some good hard thinking about what kinds of SF to request. Although I had a slight preference for social, human-centered science fiction—as practiced by the likes of Shelley, Wells, Sturgeon, Leiber, Simak, and Le Guin—I also loved some examples of high and heroic fantasy—again Leiber and Le Guin, and especially Tolkien—and supernatural and psychological horror—again the amazing Leiber, and Shirley Jackson, Blackwood, and Poe—and stories that didn't fit any categories—John Sladek, and, jumping to TV & film, Monty Python. As Peter Schickele quotes Duke Ellington, "If it sounds good, it *is* good." I figured, why choose? We couldn't offer writers buckets of money. We could offer them a chance to write from their personal vision, in all kinds of sub-genres, from the ultra-logical to the surreal, in the full patina of tones, from dark as winter midnight to light as a tickling summer breeze. We could be open, not just to categories, but to the full literature of speculative fiction. I figured that we could attract work equal in quality to that appearing in the majors by being open to a wider range of fiction.

Twenty years ago, August 15, 1986, John Calvin Rezmerski brought *Tales of the Unanticipated* #1 from the printer. It featured the marvelous cover by Erin McKee with our mascot, TOTU the three-eyed cow; included a Rezmerski poem that went on to win a Rhysling, thoughtful stories by Ruth Berman and Terry A. Garey, a solid debut novelette by Carolyn Ives Gilman, a zany tough-guy detective parody by Marc Hequet, essays by John W. Taylor (on Philip K. Dick) and Kate Wilhelm (on a writer's responsibility), and some luscious bug-eyed-monster artwork by Ken Fletcher. You could tell from the way it was put together that the editor was learning his skills, but the contents suggested that fledgling editor was right in believing there were bushels of good-to-very good stories out there, homeless. We kept going.

Over time, as I sought recommendations from a diverse, insightful, and opinionated editorial staff, a *TOTU* editorial philosophy developed, one that fit the very wide range of material we were inviting. We would work with writers, often in great detail, to help them "cut away the part that's not the horse," turning that pretty good story into a story that lived up to its full potential. But we wouldn't rely overmuch on the reams of advice out there on the one true way to write each subcategory of SF. It seemed to me that some of the advice (notably that in Damon Knight's *Creating Short Fiction*) was descriptive, and useful. But much of it struck me as prescriptive, designed not to improve the field's quality but to narrow its possibilities. The seven-point plot skeleton isn't the one way to construct stories, it's a way to construct one kind of story. Then there's the argument that you can't mix categories in a story. Of course you can. Simultaneously operating by more than one set of rules takes a knack, but people have been doing it successfully for over 50 years. Enough examples. At *TOTU* we recognize that stories do need to operate consistently by some kind of logic, but the logic need not be imposed from outside, it can be generated internally by a story's premises and approach. Rather than telling writers that they aren't entitled to do stuff, we respect what they're trying to do and try to help them do it more effectively.

The results speak for themselves. We remain quirky and scruffy and unanticipated, publishing some of the more interesting and original fiction around. And after 20 years, we're still here.

—**Eric M. Heideman**

Owning the Shadow

While musing on the topic for my editorial, I looked up "monster" on Wikipedia. The English word is derived through Old French from the Latin *monere*, "to warn." Until fairly recently, "monsters," that is, defective and malformed animals, were omens of evil, proof of demonic presences. Giant monster films of the 1950s served a similar purpose, cautioning the viewer against the modern demon of nuclear war, and mutants created by the environmental evils of toxic sludge, genetic engineering or ultraviolet radiation from a depleted ozone layer are still SciFi Channel staples.

Monsters in fiction tend to be a different breed; they are productions of the "dark" side of the human psyche. Perhaps as a side-effect of urbanization, or the influence of psychology, monsters in contemporary fiction have lost their animal shapes. The dragon and wolf of medieval times have become the vampire and serial killer—wearing Armani or Levis instead of fur or scales, they are indistinguishable from "normal" people, until they show their more-or-less metaphoric fangs. Sartre famously said, "Hell is other people," and today the devil is my next door neighbor, if not living inside my own skull.

Indeed, the most frightening monsters today not only wear human faces, but believe themselves to be heroes. While initially pursuing a noble goal, they are baffled and frustrated by resistance and end up projecting all the evil in their own Shadows onto "the Other." The wolf doesn't just look for easy meals in what was once its territory, it wants to destroy my farm, and the next step after eating my goats is to eat my children. That political faction espouses a philosophy diametrically opposite ours; they clearly want to take over the country and impose their viewpoint on us, therefore we need to take over the country first and get rid of them. After all, if the enemy is monstrous, then monstrous measures are necessary and acceptable to defeat it. In fiction and in Jungian psychology, the only means to survival and growth is to acknowledge, accept and tame the Shadow self. The question is, how do we re-humanize our real-world enemies, and how do we regain our humanity in their eyes and our own?

—Rebecca Marjesdatter

Mathoms

Our regular readers will have noticed that last issue we expanded *TOTU*'s physical length and breadth, to nearly 8 ½" x 11", and that this issue we've returned to our standard (issue #s 20-25) size. Turned out that bookstores didn't like the larger size, because it was hard to shelve. Yes, we should have checked first; we live and learn.

It has seemed to us for some years that we've been moving from a traditional magazine to something more closely resembling an original-fiction anthology, hence last issue we tried out the subtitle "The Anthology of TOTU Ink." After further mulling about we've come to think that *TOTU*, in keeping with its unconventional nature, is really a blend of magazine and anthology. Thus our new subtitle, "The Antholo-Zine of SF Minnesota."

To *TOTU* fiction veterans Patricia S. Bowne, Stephen Dedman, Martha A. Hood, Judy Klass, William Mingin, Sarah Monette, Mark Rich, Patricia Russo, Robert P. Switzer, and Laurel Winter—welcome back! To *TOTU* fiction newcomers T. Bilgen, Ellen Kuhfeld, Douglas J. Lane, Brandon Sigrist, Bryan Thao Worra, and Jason D. Wittman—thanks for stopping by! Come again soon.

This is our "Monsters" issue. Longtime readers of this publication will have noticed that I love monsters—but this is *Tales of the Unanticipated*, so we're serving up lots of different kinds of monsters, some quite visible, some hard to spot, some cuddly, some blood-curdling. See Rebecca's editorial for some thoughtful musings about monsters.

I've taken the liberty of composing a song for this occasion. You know the tune.

The Monster Song

If you're Vampy and you know it, flap your wings.
If you're Vampy and you know it, flap your wings.
If you're Vampy and you know it, then your corpse will surely show it,
If you're Vampy and you know it flap your wings!

If you're Wolfy and you know it, show your fangs.
If you're Wolfy and you know it, show your fangs.
If you're Wolfy and you know it, then the moon will surely show it,
If you're Wolfy and you know it, show your fangs!

If you're Frankie and you know it, walk like this—[arms outstretched]
If you're Frankie and you know it, walk like this.
If you're Frankie and you know it, then your bolts will surely show it.
If you're Frankie and you know it, walk like this!

If you're Mummy and you know it, wrap your head.
If you're Mummy and you know it, wrap your head.
If you're Mummy and you know it, then your ankh will surely show it.
If you're Mummy and you know it, wrap your head!

—**Eric M. Heideman, June 29, 2006**

TALES OF THE UNANTICIPATED is published at eight-month intervals by TOTU INK. Copyright © 2006 TOTU Ink, Inc., for the authors and artists. Reproduction in whole or in part by any means without permission is prohibited. The opinions expressed herein are not necessarily those of TOTU Ink. Indeed, the opinions expressed may change on rereading—you can't step in the same story twice. Editorial & Non-poetry, non-art submissions: send to Eric M. Heideman, Tales of the Unanticipated, PO Box 8036, Lake Street Station, Minneapolis MN 55408. TOTU is not an around-the-year market. Please check our Contributors' Guidelines on p. 7. Subscription service: Send address changes, subscription renewals, or new subscriptions to Tales of the Unanticipated, PO Box 1099, Minnetonka MN 55345. ISBN: 0-9760146-7-X

Contributors

T. Bilgen writes, "Living in Seattle, I don't get much exercise. Unless you count riding the bus. Not much of a sports fan either, but it's hard to resist all the passion surrounding it. My fiction has appeared in *AlienSkin Magazine*; *Aiofe's Kiss*, *Byzarium*, *Nanobison*, and *Not One of Us*."

Bruce Boston has received the Bram Stoker Award, a Pushcart Prize, the Asimov's Readers' Award, and the Grand Master Award of the Science Fiction Poetry Association. He is the author of 40 books and chapbooks, including the novel *Stained Glass Rain* (Ocean View, 1993) and the recent collection *Flashing the Dark: Forty Short Fictions* (Sam's Dot, 2006). Bruce lives in Ocala, Florida with his wife, writer-artist Marge Ballif Simon. For more information, please visit his website (http://hometown.aol.com/bruboston).

Patricia S. Bowne has no experience with the living dead outside of 8:00 a.m. classes. When not writing fantasy, she teaches at a small college with no necromancy program and no faculty possessed by demons. Additional stories about Osyth and the Royal Academy of the Arcane Arts and Sciences can be found in *TOTU* #s 23-26 and in *Year's Best SF 3* (David G. Hartwell & Kathryn Cramer, eds.).

Stephen Dedman lives in Bayswater, Western Australia. He is an associate editor for *Eidolon* Magazine; the author of the novels *The Art of Arrow Cutting* (1997), a Stoker Award nominee; *Foreign Bodies* (1999), and *Shadows Bite* (2001; all Tor); the Australian-published story collections *The Lady of Situations* (2000) and *Never Seen by Waking Eyes* (2005); and stories in "an eclectic, even motley variety of publications," including *Year's Best Fantasy and Horror, 10th Annual Collection* (Ellen Datlow & Terri Windling, eds., 1997); *Isaac Asimov's Utopias* (2000), *Asimov's Science Fiction*, *The Magazine of Fantasy and Science Fiction* (*F&SF*), *Science Fiction Eye*, *Hayakawa S-F Magazine*, *Andromeda Spaceways Inflight Magazine*, and *TOTU* #s 18-21 and 24-26.

durenda was born in palm springs, california in 1981. was attending uc berkeley but is taking time off to be with her mother who has terminal cancer. she writes to foment la revolucion against tyrannical horrors and end all levels of oppression.

Cornelius Fortune's work has appeared in *Tales of the Unanticipated*, *Nuvein*, *Black Petals*, *Excess Compassion*, *Dreams of Decadence*, *Dark Fire* Fiction, the forthcoming anthology *Mirrors in Flame*, and many others. He is the author of the horror collection *Stories from Arlington*. Visit his website at www.storiesfromarlington.com, or email arlingtonbooks@yahoo.com

Rodger Gerberding had two recent one-person shows of his work in various media; the last, at the Magic Theatre of Omaha, Nebraska, was entitled *Night Works of an Actor*. In November of 2005, he was a guest artist/speaker for the first annual Nebraska Forum for Persons with Disabilities in the Arts, at the Omaha Playhouse. In June of 2006 he served as guest curator for the second annual Midwestern Mental Health Invitational Exhibit, a nine-state gathering of art by persons with disabilities, Held at the Glore Psychiatric Museum in St Joseph, Missouri. In August, he will have a one-person show at the Michael Phipps Gallery of Omaha, to be called *The Secret Lives of a Picture*. (Natch, he continues to draw and paint, as if he had a reasonable alternative.) Too, he is currently completing his interpretative biography, *Bette Evans: An American Life*, for fall publication and debut at the Iowa Library Association's annual conference, where he will also be a guest lecturer.

By Day, **Eric M. Heideman** runs a Minneapolis neighborhood library (the one with the Science Fiction Room). He's published fiction in *Writers of the Future, Volume 3*; *Alfred Hitchcock's Mystery Magazine*; and *Best Mystery and Suspense Stories, 1988* (Walker), and around 200 reviews, essays, features, interviews, and biographical sketches in such places as the Minneapolis *Star Tribune*, *Twin Cities Reader*, *What do I Read Next?* (Gale), *MonsterZine.com*, *TOTU*, and various and sundry convention program books. Hang out with him in Krushenko's, his space for SF conversation, at Diversicon, Arcana, MarsCon, OdsseyCon, Minicon, WisCion, and CONvergence. Last year he volunteered for a city council candidate who actually won. He tries to squeeze a couple of weekends a year in Upper Michigan, canoeing and puttering around in the cabin his grandfather built in 1909-1910, off a road so rural you still can't MapQuest it. He has recently had some success persuading his quarreling cats, Boris Karloff and Johnny Depp, to just get along.

Martha A. Hood writes, "With the exception of 'Missing Piece,' in this issue, my credits haven't changed since last year; but I am working hard, almost done with the current draft of my novel, and working on a new short story as well. 'Missing Piece' was inspired by someone I knew in high school, which means I can say it is 'based on a true story,' even if I did make it up. I still live in Irvine, California, with two other humans and four cockatiels. The youngest human, our daughter, will be a high school senior in the fall. Her activities kept me surprisingly busy, even though she now drives, even has her own car. I also have to deal with the house, which is falling apart, has plumbing issues, termites, and sections of dry rot, just to start. (See 'If Only,' *TOTU* #25—also based on a true story.) But for some reason, I seem to have more time to read these days. All in all, I can't complain."

Judy Klass of New York City has had lots of stories published in *TOTU*. Her stories have also appeared in *Asimov's*, *Space & Time*, *Harpur Palate*, *Phoebe*, *Wind Magazine,* and elsewhere. Her play, *Stop Me if You've Heard This One...* recently won the Dorothy Silver Award. Judy moonlights as a country singer/songwriter. Check out her *Brooklyn Cowgirl*

CD at www.cdbaby.com/judyklass. And you can download her songs at iTunes!

Deborah P. Kolodji's eyes are greener than anything on Mars. She's a member of the Science Fiction Poetry Association and the Haiku Society of America. Her work has appeared in *Strange Horizons, Modern Haiku, Astropoetica, Star*Line, Dreams and Nightmares,* and many other places. Her third chapbook of poetry, her first science fiction poetry collection, *Symphony of the Universe,* is available from Sam's Dot Publishing.

Ellen Kuhfeld writes, "In first grade I was reading *Doctor Doolittle, Mary Poppins,* and John W. Campbell. (Some librarians put them all together on the kids' bookshelf. For almost 60 years now, I've wondered if they knew what they were doing. As I grew, science fiction was the genre that stuck. I began writing in high school, and started college in the late fifties. In college I published newsletters and fanzines. (I'm still doing it today.) I graduated with my doctorate in nuclear physics, then ran away and joined the museum world as a public-access Doctor Science. I've always enjoyed writing both fiction and fact—I claim my specialty as 'humorous technical writing.' (I had an article in the *Journal of Irreproducible Results*.) Now, in the twenty-first century, I am chronicling the more humorous aspects of the Twin Cities werewolf community. Werewolves: not just for horror anymore."

Douglas J. Lane is a transplanted upstate New Yorker who now feathers his nest in Manassas, Virginia. He's previously worked as a newspaper reporter, and currently makes hs way in the world as a Marketing writer by day. By night, he blames his desire to tell stories on Ray Bradbury, Charles Beaumont, and Harlan Ellison. He's currently at work on a handful of new shorts and the second draft of his first novel. The fruits of his other creative outlet, short film making, can be found at www.originalideafilms.com. 'Mister Eddie' is his first published short story, and is dedicated to Allie Vose, who enjoyed Poe, loved life, and is dearly missed.

Rebecca Marjesdatter is a poet and prose writer, currently living in Minneapolis. Her work has appeared in *TOTU, The Magazine of Speculative Poetry*, the anthology *Women of Other Worlds*, and a future issue of *Asimov's*. She won the Rhysling Award for speculative poetry (short form) in 2000, and performs with the "Lady Poetesses from Hell" at local conventions, sharing the stage with such luminaries as Jane Yolen, Ellen Klages, and Grace Lord Stoke.

William Mingin, a graduate of the Clarion West SF writing workshop and a member of the Garden State Horror Writers, has published 15 short stories in such venues as *TOTU, Talebones,* and *Black October,* and over 140 non-fiction pieces. Four of his stories have received honorable mention in *The Year's Best Fantasy and Horror,* and one was reprinted in *Year's Best Fantasy 3* (David G. Hartwell & Kathryn Cramer, eds.). He reviews audio books for *AudioFile Magazine*, and last year was a judge for the Audio Publishers Awards ("Audies"). He's married and lives in central New Jersey, where he runs a small book-export business in partnership with a German bookseller.

Having completed her doctorate in English literature, **Sarah Monette** lives and works in a 100-year-old house in the upper Midwest. Her short stories have appeared in *Lady Churchill's Rosebud Wristlet, Strange Horizons, Alchemy,* and *TOTU* #s 25 and 26, among others. Her first novel, *Melusine,* appeared from Ace Books last August; her second novel, *The Virtu,* should be out by the time *TOTU* #27 sees print. Visit her online at www.sarahmonette.com

John Calvin Rezmerski's poems have been published in magazines and anthologies as varied as the *Wall Street Journal, Mennonite Life, Nursing Outlook,* and of course *TOTU*. His books include *The Frederick Manfred Reader* and *What Do I Know? New and Selected Poems* (both Holy Cow! Press). He lives in Mankato, Minnesota.

Mark Rich has fiction, poems, and reviews appear in recent or upcoming issues of *Electric Velocipede, Asimov's SF, Ship of Fools, Poesia,* and *New York Review of Science Fiction,* among other publications. He is illustrating a collection of Ezra Pound stories for Spilt Milk Press, and is still playing folk and rock music with partner Martha Borchardt. The two of them live in Caston, Wisconsin.

Stephanie Rodriguez is an award-winning illustrator and a graduate of New York City's Fashion Institute of Technology. Stephanie's illustrations have appeared in many publications from around the world including *Aurealis, Cemetary Dance, Strange Horizons, newWitch, Mythic Delerium, Revelation,* and *Nocturne*. Though emotional, her work is influenced by an intense study of Expressionism, African art, jazz music, and the illustrations of Howard Pyle and Arthur Rackham. Currently, she resides with her husband Maikel and their dog Luke in Miami, Forida.

Patricia Russo drinks at least a full pot of coffee a day, smokes at least two packs of unfiltered cigarettes a day, and spends most her waking hours trying not to kill people. Her stores have appeared in *Surreal, City Slab, TOTU,* and the Stoker-nominated anthology *Corpse Blossoms.* She will have a reprint in the upcoming anthology *Best of Not One of Us.*

Laramie Sasseville is a graduate of Wellesley College with a degree in Studio Art. She has shown her illustrative work in the Twin Cities area since 1979, including one-woman shows at local coffee-houses and regular participation in art shows at Minicon, MarsCon, and CONvergence science fiction conventions. She has shown her functional art (scriptural bookmarks) at Powderhorn Art Fair and M'Or Designs. She is a three-time winner of honorable mentions in the Illustrators of the Future Contest. Her cartoons and illustrations have been printed in numerous publications of the Minnesota Science Fiction Society (MN-StF) as well as in *Once Upon a Time Magazine for Children's Book Writers and Illustrators*, *The Dream Network*, and as featured artist in *Spinning Free*.

Ann K. Schwader lives and writes in Westminster, Colorado, with her husband and one profoundly spoiled corgi. Her poetry and fiction have received several honorable mentions in *Year's Best Fantasy and Horror*. She is also an active member of SFWA, HWA, and SFPA. For further information—and a translation of all that alphabet soup!—visit www.geocities.com/HPL4ever

Brandon Sigrist writes, "When I'm not writing, I help design buildings for a Twin Cities-based architectural firm that specializes in environmental educational facilities—park shelters, visitor centers, and the like. All in all, not a bad gig. I'm a member of a local writers' group called the Ministry of Speculation, and I have one other piece of writing that will be published this year. It won the last quarter of the Writers of the Future Contest."

Marge Ballif Simon freelances as a prose writer-poet-illustator for genre and mainstream publications such as *Nebula Awards 32, Strange Horizons, Flashquake, Flash Me Magazine, Dreams and Nightmares, The Pedestal Magazine, Vestal Review*, and all but two issues of *TOTU*. She is former president of the Science Fiction Poetry Association, and now serves as editor of *Star*Line*. She has received the Rhysling Award for speculative poetry and the James Award for art. Her poetry collections, *Night Smoke* with Bruce Boston (2003) and *Artist of Antithesis* (2004) were Bram Stoker Award finalists. In addition to her solo work, Marge collaborates with her husband, prose writer-poet Bruce Boston. Their poems, stories, and cartoons have appeared or are forthcoming in *Strange Horizons, Dark Regions, Dreams and Nightmares, Star*Line, Fantasy Commentator*, and *Dark Wisdom*. They live in Ocala, Florida.

Robert P. Switzer resides in the small town of St Mary's, Ontario, Canada, where he is currently at work on his first novel. From 1998-2001 he co-edited the Canadian speculative fiction magazine *Challenging Destiny*. His first fiction sale, "Chief of the Sexy and Cool Committee," appeared in *TOTU* #26. Robert can be reached at thebobswitzer@aol.com

Bryan Thao Worra's fiction and poetry have appeared in over 50 international publications, including the *Bamboo Among the Oaks* anthology, *Whistling Shade, Urban Pioneer, Unarmed, Asian Pacific Journal, Journal of the Asian American Renaissance*, and *Quarterly Literary Review Singapore*. He has also coordinated many shows and exhibitions promoting Hmong and Lao writers. He lives in the Twin Cities, where he will serve as Special Guest at Diversicon 14 August 11-13, 2006.

Augie Wiedeman's recent work includes a lovely jacket for Wilum Pugmire's *Sesqua Valley and Other Haunts*. Personally (the art editor interjected) Augie is one of the kindest of humankind, never too occupied to call or write or send gifts of his work and others, he is astonishingly supportive, and astonishingly underrated, given both the quality of his art and his friendship. Welcome to the cover, Augie, and thank you.

Laurel Winter's recent exploits include 5 ½ weeks in Ireland and Paris, during which time she wrote 100 poems; a 6 ½ week, 8,694 mile road trip, which included beginning a new novel on November 12 of '05 (by the end of the year the word count was exactly 2K) and—after 5 months without an address—moving into the apartment of her dreams (radiators! Hardwood floors! Wi-fi! Cheap rent!) in Rochester, Minnesota, after planning and discarding various and sundry moving schemes. As this bio went to press, she was waiting (impatiently) to hear from agent and editor on 4 ½ novels. She is currently undergoing treatment for overuse of fractions.

Jason D. Wittman has published or will publish fiction in scifi.com, *Andromeda Spaceways Inflight Magazine*, and *Dark Krypt*. He is also a published game designer, with two games, Tile Chess (a form of chess for up to six players) and Spooks (a card game with a haunted house theme), both published by Steve Jackson Games. His website is www.sff.net/people/jasondwittman

Mail Orders

Prices, availability, and special offers are subject to change without notice. Please see our official website www.totu-ink.com for current prices and availability.

Four-issue subscription: $28.00, check to TOTU Ink. In Canada add $3 postage. Add $6 for international. All prices are in US dollars.

Heckuva Deal: Issues #2 through #16, issues #18 and 19 all for the incredible price of $40.00 US, shipping included! In Canada add $5.00 US. Add $10.00 US for international. (Photocopy facsimiles of #1 and #17 can be purchased separately.)

Back Issues: For a complete list of available back issues, see our website, www.totu-ink.com.

Tales of the Unanticipated
PO Box 1099
Minnetonka MN 55345

TALES OF THE UNANTICIPATED
Contributors' Guidelines

Reading submissions for issue #29 that are postmarked October 1-October 31, 2006. We will respond by March 31, 2007. If you are reading this after October 31, 2006, do not send unsolicited manuscripts. Keep an eye on our website (www.totu-ink.com) for reading period guidelines/updates. Please note that we *are not an around-the-year market*.

For questions and queries contact: submits@totu-ink.com

PROSE SUBMISSIONS—*please follow carefully*

Send a manuscript copy of PROSE submissions (with SASE) to:

Eric M. Heideman
Tales of the Unanticipated
PO Box 8036
Lake Street Station
Minneapolis MN 55408

(Eric does not assume or accept responsibility for art and poetry mailed to the above address.)

In addition to mailing us mss. copies of your prose submissions, email your submission as an attachment to:

submits@totu-ink.com

We can accept most file formats--Word, Open Office, Word Perfect, etc.--but if you are not sure, send your submission as a Rich Text Format (RTF) file. For our international contributors, A4 is OK. Size, in this case, doesn't matter. If you do not have a computer document for your submission, please email us at the above address to let us know you have mailed us your manuscript. We will let you know, by email, when we have received the manuscript by mail and email.

The editor, whose day-job involves reading huge amounts of information off a screen, will not spend hundreds of additional hours a year reading story mss. off his home screen, and *TOTU* cannot carry the expense of printing all the submissions we receive. If you want your prose submission considered, you need to send a paper manuscript copy along with the electronic one.

Please note that Eric and the *TOTU* staff put a lot of time and care into helping promising writers hone their craft. Writers of originality and vision often need help presenting their material so that their desired effect gets across to readers. That's what editors are supposed to be for. To be helpful, we think it's necessary to be honest. If you see personal editorial feedback as enemy action, please don't waste our time; we have an antholo-zine to put out. If you like getting feedback, we look forward to reading your stuff.

FICTION: Reading submissions postmarked October 1-31, 2006, for #29, a general, nontheme issue. Pays 1 ½-2 cents a word for science fiction, fantasy, horror, hybrids thereof, and unclassifiable stories. We prefer stories with personality, and originality of vision, to the factory-made brand. We will consider stories up to 10,000 words; no serials.

NONFICTION: *TOTU* pays 1 ½-2 cents a word for essays for the general reader on speculative fiction writers and themes, or speculative science essays, to 6,000 words. We're currently backlogged on interviews. No plot summaries masquerading as book reviews. Query Eric M. Heideman at the above address with an SASE or send an email query to eric@totu-ink.com with your idea before submitting.

RIGHTS: *TOTU* acquires First North American Serial Rights. We occasionally settle for One-Time Reprint Rights on previously published material, but if your piece was previously published, or is scheduled to be published elsewhere, you need to say that in your cover letter. No surprises, please. Once your piece has appeared in *TOTU*, you are free to resell it to other markets. But when it's republished please iuclude a statement to this effect: "(Story title) originally appeared in *Tales of the Unanticipated* (issue number & year)."

SIMULTANEOUS SUBMISSIONS: Because of the short reading window, we're willing to consider simultaneous submissions, but again, no surprises; you need to mention up front in your cover letter where else your submission is sitting, and you need to let us know promptly when/if it is accepted/rejected by the other market. (After several staff members have each devoted hours of consideration to a piece, it doesn't make us happy campers to learn that, in the meantime you've sold it to a market where you hadn't told us it was even under consideration.)

MULTIPLE SUBMISSIONS: Because of the short reading window, we're willing to consider up to three stories at a time; but please include a *separate SASE* for each story. Failure to include separate SASEs may result in the prompt rejection of a story that might otherwise have received detailed consideration.

E-SUBS: *TOTU* now asks for *both* paper and electronic copies of prose submissions. Electronic submissions without accompanying paper copies remain unacceptable. Please carefully read through "prose submissions" above for details. For poetry submissions, see below.

PAYMENT: 1 ½-2 cents a word for fiction and nonfiction. See above for what kinds of fiction and nonfiction we'll consider.

POETRY: *TOTU* pays $7 for speculative poetry, up to two typewritten pages per poem. Send submissions to:

Rebecca Marjesdatter
2011 3rd Av S, #22
Minneapolis MN 55404

Or email to: poetry@totu-ink.com

In the case of poetry—and only poetry—it's acceptable to submit either by email or postal mail. Email submissions are preferred. If you send your poetry submissions by postal mail, please include an SASE.

ILLUSTRATIONS AND CARTOONS: *TOTU* pays $25 for front-cover art, $15 for back-cover art, $12 for commissioned interior illustrations, $7 for cartoons and spot illustrations. For an assignment, send several clear photocopies representing the range of your work. Please do not send original copies unless asked to do so. Send art portfolios to:

Rodger Gerberding   (New address as of 2005.)
379 Lincoln Av
Council Bluffs IA 51503

Send cartoons to Eric M. Heideman at the address for fiction submissions, above.

Sarah Monette's a writer who is really going places. Witness this amazing novelette.

Katabasis: Seraphic Trains
by Sarah Monette

snow falls in her open eyes

Her name is Clair. She wears black, no jewelry, and has long straight hair, dyed a dark reddish-purple, the color of the foundries' breath against the night sky. If she feels any emotions, her eyes never reflect them. She does not talk about herself, and she has never cried. Her apartment is enormous and bare, and your footsteps echo hollowly off the parquet floor, giving the impression of even greater vastness, greater emptiness, as if you walked through a palace made of ice, cyclopean and uninhabited. The walls and the few pieces of furniture are stark, sterile white, like untouched snow. Clair moves like a shadow through the whiteness of her rooms.

your hatred, like a sleeping beast

It was a great city once, and powerful. It has power still, dark, corrosive power like smog. The foundries and factories are mostly shut down now. Those that still operate stain the sky with billows of black and gray; in some quarters of the city their roaring can be heard all night long, and they throw bruised and blurry rainbows against the clouds. A river flows through the city's heart, sullen and slow, but brown and hungry and strong. And the city itself is a snarl, a brawl, a festered wound. It seethes and roils and bides its time.

the stings of winter wasps

Beyond the window, snow fell like frozen drops of poison.

Clair looked at him, her eyes clear and pitiless. "It's very nice, Sean," she said.

"Nice?" he said. "That's it? Just 'nice'?"

"Oh, darling, I'm sorry." Her laugh, the sound of icicles shattering. "It's lovely, Sean, of course it is. I'm very impressed."

"It isn't finished," he said desperately. "I mean, I know there's weak spots, and I ...."

Her eyes were a strange color, milky gray with touches of blue and green: dirty, dead-of-winter ice. Her gaze always upset him, dazed him; in the depths of his heart he knew that it had enchanted him. Now, cold and hard and full of light, her gaze silenced him, and when she was sure he would not speak, she said, "I'm not saying you're not talented, Sean, because clearly you are. But I think you've maybe overreached yourself just a trifle. It's such an *ambitious* project. I know you're very serious about it, but I think—"

"You think it's no good."

"I didn't say that."

"But it's what you meant, isn't it? *Isn't it*?"

And she looked at him, not alarmed by his nearness, his anger. His gaze dropped first. "I think it's awfully ...traditional."

"You mean clichéd."

"Do I?"

"Well, don't you?"

"You're still young, Sean. It's all right to model yourself on the poets you admire."

"But I'm not!"

"Oh, please. Darling, I don't want to be cruel, but there's no sense in letting you delude yourself. You're dripping T. S. Eliot from every page."

"Thank you, Clair," he said with stiff irony.

"You're *young*," she said. "Give yourself time."

"Are you saying my writing's immature? Come on, Clair, say what you mean!"

"I thought certain passages were just a little ...naïve," she said, and the cold clear eyes watched his reaction without changing.

"I'd better go," he said, aware of the blood mounting to his face, aware of the hot prickle of starting tears.

She let him leave; only as he was opening the door of her apartment did she say, softly, almost laughing, "You'll be back."

silver ribbons for my love

The river runs through the heart of the city, and braiding, around and over and under the river, the city's rail system is a welter of tarnished silver ribbons. The tracks sear through the city with a fine disregard for its geography, soaring above and plunging below the streets as the whim takes them, sometimes following the lines laid by the major boulevards, sometimes running alone through empty lots, sometimes cutting a swath through residential districts so that top floor tenants could, if they were so inclined, reach out from their back windows and have their arms ripped off by the force of the passing trains.

It is said in those districts that not all the trains which run on the city's tracks are listed in Metropolitan Transit's compendious schedule. The residents will tell you that after midnight, on some nights, there will be other trains, trains whose cry is different, the bellow of some great beast fighting for its life. And if you watch those trains go past, behind those bright flickering windows you will see passengers unlike any passengers you have seen when riding the trains yourself: men with wings, women with horns, beast-headed children, fauns and dryads and green-skinned people more beautiful than words can describe. In 1893, a schoolteacher swore that she saw a unicorn; in 1934, a murderer turned himself into the police, weeping, saying that he saw his victims staring at him from a train as it howled past the station platform on which he stood.

These are the seraphic trains. The stories say they run to Heaven, Hell, and Faërie. They are omens, but no one can agree on what they portend. And although you will never meet anyone who has seen or experienced it, there are persistent rumors, unkillable rumors, that sometimes, maybe once a century, maybe twice, a seraphic train will stop in its baying progress and open its doors for a mortal. Those who know the story of Thomas the Rhymer—and even some who don't—insist that all these people, blest or damned as they may be, must be poets.

starless night

For days after Sean's suicide, Bram Bennett walked around without being aware of what she wore, what she ate, what she did. Her whole head burned with words to which no one would listen. She looked at the people she knew on campus and was dully astonished at how little she liked them. The idea of talking to her parents was merely ludicrous, and she had gladly lost contact with the few friends she had had in high school. There was no one she could tell, no one who would understand her grief. She felt like a woman standing in the aftermath of Hiroshima, surrounded by debris and corpses, the only living thing for five miles in any direction and herself dying, dying of the radiation she could neither see nor feel.

the twilight water

The subway station is a long, barrel-vaulted hall, an echo chamber for sounds which seem to have no origin. No passengers board trains here. The iron benches sit desolate, their only company the illegible sheets of newsprint which fly and flap and skitter and scuttle from one end of the platform to the other.

Those who disembark at the Court of the Clockwork Kings do not linger.

velvet death

The interior of the train car (Bram thought) was a very good imitation of a Metropolitan Transit train done by someone who'd never actually been inside one. All the colors and shapes were right, but the textures were wrong. The walls were papered with something silvery that felt like velvet; the seats were upholstered in blue satin. The floor was carpeted in black brocade, the ceiling was pressed tin, and Bram wasn't sure, but she thought the poles and safety fittings were solid silver. It made her feel small and grubby and excessively herself. Her black clothes were too obvious, and surely everyone in the car could tell she dyed her hair, that her light hazel eyes would never belong with hair that black. The rings in her ears and nose felt like something she'd done merely because everyone else did. She was morbidly certain that the black rose tattoo on her back, safely covered by her T-shirt and leather jacket, was nonetheless radiantly visible to everyone who looked at her. She sat on one of the blue satin benches, worrying that she was getting it dirty, and clutched her guitar in its case across her lap.

The other occupants of the car mostly ignored her. There was a horde of children with cat-heads—kittens, she supposed, since none of them could be more than four years old—playing some elaborate game up and down the aisle; she counted two Siamese, three brown tabbies, two tortoiseshells, and one white Persian. They were dressed like Victorian children in velvet suits with broad lace collars. Their round eyes, green and amber and gold, looked at her with perfect trust and perfect indifference; to them, she was merely one more obstacle to be incorporated in their game.

At the far end of the car from where Bram sat, there was a woman, naked except for an opal choker around her neck, green-skinned, her eyes the luminous white of clouds—so beautiful that her beauty was like pain. She was clearly watching the child-kittens, with sharp attentiveness rather than the amused tolerance of a stranger, and Bram wondered if this woman, whom any culture in the mortal world would have worshipped as a goddess, was employed as a child-minder by a group of cat-headed parents.

Just down from the green-skinned woman were a group of creatures who looked as if they were made out of tree-roots; twisted, hunched, and knotted, they huddled together and talked in high, scratchy voices, like twigs against a windowpane. Bram couldn't understand what they were saying, and from the vindictive cunning in their tiny red eyes, she was quite sure she didn't want to. Across the aisle from them was a giant, black as moonless midnight, with a bull's head and hooves, his horns brushing the roof of the car, his long, rat-like tail sweeping out into the aisle and restlessly curling and uncurling itself around the nearby poles. The child-kittens treated the tail like a hurdle, jumping over it with exaggerated, giggling caution. The minotaur ignored them completely; he was immersed in a small, crumbling book bound in cracking green leather.

At the other end of the car sat two tall, grave, chalk-white gentlemen, dressed in chalk-white business suits and each with his hands folded over a chalk-white briefcase in his lap. Bram would have taken them for angels, remembering the stories Sean had told her about the seraphic trains, except for the crusted blood at the corners of their mouths. Their eyes were of no color that she could discern; they looked and spoke only to each other, studiously ignoring everything else in the car, including, on the bench nearest them, a group of giggling young women, golden-haired and warm-eyed, dressed in old rose and gold and burgundy velvet, their ears as delicately pointed as cathedral spires. Every time Bram looked at these young women, one of them was looking at her, and she had the horrible feeling that she was the cause of their giggles.

And directly across from Bram, there was a dead girl. The girl's hair was lank and brittle, her eyes sunken, her nails dark and splintered against her pallid, blue-tinged skin. And Bram could see the ragged, black-edged hole in her temple, not quite concealed by her hair.

The fifth or sixth time Bram snuck a glance at the dead girl, she met her eyes. Red-faced, ashamed, Bram twitched a smile at her. The dead girl looked down at once, and Bram fixed her gaze resolutely on the silver pole opposite and slightly to the right of her.

And then the dead girl raised her head, and Bram's gaze was instantly drawn back to her. They stared at each other, and Bram could not help feeling kinship with this girl, the only other mortal in the car, even if she was dead.

"Your music's really neat," said the dead girl.

"Thanks," Bram said, blushing again. "Thank you. Really."

"It's a stupid thing to say."

"No, it's not. It's nice of you."

"No, really. You don't need me telling you you're good. I mean, the train stopped for you, didn't it?"

"That's not what caused it," Bram protested. That couldn't be true; she, Bram, could not have succeeded where Sean had failed.

The dead girl glanced up at her and away, and Bram felt the force of her disbelief even through the filmy congealed deadness of her eyes. "Oh, come *on*," the dead girl said. "You gotta know how good you are. What else were you doing out there playing at the trains anyway?"

"I'm looking for someone."

"*Looking* for someone? Either you're on crack or you're pulling my leg."

"No, I mean it. Someone …someone like you."

The dead girl's eyes were like stones behind the filthy curtain of her hair. "Someone dead?"

Bram took a deep breath and let it out. "Yes."

"That's fucked up."

"Can you help me? Can you tell me how to find him?"

"I can tell you you don't want to."

"I *have* to. Please."

The girl leaned forward and put her dead, grimy hand on Bram's knee. "Please, chickie, believe me. You don't want to. You want to go with those girls who are checking you out and live forever in Faërie or some shit like that. Or don't get off the train. Just go right the fuck back where you came from and get a record deal. You don't want to go to the Court of the Clockwork Kings."

"Is that where I'll find him?"

"Are you even listening to me?"

"I am, I promise, and I really appreciate your concern. But this is what I have to do."

"And I thought *I* was fucked in the head. But whatever it is you've got is way worse than a bullet. Okay. Yes. That's the stop you want. The Court of the Clockwork Kings. But, I mean, really, what good do you think it's going to do?"

"I'm going to bring him back," Bram said, articulating for the first time the plan which had sprung full-formed into her head as soon as she had seen the open doors of the seraphic train, and the dead girl, after a disbelieving moment, rocked back on the bench and went into a terrible dry spasm of laughter that sounded like someone choking to death on a bone. The two tortoiseshell child-kittens stopped a moment, staring at her with grave wonder, but the green-skinned woman called to them, and they ran to her.

"Man, you are just fucked up," the dead girl said, and after that she would not speak to Bram again.

our story crumbles in my hands

When you go to the office of the city's oldest paper, the *Telegraph-Clarion*, and ask to see their archives, you will be admitted to a room crammed to bursting with the huge black ledgers in which the city's entire journalistic history is preserved. In those grim and brittle ledgers, you will find births and deaths and marriages, records of parades and speeches—a relentless marching army of facts that will not surrender up the answers you can sense, like rats in the wainscoting, behind the bland, prosperous wallpaper of the articles' words.

But even the *Telegraph-Clarion* has not always been able to flatten the oddity out of the city's dark flourishing. In the 1870s a factory girl living in Prosper Park was reputed to tell the future. Not major events such as wars or assassinations or stock-market crashes, but predicting the number of kittens in a litter, or how many tries it would take a boy to hit a target with a stone. In 1877 she threw herself under one of the Metropolitan Transit trains and died. The brief popularity of apocalypse preachers at the end of '77 can hardly be coincidental, a fear that her tiny, trivial talent had shown her something too dreadful to be borne. But no such calamity ever occurred.

Similar cases abound: a classics professor who chased rainbows until his disappearance in 1964; Caroline Hayward, who was discovered weeping in Asherton Park in October of 1905, her hands stained with blood that was not hers. No victim was ever found, and Caroline Hayward could speak, stammering, sobbing, only of falling leaves.

And there is the story of Phoebe Gruenstahl.

Phoebe Gruenstahl was institutionalized in 1909; she was seven years old. Her parents told everyone that she had died, and in time, freed from their strange, mute, savage child, they came to believe it. She was an inmate of St. Catherine's for twenty-nine years, and then one sweltering August night in 1938, she escaped. No one, then or later, ever discovered how.

The city was in a panic for seven days. It became generally accepted that she had gotten into the sewers, and there were expeditions with dogs and rifles to bring her out again, but no luck. In fact, there were no confirmed sightings of Phoebe Gruenstahl until February 1939, when her body was dragged out of the river less than half a mile from the then newly completed Enoch J. Hopkins Bridge, the first bridge to allow the Metropolitan Transit trains to cross the river above the ground.

Cause of death could not be determined.

Everyone who examined the corpse remarked on its astonishingly beautiful smile. In life, Phoebe Gruenstahl had never smiled, never once.

your face, dark behind the glass

Sean Lacroix was born and raised in Prosper Park, one of the city's oldest and grimmest neighborhoods. When Sean was seven, his parents moved the family from their increasingly cramped apartment to a house backing onto the Metropolitan Transit tracks. Sean had a tiny bedroom to himself, at the rear of the house; if he stuck a broom handle out his window, he could bump the tracks with it. The noise and shaking of the trains bothered him at first, but quickly became a mere fact of existence.

One night in July, Sean sat by his open window, watching the trains go past and trying not to listen to his father yelling at his mother in the room below. The trains roared by, and Sean pretended they were fabulous monsters, but he knew they were just trains.

At 1:39 a.m. he heard an approaching train, although the next train wasn't due until 1:50. Curious, he leaned forward even as the train let out a chuffing yowl like the hunting cry of some great beast.

It roared past in no more than five heartbeats, so fast that Sean had no idea of it overall, but individual images, like fragments from a kaleidoscope, lodged in his heart and would stay with him until the moment of his death.

A dead woman, wrapped in a blood-stained shroud, tenderly stroking the hair of a sleeping child.

Two tall, beautiful people—whether men or women he could neither then nor later decide—dancing together, their wings trailing behind them like iridescent gossamer.

A saber-toothed tiger yanking at its chains with human hands.

Two queens, crowned and jeweled and with the heads of foxes, playing chess.

In the last car, a man with the head of a white stag. The man wore black velvet, and on every branch of his wide-spreading antlers a tiny white candle burned serenely, anchored in its own wax. The man's dark, lambent eyes met Sean's, and Sean knew, then and ever after, that that stag-headed man understood him and loved him as no one in his life ever would.

And then the train was gone.

wings, torn from cloudy moths

Lying together in the darkness.

They had just had sex, awkwardly and uncomfortably, on Sean's narrow dorm-room bed. It had not exactly been Bram's first time, but it couldn't count as more than her second. She hadn't said anything about that to Sean, but she was afraid he'd been able to tell anyway.

"Sean?" she said into the darkness.

"What?" Sean said. He sounded sleepy, maybe a little irritated.

"Oh, nothing. I just …was I okay?"

"Sure. You were fine. We aren't being graded, you know."

"I didn't mean that. It was just …." She lost her nerve and said, "The bed's pretty narrow."

"Hey, we didn't fall off. Ten points out of ten."

"Okay," Bram said, although she was only partly reassured.

But Sean was awake now; Bram felt him shifting position, sitting up against the headboard with the pillow behind his back. She stayed as she was, lying on her side, pressed against the wall, her head inadequately supported by what she would later find to be a pair of Sean's roommate's sweatpants.

Sean said, "What do you want your music to do, Bram?"

"What?"

"Your music. What do you want to do with it?"

"I don't know. I guess I'm not sure what you mean."

"Don't you have any aspirations?" Sean said, a stinging flick of contempt in his voice.

"Of course I do. I just …they're hard to articulate, you know?"

"No, they're not. Not if they're real."

"Well, what's your aspiration then?" Bram said, defensive and yet hoping that perhaps Sean was working around to asking her to read his poems.

"The city," Sean said. "I want to capture the truth of the city."

And when she asked him what he meant, Sean told her about the seraphic trains and the river and the city's tenebrous history. But he did not show her his poems.

her blood

Things Lost In The City And Never Recovered:

3 canvases by the American surrealist painter, Frank Attwater: *The Sum of All Objects in the Room*, *The Dirigible Eaten by Stars*, *The Andiron*

the diary of the novelist Susan Kempe (burned by the author before her suicide in 1988)

St. Roque's Hospital (destroyed in the fire of 1922)

the key to the secret room in the house at 549 Grosvenor Avenue

7 life-size wooden marionettes, representing Henry VIII and his 6 wives: Catherine of Aragon, Anne Boleyn (with detachable head), Jane Seymour, Anne of Cleves, Catherine Howard (with detachable head), Catherine Parr

a packet of Agathe Ombrée rose seeds

a stained kidskin left glove missing the index finger, said to have belonged to the Confederate spy Rose O'Neal Greenhow

the Maupin Boulevard subway station

the moon's pyre

Bram climbed the stairs from the subway station and emerged in the middle of a brick-paved plaza. There were benches around the edges of the plaza, and tall, ornate streetlamps; the plaza was almost disappointingly normal, except for the fact that it was underground. The air was cold, but stuffy, and the sweetish scent of dust was everywhere.

She looked up, but the streetlamps did not cast enough light for her to see if the ceiling of this place was natural or man-made. She squeezed the handle of her guitar case, for reassurance, and started to walk toward the edge of the plaza opposite the head of the stairs. She wished, a tired, aching thought, that she had any idea of where she was going.

Bram walked through the Court of the Clockwork Kings. The houses loured on either side, crammed cheek-by-jowl, tall and narrow-fronted and stern. There were no lights behind any of the windows, but she could not shake the faint, frightened impression that the houses were not deserted, that the rooms behind those staring windows were not empty, and that those who waited in those airless, dusty rooms (and waited for what?) were watching her as she went past. She walked a little faster, but that made the echoes of her footsteps mime the increasingly rapid and panicked rhythm of her heart, and she had to slow down again.

After a time—she did not know how long, and she was afraid to look at her watch—she saw a different kind of light up ahead. It bloomed like a rose against the darkness, not the right color for a fire, although it was naggingly familiar. She got a little closer and realized it was pink neon, as lurid and tasteless as anything one might see on Jefferson Avenue. Bram stopped, bewildered, suddenly afraid in an entirely new way.

And it was at that moment that she became aware of a hand on her arm.

She jerked away and turned, in one motion, and found herself staring at something that looked like a man but wasn't one. It was tall and deathly white—not the same white as the chalk-white gentlemen in the train, this was a dead white, like the undersides of rotting fish—and wrapped in trailing black that might have been a cloak or a shroud or a pair of nebulous wings. Its eyes were blood-red slivers of glass.

"What are you?" Bram said, her voice shrill and shaking. "What do you want?"

"We are the noctares," said the creature, and Bram looked around wildly, but there was nothing like it in sight; its words, though, were blurry, echoing, as if it spoke with more than one voice. "We serve the Clockwork Kings. What do you seek, you who breathe, in the Court of the Clockwork Kings?"

"I …I'm looking for someone."

Its head tilted, slowly and jerkily, like a rusty piece of machinery, to the left. It said, "You do not belong here, you who breathe. Go back. Go home. Walk beneath the sun and stars and taste the air of the world. Do not walk in this city of darkness."

"I can't. I'm sorry, but I just can't. I have to find him."

It stared at her, its red glass eyes unfathomable, and said, "If you will not go, we must take you before the Clockwork Kings. We who do not breathe and never have, we beg you: go now. Do not look back. Let go of that which does not breathe."

"Wh …what will they do to me?"

Its head tilted, with the same slow jerkiness—clockwork, Bram thought and then wished she hadn't—to the right. It said, "The Clockwork Kings do no harm."

"Then I will see them. I am not afraid." A lie, a lie, but she could not go back, not without Sean.

It bowed its head. "You have made your choice. Come with us." And its hand, as white and cold as death by freezing, took Bram's arm just above the elbow. This time, Bram could not pull away.

those cold mirrors

Clair was the only person Sean had ever loved. When she kissed him, when she smiled at him, he felt almost breathless with awe. He told her things about himself he had never told and would never tell a living soul. The first time he had seen her, the first time he had looked into her eyes, he had thought he'd seen his Stag of Candles reflected there. He had been trying to find that reflection again ever since, but all he ever saw was himself.

bone needles

Sean sat in the dusty dimness of St. Christopher's small parish library. He was working on a poem about St. Christopher's, his own parish church, for *The Stag of Candles*; he had spent the afternoon looking through the contents of a box labeled simply FROM CONVENT. Most of it was incomprehensible to him, but down at the bottom, he found an accordion file of documents relating to the case of a nun who was committed to St. Catherine's in 1942. She claimed she heard angels singing in the roofs of the transepts—this, the last in what was apparently a long history of visions and voices, some of them distinctly secular, all of them highly suspect. Moreover, in a letter written to her sister but apparently never sent, she gloried in the fact that only she could hear the angels, her tone that of a spoiled child gloating over a birthday present. When she would not recant—when she became blasphemous and violent before the Bishop—she was committed to St. Catherine's. She died of pneumonia nine years later, insisting to the end that angels had sung to her from the roof of St. Christopher's.

Sean jotted down some notes; as he was starting to tidy the contents of the box, the ancient and almost senile Sister Mary Bartholomew tottered over to the table, peered at Sean's pile of documents, and nodded to herself.

"Did you know her, Sister?" Sean asked, not hopefully.

"Her and her angels." Sister Mary Bartholomew snorted. "We all heard them—but only Sister Mary Jude was fool enough to say so."

And she tottered away again, leaving Sean staring after her. He was suddenly very cold.

long-held breath

It was past eleven on the fifth night after Sean's death. Bram crossed the campus without seeing the stark, strange beauty of the bare oak trees against the sky. She made for the nearest Metropolitan Transit stop, bought a ticket she had no intention of using, and climbed the narrow, scaffold-like staircase to the platform.

She was following Sean as best she could. Her grief was too raw and black to admit of any other course of action. But she intended her suicide also to be a memorial, a testament to the tremendous jagged void Sean left in the world. Sean had told her about the seraphic trains, had told her some of the stories about them, and she had heard the longing in his voice. She could not end things until she, too, had watched a seraphic train sweep by and leave her behind, scorning her offering.

She lifted her guitar out of its case, tuned it, and

began to play. She paid no attention to the passengers waiting for the next train, no attention to the cold air or the bad lighting; nothing existed except the music and the trains that roared and howled and gibbered their way past. Each of them was an ordinary train, and Bram kept playing.

She started with folk songs, some Bob Dylan, Beatles songs that she'd been playing since her first guitar lesson at the age of eight. She segued into her own stuff when fingers and voice were warm, when she could feel the strength of the music all the way down her spine. It would be cheating not to play her best, and she knew it would make no difference. No seraphic train would stop for her. Midnight came and went, and she was still playing. She stopped only to get drinks of water. She felt that her heart was opening wider and wider, that it was pushing open the stone carapace of grief and her music was soaring out like dragons.

There was no self-consciousness left when she started playing "Why Do You Linger?," a song she had half-despaired of ever finishing. But tonight she understood it; tonight it was as clear and brutal and precise as a glass dissecting-knife. Tonight she understood what the song was trying to say, that the truth was still beautiful, even if it came out of something painful and ugly and heart-breaking.

The song ended; she looked up, arming sweat off her forehead, and saw the train standing at the platform, doors open; there were faces at every window, looking at her, and not a single one of them was mortal.

A seraphic train had stopped for Bram Bennett.

my love waits for me in green

The Fairlawn Memorial Garden is always deserted. Funerals are held here, the grounds are immaculately kept, but, no matter when you visit, you will never see another living soul.

The Thiboudeau Hill Cemetery is noted for the yearly funeral procession of the city's fifth mayor, Henry Hamilton Carr. Cemetery workers from all over the city gather at sundown on March eleventh to watch the spectral procession, though no one now knows who the mourners are.

The city's most famous (or infamous) resident, the poet and critic Francis Burnham, is buried in St. Mary's Cemetery. Stories were whispered throughout the city of his debauched ways: his orgies, his absinthe and opium, the fortunes he squandered and the young men he ruined. He went mad at last—and the reasons given for his madness are as many and varied as the people who tell the story—and hanged himself in the cupola of his house on Grosvenor Avenue, where his last sight would have been of the city below him. His house now belongs to the city's most influential judge, who does not welcome sightseers.

The Three Oaks Cemetery, though sadly neglected, has some of the country's finest examples of nineteenth-century funerary sculpture. The weeping angel on the tomb of Hester Lyall repays the effort it takes to climb the overgrown path, and the sad, somber dignity of the family group which marks the Addison graves is undiminished by the ivy which twines around their lower bodies. Some long-ago vandal made off with Mrs. Addison's head, and every St. Valentine's Day a posy of belladonna is left by persons unknown on the stump of her neck.

The city has one crematorium, which operates only at the dark of the moon, and what is done with the ashes it is better not to ask.

singing home the rooks and ravens

Sean stood at his dorm-room window, staring out at the quadrangle. Behind him on his desk, a poem lay abandoned in the middle of a line. He was thinking about Clair.

More and more frequently these days, as he tried to work on *The Stag of Candles*, he found himself thinking about Clair. Her delicate face, her Medusan eyes, came between him and the page, leaching the strength out of his words. He was aware that he was writing less, and what he wrote came harder, and, when it did come, it was feeble, thin, twisting restlessly away from what he wanted it to be.

It's Clair, he thought, and although his eyes were looking at the fountain in the quadrangle, mute and desiccated with the winter, and his hands were clenched white-knuckled on the window sill, in his mind he saw only her, felt the silkiness of her hair beneath his fingers. Somehow, in some way he could not describe or explain, he was losing his poetry to her.

He had felt this, uneasily, not quite consciously, for months; although he could not stay away from her for long, he had been trying to find ways to distract himself from Clair. He had even, in the extremity of his desperation, started going to open-mike nights at Café Xerxes. Everyone was tremendously impressed with his poems, and although he loathed himself for it, he could not help being flattered, gratified. One of them, hero-worship all over her face, had even made a shy, clumsy, stammering pass at him the week before. He had turned her down, but not unkindly. Bram Bennett was actually a pretty good songwriter, and she was a fierce little Goth; she made a good shield against the talentless and overwrought.

But no matter how he felt about them, their reaction was so different from Clair's, the difference between water and salt. Clair let him read his poems to her, the poems that awed the children at Café Xerxes, but her cold indifference was never shaken. And that hurt—it was the slow torture of the rack—but he also knew those poems weren't his best work. *The Stag of Candles* was stronger, stranger, unafraid. But he had shown that to no one.

And he couldn't stop thinking about Clair. I have to break her spell, he thought. I have to win free, face her as an equal.

There was an open-mike at Café Xerxes that night. Sean decided he would go and read, and if Bram Bennett was there, maybe he'd buy her a drink. And maybe, when *The Stag of Candles* was ready, he would give it to Clair to read.

dead leaves

The most notorious case of suicide off the Liliard Bridge is that of Mr. Horatio Prynne. On the night of Friday, November second, 1894, dressed in complete and impeccable evening wear, Horatio Prynne started across the Liliard Bridge from the west, stopped at the highest point of the bridge's arc, set down his cane, removed his hat and overcoat, and without visible distress or hesitation, stepped up to the parapet and leaped off. A cabman witnessed the event and summoned the police; when the body was at last recovered, at two a.m. on Saturday, November third, it was discovered that the deceased was wearing a money belt laden with silver dollars. There was no doubt that his death had been intentional.

As the Prynnes mourned, the police set about retracing Mr. Prynne's movements on the last day of his life. He had gone driving with his sister in the morning, and had seemed quite normal. He had lunched with friends, who likewise testified to his calmness and good-humor. He had then gone to visit his fiancée, Miss Lucasta Fremont, and had spent much of the afternoon walking with her in the gardens of the Fremont house on Grosvenor Avenue. Miss Fremont, though prostrated with grief, explained that she and Mr. Prynne had talked of their upcoming wedding and that she had told him details of her family history in which he had expressed an interest. Nothing had occurred to upset or alarm him, and he had left very much in his usual good spirits.

The Fremont butler remarked that Mr. Prynne had appeared to be in a great hurry.

At a quarter to five, he walked into the First Municipal Bank on Sheldon Avenue. The bank-teller testified that Mr. Prynne was "visibly agitated" and "very white about the eyes." He had withdrawn four hundred dollars from his account and had insisted that the money be given him in silver dollars. The teller counted out the money, and Mr. Prynne took it away.

That evening he attended the opera with his fiancée, his sister, and his cousin, Mr. Tobias Kingsley. Although Miss Fremont claimed to have noticed no difference in his attitude toward her, Miss Prynne and Mr. Kingsley agreed that he had seemed less attentive to Miss Fremont than usual, and both of them remembered wondering if the couple had quarreled. Mr. Kingsley further testified that on one occasion when Miss Fremont's hand brushed Mr. Prynne's shoulder, Mr. Prynne quite visibly flinched. Miss Prynne had not witnessed this awkward moment, and Miss Fremont explained that Mr. Prynne had apologized in the intermission, telling her that he, not expecting the accidental touch, had believed it to be a spider.

After the opera, the three agreed that Mr. Prynne had mentioned a headache and a desire for fresh air. He told them to return home and that he would take a cab when he was ready. No further witnesses to Mr. Prynne's actions could be found until he appeared at the west end of the Liliard Bridge at a quarter to midnight.

Horatio Prynne left no note, and the final verdict was suicide while temporarily unbalanced in his mind. The *Telegraph-Clarion* described his death as a great loss, both for the Prynnes and for the city, and a custom was established of leaving flowers at the spot from which he had leapt. This custom eroded with time and had ceased entirely by the end of World War II.

In 1896, Mr. Tobias Kingsley married Miss Lucasta Fremont. The wedding was small and private, but the guests remarked that both Mr. Kingsley and his new wife seemed radiantly happy. They honeymooned quietly in the Kingsleys' summer home on Lake Michigan. It was when they returned that Tobias Kingsley's slow decline began. He became quieter and more withdrawn even as his wife, blooming and vivacious, gained a reputation as a sparkling society hostess. Finally in 1905, he was committed to a private rest-home, where he quickly lapsed into catatonia, dying in 1910 at the age of forty-two. The last words he was known to have spoken were to his lifelong friend Mr. Barnaby Munroe, who visited him in the rest-home in the autumn of 1905.

Mr. Kingsley had not spoken to anyone for a week, and for some time he did not speak to Mr. Munroe, either. But finally, as the shadows were drawing down and Mr. Munroe was preparing to leave, Mr. Kingsley looked up at him and said, "Finally I understand poor Horry."

Only this and nothing more.

lying under the gallows-tree

The noctares brought Bram to a building she recognized; she had to cram her fist against her mouth to keep back a spasm of hysterical giggles. Of all the things she had expected to see in the underworld, the absurd Victorian gazebo from Lafayette Park had surely been last on the list. But there it sat, a debutante in an abattoir, looking self-conscious against a dark byzantine tangle of girders and pipes whose function Bram could not imagine.

Then she saw the figures waiting beneath the gazebo's arches, and her laughter withered and turned to dust in her mouth.

There were twelve of them, tall men robed in dark blood-red. As she came closer, she could see that they each wore the same mask, a stark, stylized face in unpainted white porcelain. The eyeholes of the masks were empty, but behind them she could see gears and cogwheels meshing and turning. She swallowed hard and stared at the steps of the gazebo to keep from being mesmerized by the endless spinning clockwork. The noctares let go of her arm, and when she looked around, it had vanished.

One of the twelve Clockwork Kings stepped forward and said, "I speak for all." Its voice was the voice of a clockwork mechanism, full of rust and oil, dust and dead spiders and fragments of macerated time. The other eleven bowed their heads and stepped back into the shadows of the gazebo, but she could still see slivers of light glinting off the moving clockwork in their eyes.

There was silence; unlike mortals, the Clockwork Kings did not shift or grumble or even breathe. Only the clockwork, ever moving, revolved and revolved, but it made no sound.

Bram licked her dry lips and said, "I'm looking for someone. Sean Lacroix."

"And what will you do when you have found him?" said the Clockwork King.

"I want …." She had to stop, wrench her gaze away again from the whirling gears. "I want to take him back with me. To the world."

"He is dead."

"There's ways around that, aren't there?" Bram said and flinched at her own boldness.

"A few. But why should we do this for you? Why is your love greater, your pain deeper, than that of any of the thousands of people grieving in the city above?"

"The train stopped for me," Bram said, knowing it was not enough.

"It stopped for your music, not your errand." One of the other Clockwork Kings made some tiny motion, a bare rustle of fabric, and the first said, "And yet you have answered our question. Play for us."

"Play for you?"

"Play for us. And if your music pleases us, we will let you talk to your friend, and you may take him back if it is what he wishes."

Hands shaking, barely daring to breathe, Bram took out her guitar, tuned it, and began to play. She played a song of her own, "Soaring Jilly," that she'd played often and always to generous applause. But the rapture that had possessed her on the Grandison Station platform was gone; she was aware that her playing was no more than adequate and her voice was thin and strained and tending to sharp, and the Clockwork Kings were watching her with their arms crossed. She began to imagine she could hear a clock ticking, and then to be sure that she really did, although she could not tell where the sound came from; she had only a limited amount of time to catch the Clockwork Kings' attention before they would dismiss her and her request, and she would have to go back to the world, to life, alone.

A strange thing happened then, and unlike the other events of that terrible night of wonders, it happened in Bram's head. The situation flipped upside down, and she realized that that ticking clock, imaginary or otherwise, was running every time she stepped up in front of an audience. There was always that narrow window of opportunity to make them care, make them listen, and, despite everything, this was no different. She straightened up, took a better breath, and vamped her way down from "Soaring Jilly" into the song of hers that Sean had always liked best, "Cast Shadows." And now she'd got to the place inside herself where she needed to be; the music opened up and let her in. She felt the difference, and she could tell that the Clockwork Kings felt it, too; they were listening now, not judging, and she knew she had won.

When she had finished, the Clockwork Kings bowed their heads gravely in thanks, and their speaker said, "Are you sure? Our kingdom holds other pleasures."

"I want Sean," Bram said.

Again the Clockwork Kings nodded, and they all said, with the single great voice of a tenor bell, "As you wish."

the starling's path

Regardless of what you may be told, there is no phantom in the city opera house.

corrosive kisses

It was a nightclub in a city where night never ended. The dance floor was packed with writhing, twisting, gyrating bodies which did not sweat and did not breathe. They were young men and women, beautiful in death, powerful because they did not live. They made way for Bram, separating as she came near, turning to stare at her with lightless, filmy eyes, like the dead girl in the train car. Bram asked for Sean, and they shook their heads and slipped away to other parts of the dance floor. She became aware of their scent, faint and sweet and reeking.

Finally, the twentieth or thirtieth or hundredth time she said, "I'm looking for Sean," the boy she had approached, a tall snake-sinuous blond with a livid rope-burn around his neck, nodded and pointed. There were alcoves along the walls, and in one of them, she now saw, there was a group of people dancing together, creating their own world of rhythm and sound.

"Thank you," she said, but the blond boy was already gone. Bram crossed to the alcove through the dancers, aware of their dead, empty gazes on her back. As she approached, the people dancing in the alcove felt her presence and turned. There were six of them, beautiful and dead: three girls, two boys, and the sixth was Sean, like a king in their midst. There was a tattoo across his chest that had never been there in life, the stylized mark of train tracks, and Bram felt suddenly cold and queasy.

"Sean?" she said, in a tiny voice.

"Bram?" Sean's eyes widened, but they weren't his eyes—not the rainwater gray eyes, full of light, that she had loved. The rest of Sean had become brighter, straighter, more beautiful, but his eyes had truly died These were dull gray stones, dry as drought-parched earth.

"It's me," Bram said. "I …I came to find you."

"You aren't dead." Sean and his cadre of dancers drew away from Bram a little, as if her vitality might be contagious.

"No. I …." But she had to say it; Sean would figure out the truth anyway. "A seraphic train stopped for me."

"Did it?" Sean said, with a bark of laughter as dead as he was. "And you came *here*? *Why*?"

"For you, Sean." Unnerved, scared, she rushed into speech. "The Clockwork Kings say you can come back. I played for them, and they agreed to it. You can come back with me."

The silence lasted until she realized that the throbbing, thrashing music was no longer playing. She turned around; the dancers were all standing still now, watching her with their dull, dead eyes.

She turned back to Sean. There was no joy on Sean's face, no relief, no gratitude. He was staring at her as if he had never seen her before.

"Sean?"

"What? Am I supposed to say thank you? Am I supposed to fall at your feet weeping with gratitude, a good little Eurydice? Has it occurred to you, Bram, that I might not *want* to go back?"

"You don't? But—"

"No. It's over, Bram. Clair doesn't love me—I realized that at last. And I'm not a poet. I'll never be one. There's nothing left up there for me except defeat and pain, and I don't want those."

She did not know who Clair was. "But, Sean …."

"What?" Sean said. He was smiling a little. Two of his cadre came up beside him, a girl on the left and a boy on the right. Snake-like, they twined their arms around his waist, and he put his arms across their shoulders.

Bram felt the anticlimax coming and could not help it. There was nothing else left for her to say. "I love you."

"Do you?" Sean said, without interest. "And why do you imagine that matters?"

It was a terrible echo of the Clockwork Kings' question. She said, "It's love. It has to matter. Sean, look, I know I'm not like you. I know I'm not really worth your while. I'm a poser, a wannabe, wearing black like it was peacock feathers. My name isn't even Bram. It's Michelle, all right? I don't know why the train stopped for me. It shouldn't have. It should have stopped for you. But I love you, and I came here to bring you back, and don't you even *care*?"

From all the dead dancers in the nightclub, there was a long, mocking round of applause. Bram stood still beneath it, her cheeks burning, stubbornly refusing to drop her gaze from Sean's face. And Sean looked back at her, with those murky gray eyes that were not his, and said, "Honestly, Bram—Michelle, if you like—no, I don't. Your love meant nothing to me when I was alive. It means even less to me now. Go back to the world, Bram. There's nothing for you here." He turned to the girl on his left and they kissed, open-mouthed, imitating passion they could no longer feel.

Bram flinched back, and Sean's cadre moved in between them, Sean's armor against life and risk; from somewhere, the music started again. Bram was left with no options, nothing to do except turn around and leave. She stumbled through the throng of young men and women, who would never age, never be ugly, never grow, never be able to open their hearts to anyone or anything. And even as they writhed and strutted, the dead dancers watched her all the way to the door.

why do you linger?

Sean climbed out the window of his old bedroom and scrambled onto the roof of the house; it was five to midnight, but the dark didn't bother him. Once on the roof, he opened his backpack and took out a flashlight and the battered manuscript of *The Stag of Candles*. Clair's scent was still on it, or perhaps that was just his memory of what she smelled like.

He stood, holding *The Stag of Candles* to his chest, and waited for the 11:59 train.

It howled past in a stink of oil and stale air. Midnight. Sean turned on the flashlight, folded the top page of the manuscript back against its binder clip, and again waited, like a captain's wife on her widow's walk, watching the sea for her husband's sails. When he heard the next train coming, the 12:20, he began to read in a hard, clear, angry voice.

Sean read a poem from *The Stag of Candles* for each train that passed. He kept his voice level and firm, although after about 1:45, he crouched down on the roof between trains and sobbed in choking whispers, clutching the manuscript to him like a hurt child.

At 3:12, a seraphic train screamed by. It did not stop, and the people inside did not even turn their heads. Sean scrubbed his eyes with one grimy hand and waited for the next train.

He read poems about the foundries, poems about the art museum and the coldly echoing rotunda of the public library. He read the poem about St. Christopher's, and another poem about his own confirmation and the angels that did not sing to him. He read poems about the interstate, about the city's storm drains, which were supposed to prevent floods but never quite did. He read a long poem in Spenserian stanzas about St. Catherine's. He had written a corona of eight poems, one for each of the city's eight public parks, and he read the corona to the trains, which were no more impressed than Clair had been. He read his sequence of sonnets about the river. Now, nearly 6 o'clock, he was no longer stopping between trains, just reading and reading from this bloated leviathan of a manuscript, which he had been working on in one form or another since he was fifteen.

At 6:39, a second seraphic train hurtled past; the roar of its passage sounded like mocking laughter. Tears were running down Sean's face, but he kept reading, embarked now on the long narrative poem about Sophia Walters, the early twentieth-century mystic who predicted the terrible fire of 1922 and died in it.

At 7:29, Sean read the last poem in *The Stag of Candles*, a villanelle dedicated to Clair. He stood on the roof, dry-eyed now, although his eyes and throat and nose were raw. It was over; there was nothing. He had been tested, and he had failed. The seraphic trains would not stop for him. His poetry was a bouquet of dead, rotting roses, a sickness, a canker, a stupid, self-indulgent delusion. There was no worth in him.

At 7:31, the sun rose.

At 7:32, the first daylight train passed the house at 2981 Lynn Street. Still clutching *The Stag of Candles* in a white-knuckled grip, Sean threw himself off the roof and onto the tracks just before the wheels of the train.

The pages of the manuscript flew free briefly and then were swallowed by the city, which would not mourn. *The Stag of Candles* became another sacrifice.

Lost in the city and never recovered.

the company of stone-eyed watchers

There are nine sundials in Lytton Park, each purchased and installed by the philanthropist W. W. Maddox, who died in 1920. By the terms of his will, there were to have been four more sundials installed, for a total of thirteen, but as the Maddox estate was immediately and inextricably mired in litigation between his second wife and his son, each contesting the inheritance of the other, this ambitious scheme was never brought to fruition. Both the son and the second wife accused their opponent of encouraging Maddox in his passion for sundials, which the son described as "morbid" and the second wife stigmatized as "unnatural," and as the Municipal Park Board confessed that in its heart of hearts it did not desire any more sundials, that clause of the will became part of the complicated evidence adduced by both sides to prove Maddox was not of sound mind, and was eventually, thankfully dropped.

If you acquire a map of Lytton Park and plot the positions of the sundials, you will see that they form an incomplete circle. The third sundial is set awkwardly into the side of a hill, and the sixth is buried in deep shade among a stand of cypress trees. You may begin to wonder whether Maddox's beneficence had some darker, ulterior motive, but if either the second wife or the son knew anything about that, they never said a word.

Not one of the nine sundials shows the correct time.

roses she gave me, and columbines

Bram Bennett returned to the mortal world on a seraphic train that was empty except for her and a man crouched in the corner, sobbing and sobbing. Looking at the two livid, bloodless wounds running from shoulder to waist on either side of his spine, she could understand why. It was all she could do not to join him.

The train stopped again at Grandison Station in the cool, serene darkness before dawn. Bram got out. No one had to tell her that the seraphic trains would never stop for her again. She knew it in the marrow of her bones and the beating caverns of her heart.

She stood on the platform, her guitar at her side, and wondered what to do. She supposed wearily that she could throw herself under the next train to come along, as she had originally planned, but that seemed stupid and futile; even this terrible spiny knot of pain, compounded of grief and humiliation and anger, was better than the mechanical frenzy of the pink neon nightclub.

She made her way along the platform to the stairs. She remembered that she had finished "Why Do You Linger?" in the night, and it was still in her head, raw, vital, imperfect—but complete. She could go write it down; maybe later, when the mute, stupid weight of grief had lessened, she could play it. But not at Café Xerxes. She would not go back there; it was as barren and futile as the nightclub, and she realized that that was why Sean had gone there: because it might be dead, but it was safe.

Somewhere dangerous, she thought, going down the stairs. Somewhere alive. Somewhere *new*.

The oak trees saluted her with their stark but living branches, black against the luminous sky. Suddenly, laughing, Bram raised her arms and saluted them in return.

reaching for your reflection

Clair stands in front of her picture window, gazing out across the night-bejeweled city. It is impossible to tell if she has posed herself deliberately, aware of the picture she creates, or if the angle of her raised arm, the geometry of her fingers against the curtain she holds back, the tilt of her head, the position of her feet, are merely accidental. And you would not dream of asking her.

In a moment Clair will turn away, turn back to you where you watch her from the long, low, white couch, but for now she stands, gazing out at the city which is more truly her beloved—her lover, master, servant, self—than any mortal who has ever touched her.

Love as an Unstable Isotope and Other Theories

"Love is an unstable isotope
with a half-life too short
for it to be useful,"
says the physicist,
staring into a single malt scotch.

The bartender offers her own theory:
Love as a flaming drink,
pretty for a minute and poof!
it goes dark.

The vacuum cleaner salesman
on the next stool says,
"You can knock on so many doors
and never find it at all, so
better enjoy it anyway."

—Laurel Winter

a convention of the dark fantastic
September 29–October 1, 2006
Holiday Inn Express, 1010 Bandana Blvd. W.
Bandana Square, St. Paul, MN

Guest of Honor: David G. Hartwell

MEMBERSHIP: $25 THROUGH LABOR DAY 2006 - $35 AT THE DOOR - $5 SUPPORTING/$25 CONVERTING
INFORMATION: ARCANA 36, P.O. BOX 8036, LAKE STREET STATION, MINNEAPOLIS, MN 55408
ERIC: 612-721-5959 - EHEIDEMAN@DHZONE.COM - WEBSITE: PAGES.PRODIGY.NET/REKAL (PAYPAL LINK ON SITE)

Here's one of Martha A. Hood's best stories so far. It's a real page-turner.

Missing Piece

by Martha A. Hood

For the better part of a minute, Dori hugged the side of the ravine. Perfectly balanced she was, and Amy could see that she was terrified, breathing only in shallow gasps.

Such a beautiful, warm day in the mountains. The breeze blew through the pine trees and broadcast their scent. But perhaps Dori was too frightened to notice.

Amy glanced at her cell phone, then back at Dori. She gave a little shrug.

A lizard darted out from under some brush, right next to Dori's face.

For three days after Dori's funeral, Amy thought she was free. When she awakened that third morning, it was to sunlight streaming in her window and the happy belief that Dori was gone.

After she used the toilet, she stood over the sink and brushed her teeth. The skylight above her head was cracked open, and the early morning atmospheric inversion layer carried the roar of trucks and diesels from miles away. As she reached for a hairbrush, she felt an unexpected wave of dizziness, enough to make her steady herself by leaning against the sink. She picked up the brush to run through her hair, and then she noticed: a portion of her head was missing.

She wasn't surprised. Dori had tormented her for twenty-four years; she wouldn't let go easily, even for death.

Amy explored the missing piece with her fingers, a jagged-edged chunk over her right eye. Baby-blond fuzz grew in the depression and blended into the darker blond of the rest of her head.

She heard Baby's toenails in the hallway. Baby, the poodle mix, Dori's dog, though really David's, now left in Amy's care.

Baby was in the bedroom now, barking like crazy. Amy hurried out of the bathroom. It was something in the corner, there, on the floor, in front of her dresser. At first, she thought it was a dead mouse with a long blond tail, but then she saw that it was the missing chunk of her head. She froze, fearing Baby would snatch it up and tear it to pieces, like he did his squeak toys. But the dog held back, heeding some innate caution.

Amy thought it curious that the piece of her head did not bleed, nor did it ooze, but looked as though it had been neatly cut with pinking shears. She felt certain that if she could get hold of it, it would fit right back in, like the missing piece of a puzzle.

She reached for it, but it hopped away.

Baby had stopped barking. Rather, he wagged his tail, he danced, and he panted happily, looking somewhere in the spaces between the dust motes for the unseen hand that had pulled the invisible string attached to the chunk of Amy's head.

Amy started to cry. "Damn it, Dori!" She tried again for the chunk of her head; this time, she was permitted to seize it.

Trembling, she faced the mirror. It fitted back perfectly into her head.

Amy started a new school in tenth grade. The first day, a girl sat next to her at lunch and introduced herself. "I'm new here, too," Dori told her. "What do you think of it?"

The two chatted for a few minutes about this and that. Dori looked a bit like Amy, at least in general terms. Both were blonde, and about the same height and weight. Amy's eyes were blue; Dori's, a bit greenish.

Dori asked, "Who do you like? Who do you think is cute?"

Amy said she hadn't picked anyone out, yet. But Dori seemed to know she was holding back. Amy had a sudden feeling of hollowness in her belly, as if she had not just eaten, as if her belly were being turned inside out. She broke into a cold sweat; she felt as though she'd throw up.

"Are you all right?" Dori asked.

Amy had an overwhelming desire to get away from this girl. "I'm fine."

"So tell me who you like."

Amy pointed to a brown-haired boy from her English class.

Dori grinned. "Do you want me to find out his name?"

"David," Amy said. "His name is David."

After patting her head back into place, Amy saw the time and nearly freaked—here she was the boss, and she was late for her first day back to work.

Melanie and Vicky welcomed her back. Vicky patted her on the arm and Melanie chattered about all that had happened in the week she'd been gone. The main thing was that everything was fine over at Dori's shop, a few miles away. Melanie had gone there twice. The manager and the other employees seemed to be willing to keep working to keep the place open for the time being.

They were an odd pair, her two employees. Melanie was middle-aged, twelve to fifteen years older than Amy. She was fussy, bossy, and talkative. Vicky was young, dark, and not talkative at all, bordering on sullen.

Melanie said, "You should take a vacation. Go lie in the sun on a tropical beach somewhere."

The suggestion hit her with force and produced an overwhelming longing she wasn't prepared to deal with. She covered it by saying, "I'd go crazy, just lying on a beach. I have to keep busy."

More like, she had to keep running.

Finally, she settled down in her tiny office, amid stacks of unshelved stock. She turned on her computer. Really, nothing had happened in the week she was gone. Sales of toys had been steady, and sales of books, with the expected boost from back-to-school reading lists from the local schools, were up. One of the new items, a soft toddler dice set, intended to teach numbers, had done surprisingly well, and even the beanbag toys were steady.

It was good to have competent help, and good to know she could go away for a short time without everything falling apart. Once again, the longing came over her. Now that Dori was gone, the possibility of freedom taunted and teased her.

She started to feel queasy. Her computer screen swam in front of her. Why the hell had she been thinking she was free? And the piece of her head had disappeared again; she knew it even before she touched the sickening-smooth, fuzz-covered depression in her skull. She broke out in a sweat; the air-conditioning had failed again, too. She scrambled to look for the missing piece of her head, on the desk, under the desk, in the boxes of books not yet shelved. Sweat dripped from her face and onto the cover of one of them.

She was elbow-deep in one box when Melanie interrupted her, saying, "I'll put these books out. While you were gone, I...." Melanie's eyes widened. She attempted some words that came out like the whimpering of a child. Then she took a deep breath, closed her eyes, and screamed.

Vicky came running in. Melanie moved to go, but Vicky grabbed her arm and held her. Both stared at her as if she were a sign of the end times. She needed to make this okay for them.

She called up her best this-is-to-be-expected voice. She told them that she, too, had suffered some injuries in the fall that had killed Dori, including an injury to the skull. She parted her hair and flipped it over, explaining that, earlier, her hair had covered up the hairless part. Her hair must have fallen back to its original part. She supposed she should wear a hat to cover it.

It was interesting to follow the effects of her story on them. At first, both were very tense and frightened. People never liked anomalies. They wanted them fixed or explained. What couldn't be fixed or explained, the brain tried to deny.

And so, she subtly altered the facts of what they'd seen, simply by explaining things away until no one had any true idea of what they actually saw or thought. As always, this ability of hers to misdirect both excited and appalled her.

Later in the day, when they had left and she had closed the door behind them, the air conditioning kicked on and blew into the near-naked depression in her head. In moments, she was wracked with chills. Teeth chattering, she hugged herself and returned to her desk and her screen.

And there was the piece of her head, sitting in her printer tray. She didn't even need a mirror to stick it back in.

Dori stuck to Amy like glue and everyone came to see them as best friends. More than one friend commented how much alike the girls were. Dori called Amy nightly to ask about schoolwork, went out for the same activities, and worked tirelessly to "help" her get closer to David. Amazingly, at the beginning of eleventh grade, David and Amy had several dates.

The first time she went out with him, she returned home to a ringing phone. It was Dori, asking for details about the date. Amy spent fifteen minutes trying not to give her any, fighting nausea and sweats.

And when she finally managed to get off the phone, her dad said, "Tell that girl not to call so late."

Amy told her mom about Dori, but it all sounded so weird, and the parts about being sick to her stomach and the headaches that had started sounded like something made up.

"High school is like living in a horrible small town," her mom said. "You can't even tie your shoes without everyone in the school noticing. It can be almost impossible to get away from someone without being extraordinarily rude." And she assured Amy she was nothing like Dori.

At her mom's suggestion, Amy tried to lose Dori by dropping her old activities and joining new ones. She tried the hiking club, worked on the school paper, and tried out for the girls' volleyball team. But, Dori made the volleyball team, too, and got on the school paper with her. Dori hated hiking, though, and when Amy persisted in it, Dori gave her stomach cramps on the morning of each of the club's major events.

After four dates, Amy stopped going out with David. She told him she wasn't ready to be in a relationship. The truth was, she loved David, but it was no good having him with Dori always around to ruin things.

After closing up, Amy drove the short distance to David's law office. She, Amy, was the executor of Dori's estate; David had drawn up the will.

He ushered her in, saying, "I'm sorry I didn't make it to the funeral. I...I just couldn't."

She took a chair across from his desk. A tank of tropical fish lent an air of tranquility to his office. A few stacks of files towered here and there, but otherwise the space was tidy. He seemed as though he was glad to see her. Or not sorry, anyway.

He still looked the same. Baby-faced, graying but still thick hair, and an easy, poised charm.

"It's okay you didn't go," Amy said.

He nodded, looking a bit uncomfortable. "So how are you? That whole thing must have been kind of...."

There was no word to describe how it had been, so they both let it drop.

"Out of curiosity, who came?"

"Most of her employees, her neighbors, me...there were about twenty of us."

"No family?"

She shook her head. "I tried to find her parents, but every number I had was an old one. Do you know where they are?"

He shook his head. "She told me that they had died."

Amy nodded. "While we were in college?"

He shrugged. "I guess so, although I'm not sure when it would have been."

Amy laughed. "I had no idea how successful her shop was. Certainly more so than mine. But you know Dori. Stealing my idea and then being more successful with it."

He stared down at his desk as if he was seeing an omen there.

"Are you all right?" she asked.

He looked up. "Dori caused a lot of turmoil. So did I, with the choices I made."

She was struck, as always, by how nice he was. A genuinely nice guy who never acted as though he was aware of how good-looking he was.

If Dori had never existed, how different their lives would have been! She had a vision of them, the two of them, in their house, happy together without Dori.

But the vision was making her feel sick. David's face blurred as her eyes teared up.

"My God, what just happened to your head?"

Her hand went for the depression in her skull. "It's Dori," she said. She blinked and looked around. "Don't worry. The piece is here somewhere." She leaned over his desk. All those papers. It could be underneath any of them. She checked the top of the low bookcase behind her. She knelt down and checked between the books on the shelves.

David leaned against her shoulder. "Don't worry about it." He went to a small cupboard in his credenza. He pulled out a baseball cap with an embroidered palm tree and the name of a resort above the bill. "If you pull it down a bit, it should cover the problem."

She let him adjust the cap on her head. "But I need to find it."

"Do you? Look, this has to be more illusion than reality, right? She can't really be taking away part of your head. It'll come back. See? You look fine." He framed her face in his hands, then dropped them to her shoulders. He put his arms around her and they kissed.

His manner had changed completely. At first he had been friendly, but not like an intimate, not like someone she had once been married to. When the chunk of her head went missing, he became hers again.

She pushed him away. If anything, David was weaker against Dori than she, and there was something very sick about all this.

He looked at her as though his very being depended on her.

She couldn't push him away a second time.

They didn't get around to talking about the estate until much later that day.

By her senior year, Amy was so bitterly tired of Dori's ability to get herself into everything Amy did that she withdrew from all extracurricular activities. Dori still called her a lot, wanted to study with her, and sometimes just showed up at her house. Amy avoided her as much as she could, and put up with her when she couldn't.

Amy's mom asked her about Dori's family. "There has to be something wrong there," she said.

Maybe, maybe not. Dori was an only child. Her parents didn't mix in very much with the community; no one really knew them.

During their senior year, Amy, Dori, and David all were accepted at a university about one hundred miles from their town. Amy, unbeknownst to Dori, was also accepted at a private school a couple thousand miles to the east.

Amy's afterglow lasted only a few minutes. "Oh, shit." She rolled over in David's bed and covered her eyes.

When she opened them, he was propped on an elbow, looking down at her.

"We can't do this," she told him. "Dori's here, with us."

"Don't be silly," he said. "Everything's okay. Your head's back to normal."

He held her and they talked a little about the estate. Dori had left everything to Amy. She asked him if he wanted Baby. "Yeah," he said, "I love that dog." He said he was hungry. He picked up the phone and called for pizza.

Such normal-seeming behavior. How easy, to be lulled.

An hour and a half later, they were still in bed, pizza, napkins, and hot pepper flakes spread out in front of them. Her misgivings returned. "She's here, David. I can feel her."

He tossed a half-eaten piece back in the box. "I can't bring myself to believe that."

"Believe me, if it weren't for Dori….." She eyed her clothes, in a pile by the bed. "Maybe I should go to another attorney."

"No!" He startled her. He lowered his tone. "We'll just have to keep it on a professional basis."

Easy enough to agree to. Not having sex in the future was one of those things people often promised themselves, even while still sitting in bed naked with the other person.

Amy went through her first two years of college free of Dori and without David. Her parents helped her by not giving out her phone number or any other details about how she could be reached. And Amy's mom, good mom that she was, took it upon herself to tell Dori that Amy thought it best that they "developed new friendships."

Then, around Christmastime her freshman year, David called her house. Amy was there. They chatted, but Amy was cool. She avoided giving him a number at school with the excuse that she would be moving after the winter break.

Dori didn't call during the school break, which both relieved and surprised Amy.

In January of her sophomore year, Amy's dad developed health problems—unexplained abdominal pain—which was diagnosed as pancreatic cancer. He died a few hours before Amy could make it home.

On the fourth day after Dori's funeral, Amy went to Dori's house and found a hat to wear to the shop. Dori was a hat person, as Amy was not. It was a cloche style, in a soft velvet. Amy hated wearing something of Dori's, but it was better than trying to buy one and hoping her forehead remained intact as she did so.

Melanie came in an hour after opening; it was Vicky's day off. Amy wished it were the other way around. Vicky could be counted on not to want to chat.

True to form, Melanie asked if Amy's "condition" had a name, because if she knew the name, they could look it up on the Internet and find out if there was anything that could be done.

Even if, Melanie said, the condition was hopeless, Amy could contact other sufferers for information and perhaps find a support group.

Now wouldn't that be fun.

Amy thanked her for her concern.

That afternoon, David surprised her in her driveway when she arrived home. He was holding a bag of takeout Thai. "I thought I could pick up Baby," he said, "if that's okay."

They came into her house, once their house, and Baby was beside himself with happiness to see David.

They played with the dog. They ate dinner, and talked a bit about the estate, setting up an estate sale of Dori's things, selling her house, and so forth. They cleared the table. Amy rinsed dishes; David threw the take-out containers away and put Baby out on the patio.

They headed for the bedroom.

She thought about reminding him they'd decided not to do this. She said nothing.

As she neared climax, she went weak and saw something like fireworks behind her eyes. She laughed and relaxed back into her pillow. She'd never had one like that before.

Then she felt her stomach drop. Dori was here.

David touched her head. "It happened again."

Her hand went to the depression in her head, brushing his hand away. "I don't even care about that. I care about her still being here. I killed her, David. That's why she's doing this."

A cloud passed over his face. "You said it was an accident." Daring her to say otherwise now.

"It was. I was surprised she wanted to go hiking with me. She did try to change my mind by making me sick, but it didn't work. Over the years, I've developed some resistance to her stomach afflictions."

"So she went."

"Yes. Bitching about it all the way. And it started off fine, an easy hike, only a couple miles along the edge of a ravine. But there was this one part where some boulders had fallen and they'd closed the trail. She wanted to turn around, but I refused. I kept going, and she followed. She slipped. She didn't fall all the way down at first. I could have tried to reach down and grab her hand. But I didn't."

"Could you have done that safely?"

She shrugged. "Maybe not."

"What did she do? Just hang there?"

"She didn't beg. She just looked at me. I think she knew I wasn't going to help. I tried my cell phone, but we were out of range."

He looked at his hands. "So, what happened next?"

"A lizard, of all things. A little one, just a few inches long, darted out from behind a rock. She freaked. She let go or her foot slipped, I don't know which. She fell."

He sat up straight and took on his lawyer demeanor. "You didn't plan this."

"Of course not."

"And, you would have put yourself in danger, if you'd tried to save her."

"But, if it had been anyone else, I would have tried. Anyone, whether I knew them or not." Amy shook her head. "When she fell, I was so glad. So happy. You cannot believe."

David said, "You're not a murderer. Put that out of your head right now." He got out of bed, and put on his shorts. She thought he might finish getting dressed and leave, but instead, she heard him go downstairs, open the sliding doors, and let Baby in from the patio. She heard him padding about in the kitchen. She went to see what he was doing.

He was making popcorn. Baby sat at his feet, tail wagging. David looked at the dog. "He's the only good thing Dori ever did for me."

Amy laughed. "She took him away from you when you split up."

David spilled the popped corn into a bowl. "Well, that's past us now."

"But we can't ignore the past."

"Yes, we can. Worrying about all that holds us back. Worry is a waste of time."

Her head was aching now. "I can't stop feeling that we're feeding her, by being together."

He shook his head. "You're feeding her by worrying about what she wants. You need to ignore her. That's what we both should have done from the beginning."

At the beginning of Amy's junior year, David and Dori both transferred to her school. She saw David in the Quad the first week; he told her Dori was there, too. For the next month, Amy skulked to and from her classes and wondered where she could go her senior year.

And damn, she liked this school. She didn't want to transfer.

She knew she was acting crazy. Her friends worried about her. She couldn't explain the problem, and that inability to explain made her feel cut off from everyone.

When she finally did run into Dori, it wasn't at school, but at a local coffee house hangout. And the meeting was thoroughly anti-climactic.

Dori was with people Amy didn't know. Waves, smiles, a "Nice to see you," and a "We should get together soon." A little later, Dori left with her friends.

No insinuation into her life, no exchange of phone numbers. And it stayed that way for a while.

Amy started running into David, on campus. She started talking to him. Then, in mid-November, David and Amy started going out.

Dori started "running into" them fairly often when they were out together, but she regarded them with nothing more proprietary than an indulgent smile. Once during that time, Dori told Amy about some of the girls David had dated at the other school, how popular he was. Dori shared that she herself had gone out with him a couple times.

The temptation to ask David about this was nearly overwhelming, but Amy had learned a few things and was determined not to let Dori push her buttons or jerk her chain. She learned not to react.

For a while, things were all right.

Five days after Dori's funeral, Vicky came up to her at the shop as they were closing. "I'm sorry, but I can't work here any more."

Amy didn't have to ask why. The girl was creeped-out by Amy, and by her sometimes-missing piece. "This is all a bit much for you, isn't it?" She touched her head lightly. "I understand."

Vicky reddened. "No. I mean..."

Amy stifled a smile. By her own account, the girl had been quite the Goth in high school and had the tattoos to prove it. Yet, she was scared silly. "Do you think you could finish out the week?" Amy gave her an apologetic wince. "It's okay if you can't."

Vicki nodded slowly, as if her head was being controlled by an amateur puppeteer. "Sure. I guess. I could handle that."

"Thanks. That would be such a help."

Poor girl. In her right-brained and *whatever* way, Vicki received data from the world around her and attempted to make sense of it, just like Melanie, just like everyone. She was doing her best mental gymnastics to accept the evidence of her own eyes. Amy said, "It's tough for me to accept, too."

A bit of the darkness lifted from Vicky. Perhaps she didn't need Amy's affliction to make sense; she only needed to know that Amy felt the same about it as she.

Amy smiled. "You guys have both been great to me. I don't know what I'd have done without you."

"Oh, it's okay." Vicky was still beet red. "I'm sorry." She seemed uncertain what she was apologizing for.

But Amy felt more weary than ever before. Dealing with Dori in death was worse than dealing with her in life. Whatever Amy was guilty of, she was now serving a life sentence.

Amy and David became engaged the middle of their senior year. They would be married the summer after graduation, and before David went to law school.

Dori seemed to take the news well, and actually kept a bit of distance for a while. She had a boyfriend or two. Then she inched closer to Amy, careful (as seen in retrospect) not to scare her prey.

They became friends. Close friends. Best friends.

Then, two weeks before the wedding, Amy's mother was killed in a single-car crash. Witnesses said she appeared to have lost consciousness before crashing into a retaining wall. An autopsy revealed a cerebral hemorrhage as the likely cause.

David and Amy considered postponing the wedding, but in the end, they decided to go ahead with a small civil service.

Dori, immensely supportive through the entire ordeal, stood at the altar with Amy as her maid of honor. And it was there, near the end of the ceremony, that Amy caught her eye, and a chill went up her spine, as she saw some need in Dori's eyes that terrified her.

On the seventh night after Dori's funeral, David appeared at Amy's house as usual, but she pushed him away when he tried to kiss her. "You loved her," she said.

He glanced at the stairway, which led to the bedroom, before saying, "No. I love *you*."

The sad thing was, she could see he was telling the truth. "You love me, but you're in thrall to Dori. You have been, from the beginning."

His face drained of color. He stepped back, and glared at her. Then he stepped forward and grabbed her by the elbows. "Let's get married again."

"That would be stupid." She took a deep, shaky breath. "She killed my parents and our babies, David. She's very powerful."

He said, "We'll make new babies."

Just like that. "But whose babies would they be?"

He frowned. "What are you talking about?"

"Dori's alive, inside me. Any babies we had would be hers as well as mine and yours." She paused while he took this in. "I'm done sharing with her, David. Sorry."

Dori stepped in, in the days following the wedding.

She helped at Amy's mother's house, sorting things, picking up mail, watering the lawn, organizing bills, legal papers, leftover wedding details, and so forth. She gave Amy space to grieve.

This was a new Dori, a Dori who gave instead of taking. Amy had to be grateful. She had to suppress any misgivings she had. She would not have survived otherwise.

Their neighbors and friends got used to seeing Dori with Amy, with David, with the both of them. It seemed—if not normal—acceptable. Okay. Nothing funny going on, just a dear family friend. And, from time to time, Dori would go off on her own. She had a series of boyfriends, though none of them lasted long. (But, every time a new one came along, Amy would hope.)

One day, Dori crossed an invisible line, but Amy couldn't say exactly when. It might have been the ski trip, when Dori's date cancelled at the last minute and Dori came anyway. It might have been when she arrived that first Christmas morning to open her presents with them. Or it might have been any one of several other occasions.

After two-and-a-half years of marriage, Amy became

pregnant. The three of them celebrated at their favorite restaurant with champagne for Dori and David, and imported mineral water for Amy. Sadly, only seven weeks into the pregnancy, Amy suffered a miscarriage.

On the ninth day after Dori's funeral, Amy came to consciousness sitting in bed. David was sitting in her bedroom chair fully dressed. She couldn't see out of her right eye.

"What happened?" She felt her head. The piece was missing.

"Amy? Is that you?"

"Who else would it be?" But as soon as she asked, she knew. "I can't remember anything after about three o'clock this afternoon."

"It happened at work. You fainted. Melanie brought you around. When you could answer her, you were no longer yourself. You scared her so much she called me instead of 911."

His tone of voice put her off. "You make it sound like it's my fault."

"You overcame those stomach cramps you used to have. Can't you handle this?"

She threw up her hands. "What do you want me to do?"

"Maybe if you played along a little, give her a bit of what she needs."

They'd had this conversation toward the end of their marriage. "And what, exactly, does Dori need, David?"

"She's lonely. She's hurting. She feels betrayed by you."

"She ruined my life."

"And she's left you a small fortune. After taxes, it works out to about one-point-four million."

"But she's inhabiting my body, so she really left it to herself." Amy pulled the covers up around her neck.

He rubbed his eyes and sighed as if trying to summon more patience. "Okay, if that's the way you feel. I'm only trying to find a future for us." He put up his hands. "You have some other agenda, I guess."

After he left, she noticed the stickiness between her legs. He'd had sex with her when she'd been Dori.

Amy had another miscarriage two years later. And, when Amy, Dori, and David were all thirty years old, Dori and David began an affair. Amy was unaware of it for almost two years. She then had one more miscarriage, right after finding out about David's and Dori's relationship. David and Amy divorced; David and Dori moved in together. They only stayed together a year.

The next morning, the tenth day, she left a message for David to let him know she wanted to sell her business, as well as Dori's. Then she called Melanie, said she wasn't feeling well, and asked her to go ahead and open up the shop. Then she made herself a Bloody Mary and climbed back into bed. If she wasn't allowed a life, well, then, Dori couldn't have one either.

About six months after Dori and David broke up, Dori turned up at Amy's house. She cried and apologized for everything. She took responsibility for everything bad that had happened to Amy, including the broken marriage, the disastrous pregnancies, and the deaths of both her parents.

Put so baldly, it seemed preposterous. Amy heard herself reassuring Dori that she couldn't have been responsible for all those things. Dori smiled and said how lucky she was to have a friend like Amy.

She awakened, standing in the kitchen, melting butter for popcorn. It was dark outside. She was in her bathrobe, and the microwave clock read 10:59.

David touched her shoulder and looked at her. "Amy, is that you?"

She handed him the butter. Her right eye was all blurry again. "What are you doing here?"

"I got your message this morning."

"Yeah, so?"

"Then, half an hour later, I got another message telling me to leave everything alone."

"Right. So, was she pretending to be me, or did she at least have the guts to be herself?"

"She pretended to be you. But I recognized her. I decided to come over to talk to her."

Amy frowned. "What on earth is there to talk about?"

He hesitated and avoided her gaze. "Well, us. How we're going to work this out among the three of us."

She looked down at her robe. "And you've been negotiating with her all afternoon and evening?"

He tried to speak, but she waved him off. "I want you to leave."

"Your attitude," David said, "denies your part in her death."

"It was an accident. We agreed on that."

"What was your intention in letting her come out there with you?"

"How was I supposed to stop her?"

"You had a purpose in going out there. What was it?"

She touched her missing piece. "I keep trying to shake her off."

Shortly after apologizing to Amy, Dori opened a similar book and toyshop near Amy's. They dated some of the same men. Dori joined some of the same professional and civic organizations Amy belonged to. She saw the same movies, and exercised at the same gym. She even arranged to go on the same vacation package tours as Amy.

One or two people asked Amy how she could still be friendly with Dori, after all that had happened. She would start to say they weren't friends, really, but that sounded stupid, considering how much time they spent together. She said something instead about how much easier it was to try to be adult about these things and not to bear grudges.

But of course, she struggled to separate herself from Dori. What better way than to take up hiking again?

Amy came to in the middle of the following afternoon. She was at work; her head was down on her desk. Her right eye refused to focus. She put her hand to her head and found that her head was whole, but her hair had been cut short. She was wearing strange clothes. A long skirt with boots. Dori's look. She hated it.

Vicky was standing in the door of her office. "Do you still want me to reshelve these, even though they aren't going to fit?" she asked.

"Just a second." She got up to look. The shop was in the process of being rearranged. "No, that's okay." Then, "I think I need to go home."

The girl looked relieved.

When Amy dug for her car keys, she noticed a couple credit cards loose in the bottom of her purse.

Once home, she called the credit card companies. Dori had been busy. Clothing, haircut, clothes, even a plane ticket. Dori had booked herself a tropical vacation.

Fine. She called Vicky and Melanie, and told them that, due to her health, she was closing the shop and letting them go. She went to the bank and brought them each a cashier's check so generous they'd each have several months to look for work.

She awakened sprawled on her couch. David sat in the chair opposite her.

"What are you doing here?" she asked.

"You almost got arrested," he said. "Dori went over to Vicky's apartment and demanded the money back. She got pretty loud. A neighbor called the police."

"So, why wasn't I arrested?"

"Vicki refused to press charges. They wanted to send you to the hospital for observation. I convinced them to release you to me."

"Maybe a mental hospital would be for the best."

He went pale. "Don't say that." David's brother and father had both been institutionalized. "I couldn't do that to you."

Through her blurred vision, Amy looked forward to a future, unending, of this tug-of-war. She said, "I have to do something." And then she knew what. She grabbed her purse from the kitchen countertop and her sunglasses from the desk.

"Where are you going?"

"Hiking." She never looked back.

She drove—a bit too fast—toward the mountains. She had no idea how long Dori would stay out; it could be two or three hours or it could be longer.

Fortunately, it was mid-day, and traffic was light. She took more care when driving up the mountain; if she hoped to survive this, she must first reach the head of the trail in one piece.

Her running shoes were wrong for hiking. That might be good; that might not be good.

She found the turnout where the trail started. No other cars were parked there; that was good. She plunged into it. It was easy at first, wide, and flat until it narrowed deeper into the ravine. From there, the path grew steep and narrow. Once in a while, her foot slipped on the loose dirt. Once she tripped and fell to one knee. She stood, absently brushing at the scrape, barely noticing the blood.

She came to the makeshift barricade—two stakes and a chain. A hand-lettered sign told her the trail was closed. Beyond, a rockslide spilled across the trail. She stepped over the chain.

She edged over the spilled boulders until she reached a particularly difficult spot. She stopped, suddenly elated. She would simply stay here, clinging, until Dori awakened.

She noticed how many birds were singing. It seemed like years since birds had sung for her. She noticed how sweet the pine smell of the mountains was, and how refreshing the breeze was upon her face.

Her hands and her back grew tired, but she held on.

Dori's awakening came like a punch to the skull. Amy held onto consciousness only because Dori insisted.

Dori was scared shitless, and extremely pissed off. She was trapped. Then Amy saw what else there was to that overwhelming fear, that rage. Amy felt every bad feeling Dori had ever felt, every envy, every black pit of depression, every dreg of bitterness. Dori's feelings danced like demons on shoulders of her fear.

The great void of Dori's soul yawned before Amy.

Dori had no mother, no father, no sister, no brother. She had created herself from the missing pieces of Amy and others. A small core, from ages past, had rolled itself through a hundred lives to make her. But she burned those pieces like fuel, and wholeness eluded her. Even everything was not enough.

Amy fought with Dori for control of her fingers, hands, and arms. She wanted Dori's inner void to collapse on itself and suck all her pieces in with it. "You can't hang on to nothing forever," she gasped.

Amy/Dori let go.

Amy awakened in the dark, the whup-whup of a helicopter overhead. She had the sense of something missing. Dori. Dori was gone. Feebly, she raised a hand and waved to her rescuers above.

Eight months later, as proprietress of a bar at a popular tourist destination, Amy picked up a towel and started wiping some glasses.

A few big, tropical drops spattered the asphalt outside, the beginning of the afternoon's cloudburst. The bar was empty, the tourists all out playing, but it would fill up soon enough.

Through her one good eye, she saw a couple heading up the path. She turned to the scarlet macaw perched a few feet away. "Looks like the rush is starting early," she said to the bird.

"Howdy, Sailor," the macaw replied.

The couple inched their way closer and some sense caused Amy to put down her towel and watch them. Long before she could see the man's face clearly, she recognized his walk, his posture, his body movement.

It took him a bit longer to recognize her.

"I had no idea you were here," he said. "What a coincidence."

The young woman with him looked back and forth between them, from skull-shattered, hugely pregnant, one-eyed Amy, to David.

Introductions were made, awkwardly and quickly, as David's new bride—her name was something to do with plants, like Tansy or Pansy—was in desperate need of a clean restroom. She hurried off in the direction Amy pointed, but glanced back uncertainly at David as she did so.

He began with the obvious. "You're..." he said, and "It's not...."

She shook her head. "It's not yours. It's someone from here. Right after I arrived."

"Are you sure it's not mine? When was it we last...."

"It's not yours." She glanced in the direction his wife had gone. "It's just not."

He nodded, with a look of pain.

"It wasn't to be, David," she said.

"I know." He looked around the room. "So do you run this place, or...."

"I bought it when I came here," she said. "The old owner died. It was a surprisingly easy transaction."

"I'm glad this worked out for you," he said.

"Only because you didn't charge me for all the work you did."

"Oh, that wasn't anything." He frowned. "And the eye? Did they ever figure that out?"

She shook her head. "They couldn't figure out what was wrong, so they made up some nonsense about a benign cyst structure unrelated to my fall. There's no point in operating, because I'd lose the eye anyway. It's all milky and white, so I wear the patch."

"And your head?"

"I've got a steel plate in there." She touched the scarf on her head. "It actually looks pretty normal, but I couldn't resist the kerchief, the hoop earrings, or the parrot to go along with it all." She grinned. "At least I don't have a peg leg or a hook."

"I wish there were more I could have done," he said.

"David, you saved my life. You called the police when you guessed where I'd be. They got to me within minutes after the fall."

"It still seems like too little, too late."

"Don't be silly," she said, "I am happier than I've ever been, my entire life."

As Amy told him this, Tansy or Pansy returned. She looked from one to the other of them again, but recovered her poise and turned to the bird. "Is he friendly?"

Amy nodded. "Sure. Just put out your arm and he'll climb on."

"What's his name?"

"Sailor. He came with the place. I inherited him from the previous owner, who, the story goes, found him on a boat."

"Hi, Sailor," Tansy/Pansy said.

Sailor turned a reptilian eye to her proffered arm and climbed aboard. "Buy me a drink," he said.

David and his new wife stayed and drank rum concoctions until the bar started to fill up with the late afternoon crowd.

They left, and Amy suspected she would never see David again.

And that was just fine.

We're pleased to welcome Ellen Kuhfeld to our pages with this warm and witty look at the lifesytles of the Children of the Night.

Dances with Werewolves
by Ellen Kuhfeld

"My girlfriend says she's a werewolf, but I'm starting to wonder if she's not."

Len Scott smiled with the left half of his mouth. "This is a problem?" he said.

Paul Johnson shrugged. "I *like* werewolves." Len said nothing, so Paul continued. "I'm a rock-climber. I run marathons. I love the outdoors. It keeps me in good shape, makes me feel alive."

Len looked at the man sitting across his desk. He was perhaps thirty, strong and lean, tanned and vital. Handsome in a sun-beaten way. Definitely alive.

"There's nothing more alive than a werewolf under the full moon," Paul said. "That's only three nights a month, but it carries over. Most Weres live more intensely every day of the month. Why shouldn't I want to be around them?"

"There's the possibility of being eaten when the full moon rises."

"There's the possibility of falling from a cliff when I rock-climb, or getting eaten by a bear in the Boundary Waters. If I can have extreme sports, why not extreme friendship, or even extreme romance?"

Len spread his hands, and smiled with both sides of his mouth. "It's as good a reason as any. And I can see why you came to Scott and Scott. We specialize in the unusual.

"Before you hire us, we should discuss some details. Discretion, for instance. There's a lot of prejudice against Weres. Who can blame them for wanting to keep their double life a secret? I don't like to out a werewolf unless there's something pretty bad going on."

The left side of Len's mouth quirked upwards. "Otherwise, *I* could be eaten when the full moon rises."

"I can live with that," Paul said. "I just want to know if she's lying to me."

"Well, then. I'll assign my sister Lena to this. She's somewhat a creature of the night herself. Let's fill in the details…."

First Night of the Moon

Lena cruised her Miata down Flying Cloud Drive in the late-afternoon light, her short, sandy hair ruffling in the breeze. To the left were the lowlands of the Minnesota River, a haven for wildlife; to the right, sparsely-inhabited bluffs. The sun was almost to the horizon before her; in the rear-view mirror, she could see the moon rising. The air carried the scent of greenery and water. Birds sang their evening songs.

She turned onto an access road slanting up the bluff and rolled into a spot beside a black Corvette with white striping. The lot was almost full, normal for a Were bar at sunset. If Weres came later they'd be in their skins, not driving—especially the first night of the full moon. Werewolves and gasoline didn't mix well.

The Outlook was a stone building that hugged the sloping ground, with one story on the uphill side splitting into two on the downhill. There was a patio by the lower story. She crossed to the entrance, rust tulip skirt and cream blouse flowing in the evening breeze. A necklace of gold-tone Celtic beads swayed with her motion.

She waited inside the door for her eyes to adjust from sunset to dimness. She knew other eyes were looking; she was five-nine, with the build of a gymnast. Let them look.

The room was filled, and the air surprisingly clear for a bar. There was a nervous buzz of conversation. People were drifting towards the changing rooms on the upper level. One of the women looked very much like Paul's photo of Erica Schmidt. Between the stairs up was a third, down into an empty dining-room with

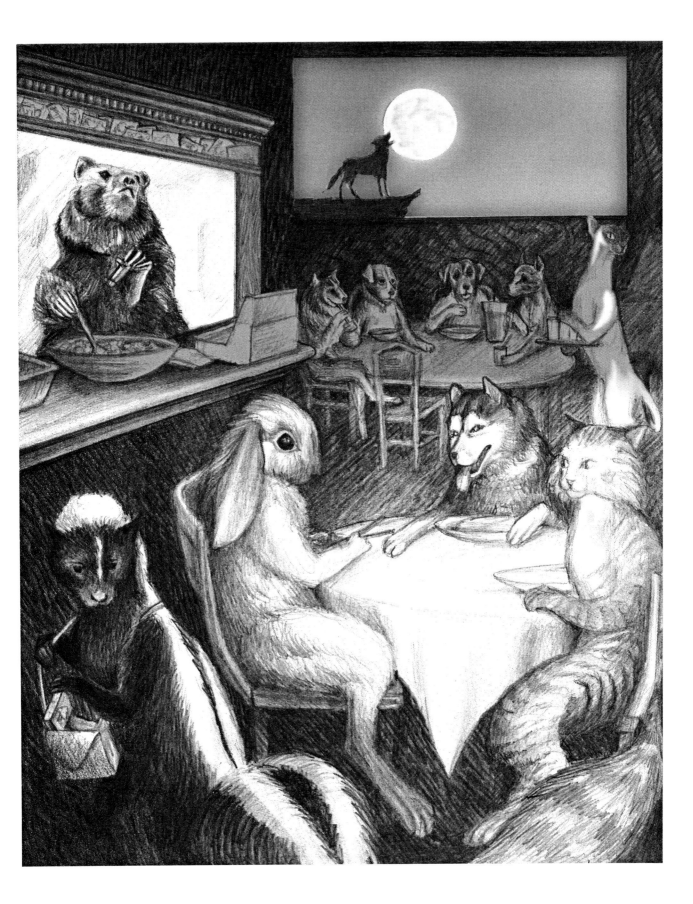

a window-wall looking out over the river gorge. Egrets were flying, sunset-red against dark waters in the evening light.

Lena went to the bar. She caught the attention of the bartender, an enormous shaggy man in a long brown tunic. *This must be the legendary Bjorn Njalsson*, she thought. "I'd like a hot beef bouillon, with a dash of Tabasco," she said.

As she sat sipping, the sound of feet and conversation diminished. Muffled growls came from the changing rooms. She squirmed uneasily on her barstool. Bjorn's arms and legs were shorter, his body longer, his head more massive. Her perceptions shifted; he'd become a bear.

He returned. "Haven't seen you here before," he said in a low, chuckling voice.

"I usually go to Hairy's," she said, "or the Townhouse. Club Metro before they closed. I'm relatively new to the scene."

"The Townhouse isn't a Were bar," Bjorn noted.

"I'm not exactly what you'd think of as Were," she said with humor in her eyes. "Consider me a fellow traveler."

Bjorn jerked his head to indicate the people still at the tables. In the dining room below, werewolves and werecats and a few other creatures were taking tables, basking in moonglow slanting in through the window-wall. There was the faint click-and-scratch of claws, an occasional screech or growl, and purrs and yips of happiness as friends greeted each other.

"You're still the same person that came in the door," Bjorn noted.

She sipped her drink. "You can never step twice into the same river, my friend. You of all people should know that 'same' is a relative word."

Bjorn shook his head in puzzlement, and reached under the bar for a bowl of raspberries. "The harvest is in," he said as he scooped a pawful into his mouth. "Care for some berries?"

She took one, popped it in her mouth, savored it. A drop of juice glistened on her lower lip. "One thing about an omnivore," she said, smiling. "You can satisfy your primal hungers without killing something."

Bjorn took another pawful, then bit into a honeycomb. "Amen!" he growled. "I see you *do* know a few things." And he shambled down the bar to another customer.

Lena finished her bouillon, then caught Bjorn's eye. "Any chance of getting a bowl of those berries? With cream?"

He brought them. She paid, and moved over to a table with a better view of the dining-room below. Erica had gone into the women's changing room. She hadn't come out, so she was probably downstairs. Erica had looked to weigh about one-forty; Lena watched the Weres below, making quick estimates of weight.

Coming up the stairs was one of the most beautiful Weres Lena had ever seen—a mist-grey Angora rabbit, carrying a salad plate. She came over to Lena's table, and gestured to a chair.

"Mind if I join you? I'm uncomfortable in a dining room full of werewolves. They eat too vigorously."

"My name's Lena. Sit and be welcome, but don't let the berries fool you: I'm an omnivore myself." Lena added, "No offense, but a were-*rabbit*? I didn't know there were any of you."

"Rabbits bite, if you startle them. Just my luck to have a pet with the virus. I've half a mind to bite her back and see how she likes being one of the Wee Folk three nights a month. But that'd cause more trouble than it's worth."

She picked up a carrot, held it, waggled her brows. "Ehhh, *crunch* what's up, doc? Call me Bugs. It reminds the wolves I'm not a safe rabbit to chase."

Lena looked at Bugs' front teeth, and agreed. They giggled. Bugs fed Lena a cherry tomato; Lena fed Bugs some raspberries. They bought a pitcher of V8 juice, and sat happily talking of shoes and ships and sealing-wax, of cabbages and kings; and what the Weres do late at night, and other curious things.

The evening passed pleasantly. Quite a few of the regulars came casually by to look at the newcomer, which suited Lena—she could look them over herself. Two of Bugs' friends sat with them a while—Mao, a were-Siamese, and Judy, a were-husky. Bugs and Mao were both about one-forty. Judy weighed at least two hundred, and definitely wasn't a candidate for *this* investigation.

Karaoke started, with Judy singing "Werewolves of London". Mao and two other werecats harmonized on a few pieces from "Cats". And Lena was in full retreat when a were-poodle started in on "How Much is that Doggie in the Window?" accompanied by yelps from the audience.

As she drove home, the moon rode high; to the right, the river glistened. The howls of moonstruck Weres came faintly from below. Lena thought of the evening. There'd been dozens of Weres, almost as many normals. Erica hadn't been seen—as Erica—after sunset. If she hadn't left unseen for the wildlands below, Bugs and Mao seemed the best candidates for Erica's other life.

She needed more information.

It was just short of midnight, and Paul had said she could call until then. She pulled into an overlook, took out her cell phone. She dialed.

Second Night of the Moon

At sundown, Lena pulled into the Outlook's lot. She walked to the entrance in the fading light. Inside she stood a moment, searching the room, then headed towards a table where a tanned man in white shirt and Dockers was waving.

Paul saw a tall woman at the door, with sandy hair in a short pageboy, and freckles. She wore a gold linen sleeveless blouse with umber slacks and canvas flats. She looked very much like Len: almost certainly, his sister Lena. He waved.

She moved towards him, growing more beautiful with each step. A slight stumble spoiled the magic, but Paul only found that, too, charming. She reached the table, held out her hand. "Paul Johnson?" she said in a rich contralto, the voice he'd heard on the phone last night.

"And you must be Lena Scott. You *do* look like your brother, though you're certainly the more elegant dresser." He hadn't taken his eyes off her for a second.

"I seem to have arrived just at the witching hour," she said as she sat. "Bjorn changed while I was crossing the room." They looked towards the bar, and a bear stood where a man had been moments ago.

"This is good timing. The dining room is just opening; let's get a table," she continued. "That'll give us a better view of the patrons."

As they went down the stairs, she thought, *and it'll give you a bit of an education.* Last night Paul had shown less familiarity with Weres and with Erica than she'd expected. He hadn't even known if she kept a pet. And hadn't known why the question was important. "Have you eaten at a Were bar before?"

"I've eaten here a few times," Paul replied. "Never at the full moon, though."

Lena chose a table for two where she could see Bjorn at the bar, and he could see her. "This table," she said as she sat. Paul sat across from her.

The room was mostly empty. There was a woman in a green-and-gold running suit at a table on the patio, chatting amiably with a skunk. Moonlight and dim fixtures lit the room, and the windows to the south looked past trees to the river. Lights moved along the highway on the far side. Now the doors from the changing rooms were opening, and Weres began to spill down the stairs into the dining room.

The room overfilled, as if dozens of hyperactive teenagers had entered—teens wearing fur suits, armed with fangs and claws. Rough-housing on the men's side turned into a scuffle, two werewolves rolling over and over on the floor, snapping at each other. Again, there were yelps and purrs of welcome; and the scuffling wolves untangled themselves before they reached the center of the room.

"I don't think they want Bjorn to see them tussling," Lena said. "It's his bar, and his tables they might knock over. Even a werewolf would rather not be disciplined by a were-bear."

A waiter was at their table—a human. *Yes,* Lena thought, *hands have their place.* She glanced quickly at the menu. "I'll have the buffaloburger, and a glass of spicy V8 with a celery stick."

"Steak tartare," Paul said, "and a stein of Beck's Dark."

"I'm sorry, sir. We don't serve alcohol during the full moon." The waiter didn't look particularly sorry. "Would you care for a non-alcoholic beer?"

Paul shook his head. "I'll have coffee."

The waiter left. Lena raised an eyebrow. "Alcohol isn't safe at a Were bar during the full moon. Poor impulse control, this time of the month? Bad idea." She folded her arms before her on the table. "Did you see Erica here?"

Paul leaned towards her. "Yes, but I don't think she saw me. She went up into the changing room about the same time as everybody else."

Over Paul's shoulder, Lena could see Bugs and Judy talking with the skunk and the woman in green. Bugs looked up at the same time, and saw Lena. She started to smile, then saw Paul and turned away. Judy hurried after her.

"If you saw her going into the changing room, she's almost certainly a Were," Lena said. "That's not a safe time and place for normal humans."

"Yes, but she said 'werewolf'. I want to be sure."

"Silly," Lena said as she shook her head. Amber earrings flashed in the moonlight. "There's probably not a single true werewolf here. You're dreaming the impossible dream."

"If werewolves are so rare, who's in this room with us?"

"Were-dogs, mostly. Where are you going to find a wolf to bite you? Dogs and cats, easy. Rabbits, even. And there's a skunk over there. You wouldn't want to meet a genuine werewolf. Dogs get along with people much better than wolves do. They like to be called 'werewolf'. But that doesn't make it so."

Paul looked as if Lena had taken away his toy.

Waiters began arriving with food: joints and chops and steaks and turkey-legs, mostly raw, and sushi. One werewolf, dancing with impatience, snatched his steak before the waiter had set down the plate, began tearing at it. There were growls and snarls and gulping sounds, and Weres glancing sidelong at each other. The copper smell of blood filled the air.

"Where's our food?" Paul said after a while. "We ordered first."

"*Our* food has to be prepared," Lena said. *"Their* food only had to be warmed to blood heat." Paul looked stricken. "And you don't want a Were getting impatient for dinner."

"Oh dear," Paul said. The waiter placed steak tartare before him. He looked at it cautiously.

"It won't bite you," Lena said. "You're supposed to bite it." She took a healthy chunk from her burger, and washed it down with V8. She wiped red from the corner of her mouth. There were crunching sounds from the next table.

Paul gulped, stood, and headed for the exit. Lena threw a fifty on the table, and followed. She caught Bjorn's eye as she passed the bar, pointed to her table. "We'll settle the details later!"

Paul was in the parking lot, standing by a low-rider Cruiser. Lena hurried up to him, saw the distress on his face, saw the reason the car was riding so low. Its tires were shredded.

She caught his arm. "Tooth-marks. Bet those tires tasted awful, too. Somebody must be *angry.* And only *your* car is damaged. This is not a good place to be." She began pulling him back towards the Outlook.

Bjorn met them at the door. "Can't take it inside, don't like it outside?" Paul glared. Lena stood between them. "Bjorn, somebody chewed Paul's tires. It's not safe for him out here. We need your protection."

"Like hell we do," Paul growled. He spun on his foot and began walking away.

"He's a damn fool," Bjorn said. "Anybody who doesn't know when to be scared shouldn't hang around Were bars."

"He's the damn fool that's paying me," Lena said. "I'd better talk some sense into him." She ran after Paul.

"Hold up," she cried. "We're getting further from my car every minute." But he continued towards the main highway. Behind her there was a rustle in the bushes, and a soft growl.

"Freeze, Paul! Don't do anything that makes you look like prey. There's a werewolf in the bushes."

A flash of motion, a gleam of white teeth, and Judy was bounding past Lena towards Paul. Lena leaned, reached, grabbed Judy by the hindleg; swooped her up into a whirl, spun three times, picking up speed and motion as she danced across the lot, then threw her in the air down the bluff. Lena ran towards Paul.

"Now run! Fast!"

There was a ruined old house nearby, with the fieldstone fireplace and chimney still standing. Paul headed for the chimney, began to climb. Lena raced after him, climbed behind him. They reached the top at the same instant. It was barely large enough for both of them.

"I didn't know you were a rock-climber," Paul said.

"I got the urge to try about half a minute ago."

Judy came loping up the road, began clumsily trying to climb the chimney towards them. She was growling low in her throat.

Lena took a small canister from her purse. She showed it to the werewolf. "Pepper spray," she said. "Your nose is a hundred times more sensitive than mine. It'd be embarrassing, getting done in by a vegetable extract."

Her eyes on the spray, tail quivering furiously, Judy began to back down. In the distance, Lena saw Bjorn heading towards them. The moon shone serenely; a nighthawk made its breathy, whistling sound. Judy bounded into the brush, disappeared in shadows.

They made their way down the chimney, and Bjorn escorted them back to Lena's car. "I'll send a wrecker for my car," Paul said to Bjorn as they left. "Tomorrow, in daylight."

Lena drove with a lead foot until they were several miles from the Outlook, then slowed. "We're in trouble with the Weres," she said. "I hope it's a hissy-fit instead of something more permanent."

"What did we do?"

"You ordered raw meat, then didn't eat it. That says 'wannabe' to a lot of Weres. And I should have realized Erica—or her friends—might think you were two-timing her if they saw us together. Or, just maybe, they realized you were having her investigated."

Lena gripped the steering wheel, looked at Paul from below lowered brows. "Tonight, and tomorrow night, you stay locked up at home. I'm going back to mend fences."

Third Night of the Moon

Lena wore running shoes, sweats, and no jewelry. It was half an hour to sunset. On the third night of the moon, that would give her an hour and a half to talk before everybody went Were. And freedom of movement, just in case.

With the sun still in the sky, The Outlook was quiet. Bjorn was behind the bar preparing for the night, and serving the occasional early-comers. Lena chose a quiet spot, sat down, and waited.

Bjorn came over. "You put down a fifty, but the tab only came to thirty-four."

"Keep the rest," Lena said. "We gave you enough

trouble last night."

"Maybe, but I should apologize too. I didn't realize somebody'd chewed up your boyfriend's tires. I don't run that kind of bar."

"He's not my boyfriend. He's a business associate. But that's something I should talk with Bugs about, I think. Is she angry? And what about Judy?"

"Don't worry about Judy. She was talking half the night about that throw you handed her. 'Almost as good as the Slingshot at the State Fair,' she said."

"It's amazing what a girl will do under the moon, in the passion of the moment." Lena smiled in the dimness.

"You'll have to explain that to me some time, if you get to be a regular here." Bjorn paused and sniffed the air, then looked thoughtful. "I might have a few suspicions, though."

"And you might be right," Lena said as she marked a score in the air with her forefinger. "And Bugs might have a few other suspicions, and she might be wrong. Think it'll be okay for me to stay and talk with her, if she comes in?"

"I don't see any problems. Not if you have a good line of talk, anyway."

"I intend to speak softly, and carry a big bowl of raspberries. Can I get a bowl of raspberries and cream, say half an hour before moonrise? And some carrots?"

"Sure."

When Erica came into the bar, Lena was at the same table she'd met Bugs at. Almost everybody had been stopping by to say hello to the woman who'd thrown Judy, and Lena had been smiling and greeting them all; when Erica passed, Lena did exactly the same to her.

By moonrise, Lena was no longer a newcomer to the Outlook.

Five minutes later, Bugs joined her. She flipped her paw at the carrots. "Looks like an invitation to talk," she said.

"We need to. There was a rather spectacular misunderstanding last night, and you and I seem to have been near the center of it."

"Moi?" Bugs said.

"Paul's tires looked like the Giant Rat of Sumatra was chewing on them. That, or somebody else with gnawing teeth."

"The two-timing rat seemed to *own* the car, not gnaw the tires."

"Actually, Paul's sin wasn't two-timing, but hiring an investigator. To find out if one Erica Schmidt is really a werewolf as advertised. I'm the investigator."

Bugs whopped herself upside the head. "Fleas are enough of a worry this time of the month, now I've got investigators too?"

"He hired me knowing I was discreet," Lena said. "And he obviously doesn't know what he's getting into. So I'll tell him only that Erica is indeed Were, and that the denizens of the Outlook are werewolves by common nomenclature—but none are true werewolves. Erica, and Paul, can take it from there."

Bugs lifted a carrot. "Ehhhhh, **crunch**—he's in for an interesting time…."

"It will probably give him a few grey hares," Lena agreed.

Judy came over to join them. "Looks like you two have made up. I'm sorry I made such a fuss last night. Bugs is a *very* good friend, and I didn't like seeing her hurt. But you handed me quite a surprise!"

"Poor impulse control," they chorused in unison.

They talked for a while longer, then Lena noted that it was time for her to be off. "Reports to give, checks to collect, things like that. Maybe teach Werewolf Etiquette 101 to Paul. I'll be seeing you both, later." She rose, and left.

In half an hour, she was at Paul's door. He let her in, motioned her to a chair. The room was unpretentious and comfortable, with photos of trails and rock formations. A sturdy end table sat next to the chair, and a good reading light.

"I smoothed things over," she began. "Erica thought you were two-timing her. That wolf last night was one of her friends, angry on her behalf.

"Erica *is* Were. But she said 'werewolf' because that's the generic. She's not a wolf, and would rather know you better before she has you meet her other half. You'd be safe, with her."

Paul wrote a check for fees and expenses, then sighed. "I didn't get my Beck's Dark last night. I think I'll have one now."

"I'll take a Bloody Mary, if you have the makings." Why *not* have a drink? It had been a tense evening.

Going into the kitchen Paul moved well, with coordination and control and a spring in his step. Lena was noticing he was a very attractive man. The refrigerator door opened and closed. She heard liquids being poured and stirred. Paul returned with a stein of dark beer, and a Bloody Mary in a tall glass. He'd even remembered the celery stick. Lena took the glass with a smile.

"You didn't seem as familiar with a Were bar as I'd expect from somebody who likes werewolves," she said after her first drink.

He dimpled, and sipped his beer. "I hardly thought of werewolves until two months ago when I started dating Erica. But when I asked her to a concert a month ago—last full moon—she said all her full moons were taken, and told me why."

"A month is awfully fast to get *that* interested in Weres."

"I get enthusiastic. It fits nicely alongside a werewolf's impulsiveness." Paul shrugged.

Lena drank, then nibbled her celery. "So why did you decide she might not be Were? Enough to pay to find out?"

"Well, I wanted to go out with her during the moon. And she was evasive. I began to wonder."

"Not only enthusiastic, but impatient?"

Lena was beginning to feel warm, warmer than the alcohol, or even the Tabasco, in her drink could explain. She looked at Paul. They'd shared danger the night before—and he'd been a damnfool to get into it, but he'd handled himself well when it counted. She remembered their eyes meeting at the top of the chimney.

Their eyes met. They were silent.

Their bodies met halfway between their chairs, and Lena didn't have the slightest idea who'd made the first move. *Darn that poor impulse control!* They kissed, long and firmly. His left hand cradled her head; she kneaded the muscles in his back. She paused for a breath, then dove back in. And four urgent hands began to misbehave.

He lifted her up, and carried her into the bedroom.

The Morning After

Paul woke slowly, languidly, to the sun glowing through the curtains. He was nude; and beside him, Lena slept on. He studied her face, thought of the night just past. Tenderly, his hand reached out to brush her cheek.

Stubble.

Green eyes opened sleepily at his touch, looked at him, smiled apologetically. "I was bitten by a woman," she said in a tenor voice.

Paul's mind whirled as his world took a new shape. "You're *Len!*" he said, backing away.

"Only since moonset," Len said with a wry grin. "For which you should be thankful. Imagine how complicated it would have been if I'd changed at midnight, like Cinderella."

"But dammit…" Paul said, "…you were Lena *before* all the other Weres changed!"

"Oh, *I* change at moonrise and moonset," Len said. "But nobody bit my clothes. Don't *you* dress ahead of time for whatever *you* expect to be doing? And you said it yourself about werewolves—-" Len's body-language and posture shifted. His voice went contralto. It was as if Lena were back.

"You can see a bit of wolf in them all month long."

neptune can't save you either

there is a sea creature who is impregnated and trapped by its mate in a den too far from even a hungry predator to be lured by its shrieking as its unborn offspring eat her from the inside out and are birthed when there is nothing left to hold them in for just a shell remains

my mother says she relates

—**durenda**

Mark Rich writes, "This is a monster story." We agree.

Beer Can Medusa

by Mark Rich

"A hoax," Harry Jones said. "They don't spend all that money for putting us on, honey."

Stephanie Jones never stopped calling Harry that: "honey," even though he was anything but. Since 1971, at least.

"What the hell kind of name is Soyuz, anyway."

"Russian."

A few days old but still being run on TV, the pictures showed Apollo astronauts and cosmonauts greeting each other. Harry had the volume low.

"Never happened."

"The doorbell," said Stephanie.

Harry straightened his slacks as he stood up from the davenport, glancing at the mirror over the mantle: dusty-road colored hair parted to one side, and rusted-nail eyes.

He laughed, a little. She knew the laugh. She turned from the counter, wiping her hands on her white apron.

In the morning she had ironed and put on a nice blue cotton dress. She felt good in this dress. She knew of no other reason to put it on. She had woken up in the guest room and peered out the curtains and saw the colors of a dream still clinging to the trees in the yard. The colors even clung to her black curls, when she looked in the mirror, for a moment. When she pulled the dress from the closet and started ironing, she looked at her hands. Not old hands, she thought.

"It's my birthday," Harry said, almost at the door.

Interference lines danced across the television screen.

"Hi, Cilla," said Harry at the front door.

A young, hushed, high voice answered.

"Hey, Stephanie," Harry said, coming back into view. The girl walked in behind him, with straight brunette hair, nice jeans, a pullover blouse. "Priscilla Grove. You know her, don't you. Well, what do you know but she's interested in coins. Isn't that right, Cilla. Heard about my collection and wants to see it. That's really something. We'll go on upstairs. Why don't you stay for supper then, Cilla. Stephanie, it isn't any problem, is it. I know you've made plenty for three. Always do."

The girl followed Stephanie's husband upstairs.

Stephanie turned back to the stove. Cilla could hardly be more than fifteen, sixteen: daughter of Nancy Grove, the first woman Harry brought home. When the two of them, Harry and Nancy, walked in the door in '71, Steph felt her head squeezing down until her thoughts could find no room inside any more.

Nancy and Harry sat in front of the TV hardly an hour before getting thick on the couch, while Stephanie Jones waited in the kitchen. She could hardly go out into the living room where the lovers were making out. Darkness pushed against the windows and stopped her from leaving by the back door. She found one thing she could do. She could wash dishes. She washed the ones that needed it. Then she took down dishes from the dusty top shelves to wash. She took out the silver service and worked away at tarnish hardly even there. She polished glasses. Midnight passed before she finished. Nancy had gone home.

She knew Nancy in high school. Even though Steph had been born in '46, and Nancy Goodwall in '44, they graduated only a year apart. Nancy had looked nothing special, though she hung around in her junior year with Jimmy Grove, Mr. Hot Stuff on the football team, and then married him the next year before graduation, pregnant with Cilla. A freak accident at the wheel shop put Jimmy in traction and then a wheelchair. Nancy found various men afterwards. Finally Harry. Harry was just finding out something about himself and what he could do, and was trying it out that night on Mrs. Grove and

Mrs. Jones.

Lines on the TV screen.

Stephanie could keep going in the kitchen. Her safe place. The lovers ate and went to a movie or Koop's Bar. Wives talked about Koop's over chain-link fences and formica table tops. Koops, where married men met their girlfriends. So they said.

She had been sleeping in the guest room for four years. She could be there and in the kitchen. Sometimes she could sit on the back porch holding a cigarette, burning her fingertips and forgetting where she lived.

The water boiled, jumping against the sides. She put in eggs first. When they were done she would put in potatoes. Her mother cooked eggs and potatoes in the same water during the Dustbowl, something Stephanie picked up. Mom had been a sweetheart, devoted to Dad. Talked so much about him Steph grew up almost knowing him, even though he died when she was tiny.

She peeled potatoes, three of them, cut out the eyes, then cleaned the counter. She had forgotten the bread rising in the oven. It had risen too high already and was slumping into itself with an exhausted look. It would never turn out right, now, although she would bake it anyway out of hopes. She kneaded it, greased two pans, and divided the dough. She set a timer to remind her when to turn on the oven. Cake could go in the same time, and come out when the bread crust was setting hard. Rummaging through the cabinet she pondered the selections. She had three mixes. She forgot to ask Harry what flavor he wanted. What kind had he had last year? Nancy, Cilla's mother, had been here for Harry's birthday two years ago. Vanilla. Last year, though, what flavor had it been? She would have to guess.

Taking the cake out she heard the footsteps upstairs. The bread would need an extra ten minutes. Not that the ten minutes would matter. The loaves had barely risen. The yeast had died. She was cooking pavers fit for the bed of the street. She looked out the kitchen door and saw Cilla on the stairs with a blank look on her face. Steph hated the blank look Harry could put on a girl. It made the girl look so useless. Steph knew no girl was useless even if Harry could do such a thing as to make it seem so.

A few steps behind Cilla, Steph's husband came down the steps looking tall and handsome for his years, wearing a new shirt. He was celebrating his birthday, on July 28, 1975, in this house in Pinville, Kansas. Harry Jones was forty.

"What's cooking?" he said, his voice big.

Steph found she had a tongue, even if only loosely connected to the rest of her. "A recipe out of the newspaper I thought we'd try. Beer-marinated flank steak. Doesn't that sound good. Was in yesterday's paper. Supposed to grill it over charcoal but you didn't start the grill outside, Harry, so I did it on the skillet."

"Wife's quite the cook," he said to Cilla.

"Table's all set," Steph said. "You can eat."

"You sit down with us, Stephanie."

"Bread's still in the oven."

"We'll say grace first."

Steph fought the electrical signals flashing across her thoughts. Even if she was thinking better than she did sometimes, the signals kept breaking her thoughts apart before they could surface. Only automatic things made it all the way to the top of her mind. Automatic things and things that hardly mattered. She felt dizzy, standing in the door of the kitchen. She could make it to the kitchen table and back, if she moved carefully and kept her wits around her.

"Cilla," said Harry, "the TV's all haywire. Whyn't you go over there and shut it off for us. Thanks, honey."

Harry would do that, Steph thought. He would call his latest his honey. She called Harry her honey.

"Let's sit down, honey," she said to Harry. It surprised her to have the words come out. Usually her mouth stayed shut.

"You like TV?" said Cilla, standing by the television set. "You watch much? Do you, Mrs. Jones?"

The girl had a hazed-over voice as if she had stolen things from the medicine cabinet. Maybe she had.

"Come on to the table, Cilla," Harry said, his back to the television set. "We'll say grace and eat some supper."

"I watch a lot of TV," Cilla said, walking to a chair. The television screen still looked a mess, the picture clearing up only now and then. She had left it on. "I remember it all. Maybe that's why I'm not so hot at school. Mom says I can remember anything, if it's on TV."

Harry looked large and calm, wearing his new plaid shirt. He had wetted his hair and combed it back. Steph's mother thought Harry looked like a big, fine man. She had approved.

Harry set his hands to each side of himself on the tablecloth and bowed his head slightly. Our heavenly father, we thank thee for the blessing of this food, amen, he said.

"What kind of TV do you watch, Mr. Jones?" Cilla said. She reached for the salad dressing and drenched her lettuce.

"Not much, I guess." He laughed hesitantly, watching Cilla nearly empty the salad dressing onto her salad. He took the bottle from her and put some on his own. "I guess I watch Joe Garagiola's baseball show

and I watch some news, but I bet you don't care about that. Stephanie here's the one for television, aren't you, Steph."

"I watch a lot," said Cilla, eating a piece of drenched lettuce. "I watch 'That Girl.' Do you watch 'That Girl'? I watch 'Rhoda.' I watch that with Mom. I watch the news and I try to remember everything. Do you think there will be another World War, Mr. Jones?"

Stephanie watched her husband pop open his Old Milwaukee, take a drink, and set it down quickly without looking at anyone. She got up to get the meat from the kitchen, and the potato salad. She had cheated on the potato salad, since she had made it so late in the day. She had run cold water over the potatoes instead of letting them cool all afternoon. Her mother would have said it was a waste of good water, cooling them that way. Steph was thinking with great clarity for all that her head felt crushed down to a baseball. She wondered at Cilla. She should hate the girl. Something stared out from behind that blank face, though. Some part of Cilla was escaping Harry and was working its way back at him. Cilla was talking television. Harry would hate that. He liked a woman in his bed before supper and then a quiet time eating without much talking.

"I heard the President on TV," Steph said, surprised again to have words come out.

"That's right," said Cilla. "Said he didn't think there'd be another World War. But I don't know."

"How're you going to believe Ford what he says," said Harry, his voice quieter but deeper than before. "No one voted for him."

"I like President Ford. Do you like music?" said Cilla. She reached for the meat.

"Pipe down a little and eat some," said Harry. "Hard to digest and yap at the same time."

"I listen to music all the time," said Cilla.

Steph's words went out, to meet Cilla's. "You know Michelle Phillips is getting married?" She tasted her words: free of meaning. Free.

"To Warren Beatty," said Cilla's deadened voice. "Yeah. I know, I don't like the Mamas and Papas. But Warren Beatty's cool."

"Whyn't you two shush. Let a man eat." Harry drank more beer. The interference on the TV screen danced ponderously for a moment. Stephanie went into the kitchen to get him another can, and said, when she returned, "The Stones are touring."

"Oh, ick," said Cilla from the table, speaking through a mouthful of potatoes. "My best friend, she loves the Rolling Stones. I like the Carpenters and Captain and Tennille and Michael Murphy."

Steph put the new beer in front of her husband, who pulled the tab without having finished the other. As he pulled it she saw how well she knew this man. She had lived with him since '63 and had never had this thought before, that she knew him through and through. She looked at him and saw a man incapable of detail who needed the rest of the world to be as silent and stupid as he was, who had a strange way with a woman and who could make her give in even when she hated him. He could twist anyone. She knew him. She felt sure now. This Cilla, this high school kid, was beginning to know him, too, more quickly than anyone else had.

The two of them could talk. Harry liked a little talk if he could talk about Joe Garagiola's Baseball World or that the Cardinals lost to the Phillies nine to four over the weekend. He could take that much. He could take only so much because of his small head. He got by all right when he could make the heads around him even smaller than his. People heard buzzings in their thoughts and the girls went to bed with him and came downstairs with empty looks wondering what had happened and whether it would happen again. They all went crazy. Cilla had gone crazy in a strange way, though. So quickly, too. She blabbed in her craziness and was egging Harry with her blabbing, and was getting out of Harry's grasp in a way so that Steph could get out, too. She had never seen this before. Harry would go batty himself, if he failed to make everyone shrink down to size. Cilla would make him. She flapped her jaws. Harry looked as though he would bust his skull. His eyes looked tiny and huge at the same time.

Steph had spent four years staring out the kitchen door at the television. She knew everything going on in the world, all the useless things to know, all the mindless facts that made up a humming background for Harry's silent, empty universe, all the assortment of things stupid and vital. It would burn him if anyone treated them as real, if they were stitched into quiet dinner time, if they were served up to him in good portions with his meat and potatoes and beer, if they were propped before him like shifting visions of the mindless set of facts he himself was. She never met another one like Cilla to know television the way Steph did. They could talk. They would drive Harry crazy, as he drove crazy every woman he touched. Steph: wife number three. There would have been more if she had cracked under having her head shrunken to a baseball every night. She hung on. Against the stupidity of it, she hung on. Now she looked back on the empty tunnel of her married life and knew why she went down through the darkness. She had kept moving, waiting for this day to arrive. Back when it started she saw no hope for breaking free. She was too weak. Harry could stare at her and freeze her up, sapping the strength out of her bones. She tried averting one eye. Then she hid herself by being in front of him at all times, a fixture in the house, a lamp, an end table. She needed no helmet of invisibility, the way Greek heroes did. She became commonplace. She flew on winged slippers, skimming from kitchen to guest room unseen because she was just there and not really worth seeing. It halfway worked, going unseen that way. Now Cilla had brought her a weapon, with her talking. Cilla could go on in such a way as to burn Harry. Talk like that would raise a wall so thick that if he tried to break through he would be thrown back on himself.

Steph kept her eyes off her husband. She knew his look without seeing. She looked at Cilla. She always knew the day would arrive when she could force him to see the monster he was, the monster named Harry, through the mirror of what she had become. When he saw the monster in himself, it would freeze him, finally, and not anyone else.

Cilla talked about Evelyn and Pat and Jackie and Gloria and Myrna on the soaps, set Steph right about the words to that great song "Wildfire," did she know that HUD lost gobs of money, six hundred million wasn't it, and look how things go so wrong, country can't take care of itself, with the crime rate up eighteen percent in the first three months of the year, you've heard that President Ford's dog is named Liberty, liberty on a leash that's government isn't it, ha-ha, but Ford's performance rating is down to fifty percent, no, said Cilla, down to forty-four percent, maybe it's forty-one percent, and Zsa Zsa Gabor has an overdue bill for fifteen-dollar shoes, I wouldn't buy fifteen-dollar shoes, well I wouldn't pay for them either, said Cilla, why's she buying fifteen-dollar shoes when the rest of the country's in the dumps, unless they're magic shoes, wouldn't it be nice to have slippers with wings on them, get out of this mess, on the news yesterday, maybe it was in the paper, they call it economic vertigo, ver-tee-go, that's what this country's in, going down a Christmas-wrapping tube, unemployment's going to stay high next couple of years, ten million out of work, that's ten million, ver-tee-go, it's amazing, but Harry's got a solid job, he's pulling in the meat and potatoes, ha-ha, heard Cher and Gregg Allman they're back together, could hop in the sack with anyone, all the Allman brothers have mushrooms tattooed on their right legs, it's a drug thing, isn't it, Beverly Sills with a deaf son and a retarded daughter, no it's the other way around, Harry doesn't like opera, looks at Dollie Parton and Dottie West and Tammy Wynette, don't you Harry, honey, you hear the music sometimes when your eyes tire out,

Harry thinks Apollo-Soyuz is a hoax, isn't that something, some people can't get it through their heads, you heard about the yellow gas, nitrogen something or other, they inhaled it, I memorized their names, Tom Stafford, Deke Slayton, Vance Brand, sick in their lungs, wonder if it's like drugs and they see weird things after coming back from space, it was lithium oxide, hydroxide, peroxide, something, wasn't that weird, go into space and meet Russians, no it was really something going into space and coming home and you land and have to breathe lithium, do you think they'll live, but you heard about the phantom hitchhiker on the New York turnpike.

"Goddamn it!" yelled Harry. The fire moved in his face as he thrust his hand forward, grabbed his beer can, and lifted it.

He threw it at Steph's head.

She sat still, watching from the corner of her eye as the beer can came at her. She felt no fear, watching it come at her head. She welcomed it. It would do some good. She had been talking at Cilla and Cilla had been talking at her and they were both trying to break out of the tiny things Harry had made of their heads. Harry could throw nothing at young little Cilla after having crawled out from under the sheets with her and after having put on a new shirt and wet his hair and combed it with her watching while she was covering her own tiny breasts. She sat at the meal table, his lover, his shield against the vision of the small thing he was. She was how he was going to live forever.

The can sloshed as it struck. The pain jolted through her. Her head went over and hit against her shoulder. How could she help that kind of reaction to being hit on the one side of the head with a beer can. She hardly minded it, just being there at the dinner table and reacting to the pressure of a beer can hitting her in the side of the head. Harry had thrown it hard. He meant business. Celebrating his birthday, and someone spoiled it: his wife, who deserved a beer can in the side of the head, thrown with a good strong arm.

The beer can was clearing her. Harry put so much into hating them for messing with his mind with their chatter. He put so much into heaving the can. So he lost them. Both of them. Steph felt the can hit and felt her head go off to the other side; and as the beer can rebounded and went to the floor her head cleared, and grew bigger again. Her head was hers again.

The freezing thing that came out of Harry's head and swept into hers and kept her small and useless disappeared. She knew where it would go now that Harry had knocked it out: back to him. It would have to. He had shaken his own bad magic out of her. It needed to go somewhere. Cilla would take no more of it. She had been knocking the bad magic out of her own head with all the gabbing. It had to go somewhere.

Harry sat there, seeing her.

She knew he saw her.

Steph pushed her chair back.

"That's it," she said.

She stood up and looked at Cilla.

She kept her eyes off Harry. Harry hardly mattered, any more.

"I'll drive you home," she said.

"No, no, I'll take her," said small Harry.

"Come on," said Steph.

"I'll go with Mrs. Jones," Cilla said, eyes wide.

"God damn it, I'll take her home. It's my—"

His words faded. He half stood, then sat down again. The beer can left in front of him sat empty. He took it in his hand. Another day he might have crushed it. He held it.

Steph picked up her purse, and felt its weight. Every time Harry had gone upstairs with a girl she packed a purse heavy with everything she could think of. She always unpacked it afterwards. The credit cards, the rainy-day dollar bills, the maps and the set of silverware and the pearl necklace and the address book and her mother's phone number: all went in, all came back out. Car keys. Papers. All this time married to a man and his contempt: he left her name on titles and accounts. He knew she would never take them away. He would die an extra death, thinking of this.

"Bye, Harry," she said, opening the front door. Cilla went before her.

"A goddamned hoax," he said. "Apollo-Soyuz. What a goddamned hoax."

He sat with his beer can. He spoke to the air, or to the can.

She knew how small he was, now. Maybe he did, too. He wore his own head, all of it, at last. He had cast parts of if out at others, over and over again. Now all the parts were back, returning him to the mindless thing he had always been. A big body with a tiny head of stone.

She reached the turnpike an hour after dropping Cilla off at the apartments where her wheelchair-bound father Jimmy Grove had been living the last couple years. She had called a high-school counselor, had stopped at the bank. Then on the highway she remembered the loaves of bread. Burning, by now. She forgot to turn off the oven. Harry would never step into the kitchen. He might stare through the kitchen door at the oven with the loaves in it. He would reach for his beer, and try to get his tiny head around what was going on.

The loaves had not risen, and being so dense would not burn right away. Later, maybe smoke would pour out. Maybe flames would shoot out. Maybe the house would go. Maybe Harry would think to get out. Maybe he would breathe in smoke.

It takes time for things to burn, Steph thought. Things get drier and hotter and sit looking as if nothing is happening, as if nothing would happen for a long, long while. On the outside something can look as if nothing is happening inside it at all. It can take a while for a fire to rise, out of that kind of looking like nothing.

The oven door, she could see from the flying car, stayed shut. She saw it stayed shut for good.

HOMUNCULUS

We always want to make
Little men, playing around
In the kitchens of the gods
We made and prayed to
When midnight lightning
Could not be expressed
As a simple one plus one
Equation to the Children
Of Oceans.
Their heirs, the Turning Wheel,
Today give snide smiles
To antique alchemy in
Favor of the clones we pray
Will surpass their aging mold,
A step short of immortal,
As righteous as the Zero.

—BRIAN THAO WORRA

You Can't Judge a Squid By Its Cover

"You'd be surprised how hard it is to find a good basic book about squid."
                                      —Eleanor Arnason

A book of squid? No, no, a school of squid. Or a grip of squid. Or a tangle.
James Lipton's wonderful book has no term for them. So, who knows?

All I know about squid, from *Loligo* to *Architeuthis*, I learned from books.
Jules Verne, the Kraken, *Believe It Or Not*, recipes for calamari—that's what I know.

The National Museum of Natural History has assembled a National Squid Collection.
Their Squid Squad will eventually publish a book of everything you want to know.

Vampyroteuthis infernalis is jet black with blood red eyes and luminous mucus.
Its costume is more frightening than its bite, if you must know.

The giant squid is rarely seen. The infant squid's too teeny to bear watching.
The average squid is the size you see on ice at the fishmonger's—you know.

Commercial species gather near the shore in millions, mate, lay eggs, and die.
The male deposits millions of sperm on Ms. Squid's head in mortal carnal knowledge.

To the outside observer, the squid looks pretty simple, all squirt and squeeze.
Inside's the equipment that a squid uses to assess what a squid knows.

—John Calvin Rezmerski

Reader, be warned: this one's disturbing.

The Lady of the Lounge
by William Mingin

I shouldn't've asked Terry to go to the bar, but who knew two guys out for a beer would meet a man-eating lounge singer?

The Apple Orchard sits on an empty stretch of road where there was an orchard maybe sixty years ago, a rambling building in sparsely wooded fields, with the low-slung Apple Orchard Inn, a no-tell motel, maybe fifty yards away. In late October, in upstate New York, the fields were cold and wind-swept, the trees leaf-barren.

Her voice was just right for a lounge singer, clear higher up, with a soft plaintiveness on the off edge of a tone, smoky and intimate on the lower notes. Never too loud, sometimes so soft you'd swear she was whispering to you. When we came in, she was singing an oldie, "Gimme a Kiss," to a piano accompaniment. First time I'd ever heard it done slow, like a long embrace, especially at the stomp, where she repeated the chorus in a languorous, accented rhythm:

"Come in the mornin',
Stay till it's late,
Never stop cuddlin',
And don't hesitate—
Cause you got the power
To put me in bliss—
Gimme a kiss."

She was in her late twenties, about five-six, hair a shade off auburn, thick, wavy, down below her shoulders; powdery white skin. She moved sinuously to the music, like she was painted on something that rippled. The tight sheath of her dress, so dark a purple it was almost black, accentuated her hair and pale complexion. She looked straight ahead as she sang, into a distance only she could see, with a sad longing laced with desire.

Watching her, I felt the mingled regret and itch you feel when you remember bedding a lost love. Terry's reaction wasn't as nuanced, but he's ten years younger than me. He looked like someone had tapped him between the eyes with a ball peen hammer. He was breathing through his mouth.

Terry's fiancee, Mary Lynn, is girl-next-door pretty, squeezably-soft and feathery-blonde. But when you stood next to her, you could hear plans whirring in her head: house, yard, fence, kids; his whole career laid out, salary increases, savings, what dull patch of warmth they'd retire to. I think she had names picked out for the grandchildren.

Terry sat close to the stage, which was no bigger than two dining room tables. I followed. The singer had gone from "Gimme a Kiss" to "I Close My Eyes (And There You Are)," more up-tempo, but in a minor key:

"I see you in all my thoughts and I dream about you—
How else can I ever live without you?
You left me all alone, but I'm not lonely—
My one and only—
I close my eyes and there you are—"

There was a lot of applause for a small joint just outside the middle of nowhere, and not a few wolf whistles. Terry's made me clutch at my ear. She half-smiled at the whistles, bowed once, and went off.

Terry rushed over to accost her. I couldn't hear what they were saying, but saw her coy smile, the tilt of her head, the way she batted her eyes. She was a stranger in a car offering candy; and she was the candy.

As they headed off, Terry turned back and gave me The Look—the look your buddy gives you that says "How about this?" and warns you not to follow. He's your ride? Settle in for a while. The Look is sacred.

I figured what Mary Lynn didn't know wouldn't hurt her. I'm not proud of that.

But I *was* teed off. I went over to the accompanist, who played on softly, with a chip on my shoulder.

I was stopped first by the way he played. His hands drifted over the keys like articulated smoke. He leaned in to the keyboard, leaned back, working without effort, an endlessly patient gigolo arousing a sleeping empress.

Then I saw his face. Ever been stopped cold by a piece of bad news, so that you just sit and blink? Good thing for him he sits off in a shadow, I thought.

Then, still irritated, I said, "What's up with your friend?"

He finished the song with a flourish. "My friend?"

"The singer. The guy I was with talks to her for ten seconds, and she goes off with him. She earn extra cash that way?" I wasn't normally that nasty. I was getting a bad feeling. The guy's looks were spooking me.

He smiled sadly and shook his head. "Nothing like that." His tone registered no offense, just a kind of regret.

My dislike of him began to evaporate. He looked withered; there was nothing there to *be* angry with. And then there was that playing, way too good for this place. I offered to buy him a drink, to make up for the nasty comment.

"Wasted on me," he said, so I supposed he was one of those that don't feel it.

"What's your name?" I asked.

"Ray," he said, like remembering a loss.

Yeah, little sunbeam. "Maybe you ought to hit your own room," I said. "You look about done in."

He shook his head. "My room *is* her room."

My irritation and distrust came back. "What is this? An 'open marriage?' Or you one of those voyeurs, sends his wife off with someone, then gets all the details?"

"Nothing like that, either."

"Pimp?"

Even then he didn't get offended. "Nothing—"

"Yeah, I know, I know. Well, what *is* it like?"

He looked like he was considering a big decision. I could see him make it.

"You're going to have to help him," he said, looking up at me, his face drawn and sorrowful. "I might have tried to warn him, but he'd never have believed me."

"What are you talking about?"

He looked at me appraisingly. "No," he said, "you won't believe it either, without seeing. Come outside a minute."

We walked around back of the club. In a place away from sight but exposed to the moon, he unbuttoned his vest and shirt and opened them up.

Just for a second I thought, don't tell me he's one of *that* kind, but then I saw—

You know when you eat spareribs, when you're done there's moist bone, some gristle, a thin layer of skin or cartilage that lays against the bone, and tiny bits of gnawed flesh you couldn't quite get to? In some spots, Ray's ribs shone like newly polished dentures, but some of the crevices still held meat. Within the cage of bones were, as far as I could remember from high school biology, *some* of the right organs suspended in a thin membrane, but not all of them. And some of those remaining were gnawed or hollowed out.

I puked for the first time in a long time, turned and up it came. It wasn't just the sight of all that stuff that should be interior and unseen. It was the impossibility—the sense of all I knew of normal reality knocked out of me, like a sucker punch to the midriff.

Thank God he only showed me from the waist up.

He buttoned back up while waiting for me to recover. I turned to him, wiping my mouth. "How the hell did that happen?"

"Come with me." He led me over to one of the motel rooms. A light was on inside, and there was a gap between the curtain and the end of the window.

"Curtain won't stay closed," Ray said.

I bent to look into the room.

Terry lay atop her, his face contorted. I suppose some of it was pleasure, but a lot of what I saw had to be pain. I'm not sure, right then, he knew the difference.

She was bent upward, gnawing at his chest. I saw her loosen a piece, using her tongue to help strip it away so that her teeth could get a good hold on it and tear it off. She lay back and wolfed it down. When she came up to lick at the bloody wound, her hair hung lank and matted with sweat, and her breasts bunched up. Only her top two breasts were visible. When she lay flat again, the smaller mounds and nipples of her lower breasts came into view, four more trailing down her belly.

I threw myself against the door, but it was pretty solid. I don't think they even heard me. I looked around for something to smash in the window.

"Forget it," Ray said, grabbing my arm. "If you break in while she's feeding, she'll tear his throat out. You can't stop her. I don't know if even bullets could stop her. Silver, maybe," he mused. "Anyway, it's almost over."

He was right—they had disengaged, and Terry was slumped against the head of the bed, looking dazed. She was kneeling over him, licking at the wound she'd made, dugs hanging down.

"What the hell *is* she?"

"I don't know."

"Is that what she did to you? How come you're not

dead? No offense."

"S'okay. Somehow you don't die. It doesn't bleed, it doesn't fester. It holds together."

"Does it heal?"

He shrugged. "I never got the chance to find out."

Just then Terry came out, staggering a little, his clothes still half-undone.

I grabbed him and pulled him away from the door—not too roughly, in case he was still bleeding. I looked back into the room. It was empty. I heard the shower running.

"Come on," I said, "I'm taking you to a hospital."

"Why?" he said. "I feel great."

For the first time I noticed that he sported a loopy grin. I pulled him over to face me. "You're lucky to be alive!"

His grin got wide and sly. His eyes were drunken. "Yeah, she is *amazing*," he said.

I barely stopped myself from slapping him.

"It's like that," Ray said from the shadows. "Partly it's the call that does it—her singing—and partly...well, you know. The feeling is...overwhelming." He was quiet a moment. "And maybe the saliva. It's not just an anesthetic. It gets in your blood. You feel like you're king of the world."

Even if there was a hole in you that you could keep your wallet in. "We're getting out of here," I said, pulling Terry along.

"See you tomorrow," Terry called back to Ray.

"No you *won't*," I snarled at him.

"Hey, I got a date for tomorrow."

"You idiot! She just tore off a piece of your flesh and ate it!" I tapped him hard in the chest.

He didn't even wince. "So?"

"She's not human! She's got canines like a dog and six dugs!"

Terry looked at me in irritation. "Frank, you want me to reject a woman because she has *extra* tits?"

I reached for the last weapon in my arsenal. "You go near her again, I'll tell Mary Lynn."

"Shit," Terry said, suddenly sobering.

I was afraid it wouldn't hold him for long. He was already arguing himself out of caring what Mary Lynn thought before I got him home. He refused to go near a hospital.

After that, he didn't answer the phone or return my messages. I figured he was screening his calls to avoid me. When I went by his apartment, he wasn't there. Anyway, what could I do, sit on him?

So I decided to work it from the other end.

I got to the Apple Orchard in early evening, the blue part of the day. Ray was playing, Happy Hour was on, there was a fair crowd. I waited for him to take a break. Walking over to him made my flesh creep, but he was the only one who could help.

We sat at the bar. After a minute or two of small talk, I felt at ease again. There was something unassuming and humble about the guy that just naturally made me like him. I offered him a drink—we *were* at a bar—and he said, "What the hell," and ordered a bourbon and water. I ordered a beer.

I didn't know how long we had, so I got right to it. "I've got to keep Terry away from her."

"Good luck. I gave it my best shot last night, by letting you see."

"Well, maybe you could show him what you showed me."

He shrugged. "I will if you want. But he won't see it. The guy before me tried to warn me off." He smiled wryly. "I couldn't see anything wrong with him. I thought he was scared of losing her to a younger guy. It made me cocky."

"You saw this"—I gestured vaguely to his chest—"and you still hooked up with her?"

"Yeah," he said shamefacedly. "Her voice hooks you like a drug. That's why she works as a singer. I mean, sure, it keeps us in food and gas, but it's really her mating cry."

"What happened to the other guy?"

"She picked him clean. Just left his hands and face. His ears were the last to go. Well—next to the last." He was silent a moment. "He was bones from the ground to the collar and down to the wrists. She threw him out and shut the door on him. You could hear him scrape against it like a big bug. Then he wandered away."

"Jeez," I said, shuddering. "*You've* got to get away from her."

He slowly lifted his whiskey, sipped, and shook his head. "I can't." He gestured to his frame. "I'm too far gone. Anyway, I couldn't leave her. I...need her." He sipped again and gave a tiny shudder—at the taste and the burn, I guess.

"You need her for what? To eat your life away? How long can this go on?"

He looked down at himself ruefully. "Soon I'll barely be an appetizer." He stared off and said, "When I'm picked clean, I'll wander out into a mist. I'll cross the line between life and death and keep wandering, not really dead and not alive. I won't know where I am or maybe, after a while, who."

"Jeez."

He came back from wherever he'd been, shrugged, and sipped his drink. "I've had time to think about it. Been doing a lot of reading." He flushed a little—God knows how. "Self-help books."

"Do they help?"

"No, you have to do it yourself. I guess that's why they call them—"

"Self-help, yeah."

"I read those M. Scott Peck books, *The Road Less Traveled, Further Along the Road Less Traveled*—"

"*Truck-Stop on the Road Less Traveled, Road-Kill on the Road Less Traveled*," I chimed in.

"That's me: Road-Kill on the Road *Way* Less Traveled." He smiled wryly. "Anyway, according to him, the Bible says, 'The Kingdom of God is *among* you,' not '*within* you.' This thing between her and me is like that. She's not evil. I'm not evil. It's just different kinds of hunger, feeding on one another. The evil is *among* us. So I'm in...the opposite of heaven. But maybe someone can still see that far down." He looked at me shyly. "Since I *know* there's evil, I believe there's good, too."

"You've *got* to get away from her."

Sudden tears came into his eyes. "I can't. She *owns* me," he whispered. Then he looked down at the floor. Something was dripping from his pants leg, starting to make a puddle. He opened his coat. His vest and shirt were soaked. "I like the taste and feel of drinking," he said, "but this is what always happens. I got to go." He got up off the stool.

"Ray, don't worry, it's just a little puddle."

He shook his head. "Not that. I got to go. She's calling." He gave a sickly smile. "Maybe I should change my name to 'Igor.'" He started off, then turned back. "Save Terry," he said. "Maybe it's not too late for him." He looked me in the eyes. "And save yourself," he said, and left.

Myself? What danger was *I* in?

A half-hour later Ray, dry again, sat at the piano. She came out, nodded to the audience, nodded to me, and began "The Cry-Baby Blues:"

Sometime they'll take your heart and break it,
And you'll just sit and take it—
What's the use of crying
When no one can hear?

In her rendition, it was a plaintive wail. It got to me; I could feel it vibrate inside me like a trapped bee. I began to vibrate with it.

It was a short set. Ray stayed on to play background. He nodded once to me, without looking up, as I went over to her, beginning to tremble.

I extended my hand, my breath coming fast. "Hi, Miss...?"

"Veronica, please," she said, smiling a long, soft kiss of a smile.

"Veronica, thanks. Frank Polo." We shook. Her hand was warm, small, supple. In her violet eyes was a beyond I'd never known about until I saw her looking out from it. "I was wondering if I could talk to you for a minute? About Terry," I hastened to add.

"I have a while until my next set," she said, smiling again. "I usually go back to my room and relax. Come with me?"

"Sure," I said, the breath as harsh in my throat as tobacco smoke. It was how I'd felt the first time I followed a girl up to her room, knowing what we were going to do. Why did I feel that way now? I knew what she was.

In her room she motioned me to a chair near the bed. "Let me just get out of this dress—it wrinkles too easily."

"Sure." The one line I'd mastered.

She went into the bathroom and came out in a silk robe, drawing a tie around it. She sat on her bed, curling her bare legs up under her, and smiled at me in a familiar, almost intimate way.

I couldn't help looking down at the robe. You could tell she was a little chilly. In six different spots.

"So, you came to see me—because of Terry?" An opening, if I wanted to be there for something else.

"Yeah." My voice creaked. I swallowed and tried again. "Yeah." Only because "sure" didn't fit.

"Terry told me you two go way back."

"I've known him since he was a kid. I kind of look after him."

She raised one eyebrow. "Does he need looking after?"

Yeah, I thought, he needs looking after. And so do I. Even in mockery her voice sounded like it was coming to you in the dark from the next pillow. I was getting drunk on the look of her, curved into an S on the bed, and her scent, sweet and musky. I was sweating. I tried to calm myself. I managed to say, "Look, Veronica, maybe I'm meddling, but Terry's already spoken for."

The eyebrow, a half smile. "I think he's old enough to speak for himself, don't you?"

Her voice curled around me like smoke, teasing. I burned inside and out, like breathing next to a furnace. "I don't know what you think you're doing with him—"

She gave me another mocking look. "I think you know, Frank, don't you?"

In spite of everything, I wanted to give in to her. But the very sense of surrendering kicked in my panic. I couldn't give in; there was more at stake than me. I had to get away from her, and the only defense I knew was anger. "Well, I know what men and *women* do. That doesn't give a man welts and strip away his skin. But what you do to Terry—I've *seen* you—"

She smirked at me teasingly. "Jealous? Isn't that why

you're really here?" There it was. The offer.

Suddenly revulsion and fear popped me back into sanity. I laughed harshly. At her.

In an instant, she changed. Her eyes hooded over. Even her scent was different. "You think you know an awful lot, don't you." She turned away, saying, "I don't know why you're trying to insult me. Terry and I are adults. He isn't married. If we see one another—and what we do when we see one another—is no one's business but ours."

So, I'd committed the unpardonable sin. You were supposed to be sapped and will-less. Her voice, her beauty, was the scent of a flower and the venom of a spider combined. She'd turned it on, and I'd laughed. Did she lie to herself? I wondered. Did she think she was like other women?

Now I wanted to take her throat in my hands and squeeze. I clenched my hands at my sides, afraid of what might happen, and I stood up. "If you think I'm going to stand by and watch while you chew up my friend—"

She examined her nails. "I don't recall anyone inviting you to watch, Mr. Polo. Even if that is the kind of thing you like to do." She looked at me with cold deadliness, then got up and walked into her bathroom. "Good bye, Mr. Polo," she said, and shut the door.

I stood a moment, wondering if I should try to kill her right there and then. What if the law got involved? "I had to kill her, officer, she was a man-eating were-singer. I saw her eating my best friend. Uh, no, not like that." Yeah, sure.

I went back home.

I hadn't given in, but now every atom of me wanted to give up, my other favorite habit—why I lived alone in a backwater, with a dead-end job. Give up and let my friend be savaged into a living damnation, if that's what he insisted on. But I *couldn't*. Even Ray hadn't given up totally. Telling me all he had, trying to save Terry, was like him setting out a beacon, hoping God might still find him. For once in your life, I told myself, go to war for something. *Do* something. But what?

Would bullets work on her? "Silver bullets, maybe," Ray had said. I thought that was bullshit about silver bullets, or bullets dipped in holy water. Like a bullet killed you some magic way, by carrying a spell to you, or like it needed magic to affect you. If it was magic that got you, you wouldn't need the bullets, and if the bullet could get to you, it didn't need any help.

But I didn't have to kill her. I just had to get Terry away from her.

I put some hammers, including a sledgehammer, in the trunk of my car, with spikes, stakes, a hatchet and a nail gun, and I put my shotgun in the front—the pitchfork and torch for my one-man peasant mob.

They were my whole plan. I never said I was clever. But I was determined.

Third time at the Apple Orchard in two days. Every time felt worse. I was sweating and my stomach writhed like it was trying to escape the grip of a giant fist. The shotgun, propped up on the floor, gleamed like the horns of a devil.

After I parked I had to sit for a minute, wiping my hands on my pants, calming my breathing. Fights are always worst just before you start. Trying not to think, I grabbed my diabolical companion and walked around back to their room.

They still hadn't fixed that curtain, or was Ray trying to help me out? He was sitting in the chair reading the paper. Seems he needed half-glasses. Without his jacket and vest, with his shirt open at the neck, you could see the chewed part all the way up above the breastbone. Some of it looked newly raw. Appetizer. Ray tartare.

Not six feet away Terry lay atop her, hips locked to hers. Her legs were around his lower back, her jaw at his breast. I guess now that Terry was initiated, it didn't matter that Ray was in the room.

Should I shoot? Break the door in? Knock? The sledge was still in the trunk.

I thought of all those movies where someone rushes a door just to find out it was unlocked. I held the gun over my right arm and tried the knob. It opened.

I looked to Ray first. He didn't seem surprised. He sighed and folded his paper.

The other two didn't even notice me, so I walked to the bed and—with a certain satisfaction, I have to admit—gave her head a sharp tap with the barrel, to dislodge her from his chest.

She snarled and snapped at me, but either couldn't get up because of Terry, or didn't want to. He swore and swung at me, ineffectually from that position.

I eyed the back of his head, gauged the force needed, and punched him. When he went limp, she pushed him off with a kind of convulsive force and lay there before me, eyes wide, tongue out, legs spread, face and bosom flushed, all six nipples erect.

I looked into her eyes, wide, fierce, violet, and saw not anger but invitation, urgent now—the offer, the dare. I noticed the blood on her lips and teeth, the flecks of blood dappling her breasts. Yeah, I thought, hot, wet, ready, and willing, every boy's dream. I swung the shotgun toward her.

She stayed still. That was good. I reached down and caught Terry under one arm, dragged him to the floor, trying not to dump him too hard. I said to Ray, "Wrap a sheet around him." Ray pulled off the top sheet, which was down at the foot of the bed, and got it around Terry, while I kept both barrels on those wide eyes, purple as the sky after sunset, now with a look of innocence in them, like *"What's all this about? Why are you so mad at me?"*

Then she laughed. "A gun," she said lazily, stretching her arms up above her, her breasts pointed upward, her legs stretched down, so that her sexual display was hidden. "If I wanted to stop you, do you think that gun would save you?"

"Right. You're just letting us go."

"I still have hopes for you, Frank. I don't want to hurt you. I want to make you happy."

She stretched again, but luxuriously this time, then reached down to idly stroke her top right breast. "You don't think bullets would stop me, do you?"

"Not normal bullets," Ray chimed in, shaking his head.

"Oh, yeah, I forgot. Supernatural monster needs silver bullets, bullshit!" I spat, so mad and scared I wasn't coherent. "This shotgun tears things up fine. And I've got a sledgehammer and a hatchet in the car, if I need to finish the job.

"I'm taking Terry home, but I'll be back in an hour. If you're still here, I'll show you something supernatural. I won't leave enough of you to feed a small dog. Silver bullets my fat, hairy ass!" Shows you how upset I was. I'm one of those typical no-ass guys. "If I *can't* kill her," I went on, talking to Ray, but knowing she was listening, "maybe I can maim her enough to keep guys away, no matter how she sings. If I can't do that, I'll kill you and Terry, too, if I have to."

"Not if she kills you first," Ray said, like pointing out a different way of financing your mortgage.

I ignored that. "And after I kill you two, I'll make sure people know about her. You think the publicity will help her career?"

"Who's going to believe you?" he said.

"By then I'll be a notorious killer. Lots of people will listen, especially after they see your chewed-up ass."

"I don't believe you'd kill us," Ray said.

I looked at him, thin-faced, worn-looking, spooky and quiet and sad, and I was sorrier for him than I ever could have been about Terry. But by his own admission he was already a goner, and I had Terry to save. Maybe that was part of my anger: having to give up on Ray.

I hit him in the ribs, and he fell. I heard one or two cracks when he hit. I was afraid I'd shattered him and had to hold myself back from helping him up.

"One goddamn hour to get the were-cunt caged and out of here," I gritted between my teeth, my voice shaking.

Ray looked up at me with such a sense of lost hurt that if my anger hadn't been stirred up, I'd have let them do whatever they wanted. Up until then he really had been hoping. Now I saw a light of understanding gleam in his eyes and a smile of resignation on his lips. He nodded, looking down.

I dragged Junior to the door by the scruff of the sheet, then bent and put him over my shoulder, fireman style. She watched but let us go. You could see she still wasn't used to someone standing up to her, rejecting her. She was smiling at me, still available, still hoping the way predators hope, with endless patience; none of that pride I'd met with last time. I'd pulled Terry away before she was "done," so neither of her appetites were satisfied. I guess being aroused and hungry made even *her* stupid.

So I said, "You're never getting me, you pathetic animal. Can't you understand that?"

I guess she could. She sprang up from the bed, screeching. I went through the door and slammed it behind me, hurrying as best I could toward the car. But she didn't follow. I guess Ray had some kind of influence over her after all.

By the time I got Terry to my house he was already roused up and starting to complain. Same old song and dance: he wanted her, he had to have her, I was just jealous.

I told him, "I have to go back out. If necessary, I'll tie you down, and I don't think you'll get loose before I get back. But if I find you outside, I'll run you down. If we're lucky, I'll only break both your legs. If you go to her, I'll hunt you down and shoot out the back of your goddamn head."

It wasn't the threat itself that pulled his eyes to me, it was that I meant it, that I'd just as soon see him dead. His eyes unglazed, as if he were coming out of shock. He looked at me with a sudden sense of loss, like everything bright in the world had just gone dull, all possibility for joy and excitement extinguished—about ten years of growing up and surrendering illusions in seconds. He nodded soberly, somberly. "I'll be here," he said.

I didn't know if Ray believed me literally, or if he thought he could dally, since he was hurt. But I knew I *had* to be back in that hour. I hoped—I was sweating, I was hoping so hard—that he'd taken me for real.

Ray and the thing were gone. For a second, I was

almost disappointed. I said to myself, "Jerkwater town—jerkwater monster. What do you expect?" Then I thought, Was she *really* so fierce? Poor Ray! I could see why he would want to think so, would want to believe he couldn't get away, couldn't stop her. What if all you had to do was walk?

I put the gun, hammer, and hatchet in the trunk and leaned against the car, starting to cool down. Maybe she hadn't been so ferocious, but I was shaking. With no one there to see me, I—

But if I told, that would be like someone seeing me, wouldn't it?

I was at Terry's wedding a year later, and I'm his little girl's godfather. Mary Lynn's not so bad; she eased up when she finally got what she wanted.

I thought I was too old for that kind of thing myself, until I met Janet about three years ago. She has two boys, and the warmest heart I've ever known. I knew she was solid when I saw how good the kids were. I might have shied away from the arrangement in the past—my nature, my age—but when I thought about Ray, my urge to wander dwindled. "Save yourself," he'd said. Janet and I will get married soon, and I'd like to adopt her boys. She's only thirty-two, so who knows, we may add to the brood. I've got a better job now; I can support them.

Last year I was walking through the park near my house when I saw some resiny insect shells clinging to the tree bark. There were some in the path, too, translucent, articulated. I accidentally stepped on one of the filmy, crunchy things. I thought then of Ray, wondered why, made the connection, and puked behind a tree, into the fallen leaves.

ANGERBODA'S CHILD

Discard from heaven,
malevolence grows in dark seas.
Jormandgund circles the earth.

Son of a trickster,
one long calm wave grows.

A safe harbor
becomes churning chaos,
tsunami of evil.

Swallowing serpentine tail,
he circles the equator—
scaly body forming
the world's noose.

—DEBORAH P. KOLODJI

Since TOTU *#23 (when she wrote as A.B. Ming), Patricia S. Bowne has been entertaining us with her "Osyth" stories of academic life in a world underpinned by magic. This novelette's set in that same world, but it moves off campus to the gritty life of downtown. No animals were harmed in the publication of this story.*

Raising the Dead
by Patricia S. Bowne

If I have to sit through one more meeting, I'll die," I told Edmond, and everybody laughed except the office manager. But I didn't die. It was Edmond who died; of all the nice things he'd done for me, that was the one I appreciated.

I didn't know what it was at first, just that something breathed a wave of strength into me. I felt happy, giddy, almost manic, and when I looked around the table Edmond's slumped figure shone to me the way he never had when he was alive. As I watched, the sparkles went away; the man next to me turned towards me, looked where I was looking.

"My God!" he said. "Edmond—call the ambulance, Elaine. Get a sorcerer." I did, but I knew it was too late. Edmond had left the meeting.

I'd known I had a talent ever since the tests the year before, in my senior year of school; I'd been playing around with witchcraft and enchantment, but light magic had never given me this kind of rush.

I took my license through the College of Sorcery at the Royal Academy, and I was a free-lance Necromancer by the year I was twenty-five, part-time Crown Prosecutor's Assistant. I liked funky keyboard, music with a beat. I liked smoky nightclubs and making my own money on my own schedule; I wore stockings of real silk and made them mend themselves under the table whenever a moth died in the candleflame, and danced them into holes again when the lights got low and the music hot. I swung with high rollers in low joints. I was a career girl.

Maybe midnight, the CP's office would call me at one of the bars. All the waiters knew to bring the phone right out to the table where everyone could see me take the call. A floater, they'd say, or a body in some back alley. I was cool. Got to go, boys; just one more whiskey, down like medicine. The boys get quiet, except one or two rowdies—hey honey, take me along, whatta way to go—and then a moth flies into the flame and they all shut down, hear the sizzle.

Coroner's basement is white and steel, but dark all the same. He keeps a cage of rats down there. Take out the bloodstones, hold them over the cage to see which one sings for its supper. Pull out the rat, kill it with one quick whirl onto the table-edge. The bloodstone fills up with you and you can feel your power pushing at the port it makes, eager to get out of you and work magic on the world.

Just looking at the body is like waiting for sex, but don't touch it now. No matter how good you feel now, running the dead body and your own can kill you—you have to wait, to draw the pentacle that keeps out the other things that'll want the body once they see it move. You have to recite the charms and sprinkle the powders. You have to light the hand of glory and burn the mandrake root over it, the plant that can give its own motion to the body as it twists and squeals, and then you can touch.

You take hold of the real world when you touch a body; put everything out of your mind except what you feel under your hands, because this is as close to touching the truth as you'll ever get. It opens its eyes, it looks at you without judging. It doesn't size you up, scope you out, plan how to manage you. You can put everything you have into a body. Let all the guards down, let the power flow out of you as easy as it came in; the eyes see what you really are but they don't care. The ears hear your questions and another dead hooker gives her testimony, so much better than a live woman's, protecting nobody.

What I liked was taking bodies into court. The defendant's face when he sees her, cleaned up dead, when

he hears the voice without outrage or fear. The one that was supposed to feel the hurts and burns doesn't cry now, looks at him with nothing in her eyes. That's what I like to see, when they get small and know they're the only ones left who care about their rage and fever. I look at them cold, make sure they see me turn away.

I knew it was trouble when the boys went quiet on me in spring—one, two bars in a row. "Lookin' for you," was the mutter, backing away from the table. Looking where? Every club on my list, and me following behind looking for him, afraid of nothing except that empty table. Smoky in the quietest bar, slow music, not in any back room or booth but at the bar itself, polished wood and crystal all around him.

He was a sexy man, Cleophilus Eleuthra. Oh, a sexy man, a single man, a rich man, he knew how to live, though the rumors about him were bad. But the rumors about me were bad, as well.

Cleophilus Eleuthra was the first necro who sold anything except his power—the first who made consumer goods out of death. It shouldn't be legal, said all the pros I knew. But Cleo was out of the mainstream, doing things daytimers and mundanes hadn't thought of; laws were made behind him, about things he'd already taken his profit from, and his business shot up like a mushroom.

By the time I saw him in that bar he did most of the decorating in Osyth, for people who could afford the best. Wood, fine leather, ivory, and silk brocades—those were the things people came to Cleo for, without asking too much about how he made them or where he got the power. Cleo sold you your dreams, and if you couldn't tell what you wanted he'd dream it up for you. He was the color of strong coffee, his body smooth as if there was something under his skin that wasn't fat or muscle or bone. As if he was made of something new and better. He remade everything he touched.

Nobody ever saw Cleo out on the town with a date, showing off to make other men jealous. He only had to show himself to make other men jealous, and he only had to look at their lovers to make them think they had second-best, but none of us knew who he slept beside or how warm his bed was. Maybe the rumors were true, that he only liked dead people he could make over to suit himself.

But that gossip blew away like dust when I saw Cleo the first time, sitting at that bar with luxury pooling around him. He looked at me with his head on one side and then he got off the stool and stood waiting for me as if I was a person, not a trophy. It made my voice scratchy and my manners fierce.

"What d'you want?"

"I want to buy you a drink," said Cleo. "We're the only freelance necromancers in town. It's a lonely business."

"I wasn't lonely until you came along," I said, but looking at how Cleo had remade that dive, I knew just how lonely I'd been to ever come into it. And when he said, could we go somewhere else, I knew it for sure. I couldn't take him back to my two rooms without even a picture on the walls. I couldn't ask Cleo to sit in one of my plastic-covered chairs and watch my cage of crickets.

"How can you not be lonely," said Cleo, as if he was talking to himself, "when everyone you know is dead? I need a friend," he said. "Not love, not business—just a friend."

"I'm not in your kind of necromancy," I told him. "I'm with the good guys. I can't play both sides of the fence."

"I'll be here Thursdays," said Cleo, "whenever you decide to come."

It was three Thursdays before I went back. By the second week I was hearing about it everyplace I went, how Cleophilus Eleuthra was sitting in a bar on Grive Street waiting for me. Not drinking, not taking up with anyone else. Speaking when he was spoke to, even to gawkers who came in to see the great necromancer. That was what got me, him talking to them. If he'd been sitting there proud and superior, self-sufficient, I never would have gone back. The third Thursday I went down to the bar about eleven at night, and he was there just sitting, letting everyone see he wasn't too good to wait for me.

"So what did you want?" He swung round just eager enough to let me feel how important it was. He started to get up, but I sat down before he could. I wasn't going to make it that bad. "Brandy," I told the bartender.

"How was your week?"

"You didn't sit here all month to ask me that!"

"I told you I wanted a friend," he said. "Someone I can ask that. If you want deeper questions—what's the biggest thing you ever killed?"

"A beagle," I said.

"A beagle! You killed a dog?"

"Like you've never killed something!"

"Not a dog," said Cleo. "Man's best friend." Friends were big with him, I decided.

I saw Cleo every week after that, through the summer and fall and the long dark winter evenings. First it was Grive Street, or a restaurant; then he started taking me home to his penthouse apartment, where we could see all of Osyth laid out below like a blueprint waiting to be revised. It was different. Not like being with daytimers and pretending to be no more than they were, but not like being with the dead and not having to pretend about anything, either. The good times, it was like living in a dream world, where all you had to do to get something was wish for it. And Cleo was exciting. I liked the way his mind worked, the way he saw things and went for them. It was easy to play that game with Cleo, to sit all night dreaming up new ideas. Catering? Temps?—you can make anything out of dead stuff, if you once get thinking that way.

He'd slip it in, every now and then—come down to the factory, you'll like the work, better pay than waking up hookers and no defendant cursing you, no bad-ass laying for you after he gets out. Nobody minds what you do with dead dogs from the pound. Nobody hates a man for turning beef byproducts into fine leather, or chicken feathers into down. He'd ask like he was doing me a favor, but I always said no. That's when he got evil, as if I'd let what people really thought of us into the dream. Like all the world was against Cleo, and I was one more looking down on him—all that from a "No thanks, not now."

Those times, I hated him and his made-up world. We'd fight, yell, throw things; I'd run back to the bodies in the coroner's basement, the people who'd dumped their baggage and stopped pretending. I'd look round at the toe-tags and wonder what he'd do in my place. Have them tap-dancing, no doubt. Still, I always went back to him. It was lonely down there after you'd been with someone warm. And after all, you have to make allowances for live people.

We had one of those fights just before the Vernal Equinox. The next Thursday was the big day; I went down to hide from it all in Grive Street, and Cleo wasn't in the bar when I got there. I couldn't remember whether to expect him or not, and after a few minutes' thinking I decided I didn't care. I sat at the bar, giving him half an hour. The bartender was down at the other end of the room, looking out the door at the fireworks.

There was only one other person at the bar, staring into his drink and ignoring everything else. I gave him the once-over to pass the time, and just to act out that I was mad at Cleo. I hadn't checked out new talent for almost a year, and when I looked at this stranger that way I started thinking old thoughts. I didn't like it, so I turned away. But the picture of him was in my mind.

He was a thin little man, maybe forty, blond starting to go gray, and underdressed for the place. He had a wiry, cowboy sort of build, like someone who did manual labor, but I could tell that wasn't his field. That was what really caught my interest—that even with his build, his scratched-up hands and dirty fingernails, he still had the desk-set professional look. You can always tell it, even when they've been dead a week. But this guy was alive. He was angry, too. He wasn't just looking at that drink, he was telling it off. He'd glare at it and his chin would move, the way it does when you're talking inside your head without opening your mouth, and then he'd swirl it so hard it slopped over the edge.

The bartender came back in, fireworks over.

"Hey, Elaine," he said to me. "Where's Cleo?"

"Wherever," I said, tipping my chin up. Not going to worry about Cleo, not like that guy two seats away, making up what he'd say to someone who wasn't even there—more likely, what he'd never have the guts to say. I could do better. I gave him a look that told the world I could do better—and he was giving me the same look.

Then he shifted it away from me, like he couldn't just do better than me, he was too good for this bar, this street, this city. Maybe even this plane, because when he turned his T-shirt pulled tight over his chest and I could see a texture through it, rings about the size of keyrings. Eight, ten of them, like a necklace. Crystal holders, for someone who had enough magic inside him to charge crystals.

That was daytimer magic, and Cleo and I made fun of it. But seeing those crystals knocked the fun out of me. Some people didn't have to kill things to get a charge—that's what those rings meant. Some people got a charge just from living, as if they and the world were friends. But they still ended up in bars alone, talking to their drinks.... I ought to go look up Cleo, I thought. Make up with him. Stick to my own kind.

The little guy kept looking around the bar and I could feel the power coming off him—a dense, angry feeling, thicker and heavier the longer he looked around. But then it started to change. It turned into the same feeling I had when some demon hung round outside the pentacle, hoping to get the corpse I was working with. Magicians called that the cauld grue, and it was like being packed in live ice.

The new feeling wasn't centered on the little guy, but on the stool next to him. I could tell he felt it too. He jumped up and backed away from the bar, and he wasn't mad any more. He looked more like he was going to cry.

The bartender noticed it, as well. He grabbed the fire extinguisher, sprayed the stool and the bar in front of it with a thick gray stream, half foam and half bittersmoke. The bittersmoke was the really awful stuff. It got up in my nose, in my hair, drained the power right out of me; I thought I was going to pass out, or throw up.

"What the hell do you think you're doing!" I screamed, scrambling off my stool. "You could kill someone with that thing!"

"Sorry," said the bartender. "Are you all right? Come in the back room, and I'll find you something." He meant something to kill, and I wanted it; but I couldn't walk through that smoke into the back room. I couldn't even get back to the bar for my purse. The cloud was spreading, and I had to back away from it.

"I can't," I said. "I've got to get out of here." The air was better in the street. I looked around for something to kill, but there was nothing in sight but moths flying round the streetlight, too high for me to reach. The little guy came out after me, with my purse, and found me leaning on the pole wishing for them.

"That was my fault," he said. "Can I get you something—help you get home?"

"I want those moths," I said, and he looked blank. "I'm a necromancer."

"Oh!" said the little guy. He looked up the pole. "I guess I can manage that," he said, in a sort of flat it-must-be-done voice. He'd almost conjured a demon into the bar, but he thought killing a few moths would be worse. We didn't look at each other. He shinnied up like an expert and caught the moths, tied them up in his handkerchief, threw it down to me. I had them crushed and out of sight by the time he got down, and I was feeling better.

"You must be from the Academy," I said to him. "Magic, right?"

The College of Magic was another part of the Royal Academy of the Arcane Arts and Sciences. The sorcerers I'd studied under told horror stories about what went on in Magic. So I wasn't complimenting the little guy when I said this, and he could tell.

"What, are you from Sorcery? I thought Klimt was their only necromancer." He waited a little while before he realized he wasn't going to get chitchat. "I'm in the Demonology department," he said then, a little shamefaced. "But my real field is Natural Philosophy. Hiram Rho. Everyone calls me Rho."

"I'm Elaine Hale," I said. "Crown Prosecutor's office." It didn't mean a thing to Rho, I could tell, and I liked that. He didn't care who I was or what I did any more than the dead did. Restful. Something caught his fancy, though, because when he could have walked away he didn't. He made offers—a ride, a drink, a dinner. I took him up on them. I needed food. It wasn't every night I could get a free lobster dinner, either, especially in one of those nice places where you can pick out your own live lobster in the tank—but you have to get a table right by the kitchen door so you get the best part, when the cook drops it into the pot. Rho knew that without my telling him.

"You probably want to know about the demon," he said, when we had the food in front of us. "That's what it was, in the bar."

"Not my business," I said. If he could be cool about my life, I could return the favor. "It's not coming here, is it?"

"No, it only shows up when I'm disgusted."

"Well, whatever," I said, eating lobster. Ought to scratch him off my list, I knew. A man who calls up demons when he's peeved is nobody's bargain. But there was something about him telling me all this. Telling me the truth, when it couldn't do him any good. Like we were going to be friends from the ground up. Rho went on with his story.

"I picked it up at a conference in Selanto," he said. "Literally. One of the presenters called it up to kill another presenter, and the security officer enchanted it into a piglet. I was inside the pentacle, watching the lines, and I thought it was a real pig. So I picked it up to keep it from running across the line. I let it through my wards—once you've done that, you can't shut it out again."

"Everyone knows that," I said. "But it still seems pretty dim. Why would you expect a pig at a conference?"

"It was a session on veterinary lechery," he said stiffly. "How was I supposed to know no one had a pig with them? Besides, if it had broken the lines, plenty of people would have been killed."

"Whatever," I said again. "Why are you telling me all this?"

"You weren't scared. Not of the demon, at least. Most—well, everyone I know is scared of demons."

"Oh, I'm used to them," I said. "They always come around after the bodies I work with. It's just another nuisance, like fleas."

Rho grinned. "Fleas!"

"Well, fleas are really worse," I said. "They jump off onto you."

"I suppose you could say it jumped off onto me," said Rho. "In a way."

"So what were you doing taking your demon out to a bar, anyway?"

"I had a bad day. I needed a drink," he said. "I thought if I was out with people, I wouldn't get so disgusted. I forgot it was Vernal Equinox, and the traffic was lousy—I almost got run over three times, and some jerk flipped me the bird for crossing in a crosswalk, with the light...!"

"That calls for demons," I said. "You should have sicced it on him, not the poor bartender."

Rho laughed. "If it was convenient, it wouldn't be a demon. Anyway, I'm sorry I ruined your evening."

"You didn't ruin my evening," I said. "Not unless the guy I was waiting for sees us having dinner together." I hadn't thought until that moment that Cleo might be the jealous sort. I wished I had never thought of it. Rho wasn't pleased, either.

"Who were you waiting for?"

"Cleophilus Eleuthra." I didn't like saying his name when I was with someone else. And I didn't like the look on Rho's face, either. Now, he was thinking, he might really have a problem. But he got over it.

"Why don't we go up to my place, instead of sitting here? I can show you my pigeons."

"That's some line."

"No passes," said Rho. He held his hands up like an umpire or a traffic cop. "I just don't want to sit there alone."

"I don't cheer people up," I said. "You want attitude adjustment, hire an enchanter."

"Whoa!" said Rho. "I'll take care of my own attitude! I just don't want to think about that blasted department meeting. I'll show you the place, we can have a drink, look out the window and watch the sunrise. It'll only be a few hours."

I poked in my lobster shell, but like I said, his picture was in my head. "I could handle a pass," was what I said, after a minute.

Rho laughed. "I couldn't. Not after that bittersmoke."

"How do you get a charge, anyway?"

"Sunlight," he said. "I'll have to wait till morning." It sounded like a promise.

I'd always admired the Magic Department's castle with its turrets, rooftop walkways and the moat, or at least a pond, against one wall, reflecting the mossy stonework. It looked like the cover of a romance novel in the moonlight, right down to the one lit window in the East tower that was Rho's room.

Inside, it was a maze, the big castle chambers chopped up into a warren of little offices and labs. Old buildings on the ley-line pick up so much magic that nobody can dismantle them. Whoever tries it has accidents, run-ins with heavy objects that don't want to leave their home. So remodeling's the game. Flimsy remodeling at that, made of stuff that can't fight back when you decide to take it out again. Even that carpeting and sheetrock and plasterboard picks up too much magic to ever be plain rubbish. It brings a high price on the waste market.

Cleo bitched about the Academy remodeling. He wanted the contracts, he'd have done a better job than what I saw there that night—but who knew what the ley-line would have done to his stuff? Maybe one midnight it would've all turned back into chicken bones, all the little dens the magicians had cut their castle into.

Rho's tower was one round room cut across by a new wall so he had a bedroom and a workroom, with temporary-looking plumbing in one end of each. The view was the best thing about it, and there were pigeons as promised, looking in the window when we came in and making throaty noises about us. Rho told me all about them during the two-minute tour. Then we sat at his big table under the window.

"How did you know you had a talent?" he asked, but I turned the question back at him. People only ask about you to be polite, before they start talking about themselves.

"It was pigeons," he said, waving at the window. The birds snuggled against the screen in a feathery heap. Every few minutes one of them would move, stick its head up and peck a neighbor. "One of my father's friends raised them, and hired me to take care of the loft," said Rho. "I found out I could understand the birds about half the time."

"Is that what Natural Philosophy is?"

"Mostly," said Rho. "We all talk to different things, though. I'm good at birds, but I can't do plants at all."

"What about insects?"

"Sure," said Rho.

"Crickets? Lobsters?" He nodded. "Then how could you buy me that dinner? Don't they holler?"

"I can't hear them all the way from the kitchen," said Rho. "Besides, they're nasty. Just listen to the ones in the tank sometime. Stupid and nasty."

"I thought Natural Philosophers loved everything, except maybe people."

Rho thought about that for a while, looking out over the campus. The first bit of sunrise made a red smudge along the horizon, and a big white star hung in the sky above it.

"The saving thing about animals," he said at length, "is that they have really bad memories. They don't hold grudges. If a lobster does something nasty, it's just a response; the lobster hasn't been sitting there planning it for two weeks, or keeping score about who was nastier to whom. Plants are even better, they say—plants don't even notice most of what other critters do."

"That's the attraction?" I said, looking hard at the sky. I don't know why I asked another question, because I wasn't listening. I was over-conscious of the morning, full of little living things without memories, as clean as bodies. Things that were going to wake up and see a fresh new world, look at it through eyes instead of through agendas. Things that were themselves without having to be dead. When I started listening again, Rho was in the middle of something.

"That's what they like," he was saying, "at least that's what mine tells me they like. It could be lying. But that is when it shows up."

"I'm sorry, what?"

"All that thinking. Stewing. Making up speeches, or rehearsing why you're right and someone else is wrong. That's what the demons like about people. That's why they get trapped if you conjure them into animal forms; they can't remember enough to work up a good head of steam."

"Then why do they want the bodies I work with?"

"I don't know. Still, you start the brain up again, don't you? A demon could use a nice brain, perhaps."

I didn't like that thought; a demon getting into one of my bodies, filling those eyes up with plots and plans. Making it live again. "Being human is nobody's bargain," I said.

"I think being a demon is worse," said Rho. "You know, sometimes I wonder if they can perceive anything at all outside their own minds. I've thought about this a lot," he said, settling back in his chair, "and it seems the way creatures in the arcane realms would develop. Because nothing there is solid, if you have enough power to change it. Paying attention to what exists now would be pretty useless, if someone stronger than you could change all that in an instant."

What a different world it looked like from these windows, as if some demon with enough power had taken Cleo's sharp-edged city view of Osyth and turned it into fuzzy campus trees. Rho's windows were half-open and the world outside came in and out with the soft air's movements. It was as if we hung our sentences on the breeze and let it carry them back and forth, and none of them mattered any more than the leaves that the same breeze was rustling in the trees below.

"Dead people can remember things," I said. "They just don't care." And I didn't care myself; I shut my eyes, and felt the air, and imagined I could feel the world turning under me. We sat for a long time in the growing light. It was very quiet.

"How much power would you get if you killed a demon?"

Cleo was ambitious.

"Lots, I'd imagine," I said. "If you can even kill a demon. He might not let you, though. I think he's sorry for it."

"I think he'd be glad to get rid of it," said Cleo. He paced back and forth in front of the windows, with the cold view pressing on them from outside. "I have an idea that could make us both—" he gestured, as if there were no word for what his idea could make us. "I'm talking pure power."

"What?" I could only think of souls—though how anyone could get the power out of them was beyond me.

"Oil," he said. "Fossil fuels. Hydrocarbons."

"You can't be serious!" Oil, you see, is far too long-dead for necromancers. Alchemists can handle oil, just a little bit—but alchemists don't care what they do, what they mess up in the arcane world. Overall, oil is mundane. Not because magicians scorn it, but because none of us can control it. "It's just not possible," I said. "What's next, plastic?"

"Perhaps," said Cleo. "Nothing would be beyond me. Coal, chalk, limestone—I could manage anything that didn't come straight out of a volcano." He looked past me for a minute, into the future. "Oxygen," he said, more slowly. "Carbon dioxide. Water. Why not? They've all come from something that died.

"Just ask him to meet me," he said. "It's a win-win situation. He gets rid of the demon, and you and I get whatever we can make out of it."

It just didn't grab me. Oil. Too dead—so dead there wasn't anything dead about it, if you get what I mean. It was just stuff for Cleo to make dreams out of, the way Rho's demons made a world up around themselves. The penthouse, the view, the city outside all looked unreal, as if only Cleo's wanting them kept them here.

"Don't brood," said Cleo. "I got us a treat, to celebrate."

"Celebrate what?"

"Our anniversary," said Cleo. "A year today." He turned away from me, leaned over the back of his couch and made psst psst noises, and after a second his treat stretched itself, came sliding out from underneath, and jumped up on the couch-back between us. It was a white cat, the alley sort, with what looked like old oil stains on its rough coat. I could see that someone had tried to wash it, though. It had a fat round belly hanging down between its skinny legs, a contented look, and tuna breath.

Cleo shifted over until our legs were touching and patted his lap, and the cat jumped down as if he was its friend. He petted it, rubbed under its jaw and around until he was scratching the bubbles behind its ears, where cats love to be tickled, and it had stretched out its neck with a silly smile and tensed up its hind toes. I could see the claws dig into Cleo's knee as he squeezed harder, crushed the base of its skull with one gripe. Its feet relaxed and he let the head settle down while we both shut our eyes and felt the power come into us.

Then he did something I'd never seen before; he stroked the body one long caress, and it sat up on his lap, dead as it was. Cleo petted it again. I could see it plumping out under his hands; thick fur, pink ears. Pads soft again, like it was a kitten. It purred and paddled on his knee.

"I like to give something back," Cleo said. "Happy anniversary, Elaine, and many to come." He kissed me, but I could feel the warm cat between us and I wondered who he was fooling. It was a dead body. We didn't mean anything to it any more.

"Don't do that," I said, but Cleo acted like he didn't hear.

"You ever do a cat before?" he asked. "They're better than rats. The cold-blooded animals aren't worth a thing. You'll never go back to crickets after you've gotten used to mammals."

The cat was still purring and it stretched out a paw onto my lap, like it wanted both of us together and everything would be just fine. The cold would stay outside, and we'd all be warm in our little nest, the way the world should be. It inched another paw forward, an elbow onto my leg, purring all along, and with those empty eyes half closed, contented—eyes that should have looked straight through me at nothing but the truth. It was the first time I'd ever thought a dead thing was horrible, those warm toes...I wanted to jump up, scream, shake it off me.

"Stop it!" I said. I took hold of the cat's shoulders, twisted its head up to look in its eyes, spoke to it without any charms or pentacle. "Lie down, you're dead," I told the cat, and it went limp in my hands, turned back into a true body. Scraggly, horny-toed, stinky mouth. Cleo just laughed, and I didn't know if he had made it happen, or if I had.

I did jump up, then. I threw the cat at him, right into his laugh, and that got him off the sofa.

"You bitch!" he said. "You raise the dead every day—where do you get off—"

"I don't make them pretend to care!"

"You make them pretend not to," Cleo yelled. "You're the only person in Osyth who could give a dead body tips on how not to care!"

Then, right in the middle of it, he gave me a look I hadn't expected. I was waiting for him to yell at me and tell me more about how I was in the wrong, but instead I could see him thinking it wasn't worth it, that he needed something from me that was more important. Sizing me up, scoping me out, figuring how to manage me.

"Just ask Rho to meet me. Wherever he feels most comfortable. I don't ask you for that much."

It was a long summer. Dog days. Nasty sticky hot days, even the bodies sweated. I let the tape on my answering machine fill up, told people it was broken. No way to get hold of me but the pager, no calls from anyone except folks who spoke for the dead.

I didn't see Rho again until we met at the courthouse one day in August. I re-met a lot of people that way. They got into strange territory, saw me, acted like we were best friends just because mine was the only face they knew.

I didn't want to re-meet Rho, but when I saw him in that stuffy building it was like seeing an old friend—someone you let go, thought you'd never miss, but then you see them and remember why you liked them. He'd changed, though. He looked grayer, thinner. Bad look in his eyes, a tired look.

We only got to talk a minute before one of the smooth lawyers—Ellis, from Grant, Ellis, and Howe—came bustling over to break it up. Two young fry from his firm stood down the corridor, looking at us, and they had four other people with them in jackets with patched elbows. Academy types. Rho didn't move, even when Ellis took hold of his shoulder.

"You on the jury?" I asked him. Ellis glared.

"I'm a witness," said Rho. "A hostile witness." He wasn't fooling. He looked just as mad as he had in the bar, but tireder. Like he'd worn himself out with it. The lawyer had a fit.

"You're enjoined to keep your testimony confidential," he said. "This is a closed hearing."

"I'm not talking about my testimony," said Rho. "I'm telling her how I feel. I hate everyone involved in this case," he told me, "and I wish they would just kill one another and get it over with."

"Yeah?" I said. "Well, if you kill them, get rid of the heads. That way, I can't call 'em back to identify you."

"Dammit, Elaine!" said Ellis, tugging harder. Rho grinned and let himself be pulled away.

"Dinner," he yelled. "Lobster. Eight o'clock!"

"You look like hell," I said.

"Hell is other faculty," said Rho, as if it was a quote. "Let's talk about something else."

"Fine," I said. "If lobsters are so stupid, what do they talk about?" Rho leaned toward the tank, gazed into the distance.

"Stop shoving," he relayed. "You're in my space. I'm under this rock, you keep out! Good, at least she's gone -" the waiter's assistant reached in and pulled my dinner out, and the other lobsters applauded by waving their claws with the rubber bands around them. Rho stood up straight.

"I thought we were going to talk about something else," he said.

"Did monsieur want a lobster?"

"Yes," said Rho. "The one under the rock."

"So," I said. "Any demonic visitations lately?"

"Dammit," said Rho, "are we ever going to talk about something else?"

"You come up with something, and I'll talk about it," I said. "D'you want to hear about the latest murders?"

"No. What's Eleuthra up to these days?"

"I don't know," I said. "We broke up." Maybe I was just catching it from Rho, but it seemed like everything was about fighting. "Cleo wanted to kill your demon for you," I said. "He wanted the power from killing a demon."

That got Rho's mind off department infighting, all right. He looked at me with his mouth open. "You're kidding."

"Cleo never jokes about business. Didn't he call you?"

"No!"

"Well, are you interested?"

"I don't know," said Rho. "I've had it for twenty years. I got rid of it once, but that didn't last." He didn't have much to say while we ate. I thought he needed a more lively date, someone who could make people laugh and forget.

"Well," he said at last, "It can't hurt me to talk to him. If you'll be there, too."

It was strange to be in Cleo's penthouse again. I stood near the windows and watched the men together. Cleo was his same self, like someone's dream of a magnate. Rho had made an effort, and looked worse in an old shiny-assed suit than he would have in tee-shirt and jeans. I felt closed out, as if two worlds had met and I wasn't inside either one of them.

Cleo gave Rho liquor, and I could tell Rho hadn't had anything like it before; he drank too fast, like someone who's used to rotgut and can't believe the smooth stuff really has alcohol in it. Cleo refilled his glass, and set the bottle next to him, and then they got to talking about the demon.

"You don't deserve to have something like that hanging over you," said Cleo. "You have to have bigger dreams for your life than sleeping alone in a tower with wards all around you. It's not even safe for you to go to a bar when you're down, is it?" His voice was so understanding. His hand moved, the way it had when he petted the cat that last time, but Rho didn't see it. "I know what it's like to be alone," said Cleo. "I used to tell Elaine that everyone I really knew was dead. But that's better than having the only person you really know be a demon."

"I don't know..." said Rho, looking at his hands.

"Why? What is it?"

"When I first had it, it used to come all the time," said Rho. "Now, I hardly see it. Except right now, things are rough. Mostly, though, I've learned not to get upset—not to care about things so much. If it wasn't coming—what would I do—would I start being mad again, all the time, fooling myself that it was all right? It's not the demon," he said firmly, putting down the glass. "The demon's nothing. It's the being mad that drives me crazy. At least the demon takes up some of the power. I used to hurt people when I got that mad."

"Are you living the kind of life you want? Locked up in that tower?"

"I'm living the kind of life I live," said Rho, defensive. "Nobody lives the kind of life they want. They just make themselves miserable wanting it."

"That's crap!" said Cleo. "Take away a man's dreams, and what you have left might as well be dead. Life gives you raw material. It's your job to make it into what you really want."

"That's not how I see it," said Rho. "I can't make my life over, but I can learn to stop being upset by it. Maybe I need the demon, just to remind me what life's like when you only see it through your own dreams."

It was as if Cleo decided to get angry, like a plan. He sneered at Rho. "That's slave thinking," he said. "A man dreams. He takes a chance. Maybe he gets hurt, but he gets hurt trying! You sit in your ivory tower and make fun of dreams. You sit there in front of a full plate, with clothes on your back and a roof over your head, and say people should get used to the lives they lead—"

Rho stood up. "You're right," he said humbly, but it was a surface apology. He was somewhere inside, leaving the polite body to do whatever would get him out of here. Cleo glared at him.

"Don't patronize me," he said. "You need that demon. It's your excuse for staying cooped up with pigeons. The real world's too dangerous for you. You might find out you're not as important as you think you are, with your research grants and your little publications that nobody buys, and the pretty awards you give one another." There was the beginning of a grue in the room, I thought. I looked at Cleo, but he didn't seem to notice it. "Go on," he said, opening the door. "Go back to your toys. Stay in the academy and pat each other on the back."

"I will," said Rho, very stiff and dignified. I moved to go over there, but he froze me out too. "Goodnight, Elaine; I'm sorry I wasted your time." Cleo closed the door after him, and glared at me.

"Well? What are you looking at?"

"Nothing," I said. "I—I don't know."

"I do," said Cleo. "You're looking at yourself, but you can't deal with it. You can't face what your life is made out of. I gave you everything you could ask for, and you took it all, as long as you could keep your hands clean. Do you think he's innocent, with his helpless act? The only innocent people are dead. You'd better go, before I give you that too."

I caught up with Rho a half-mile north of Cleo's building, just outside the East Gate where the city wall shut out the Academy grounds and there was nothing across the street except a big blackness of wasteland, leading down to the ley-line. He was leaning against the great arch of the gate—no, he was pounding his head against the stones, with the grue all around him. "No, go away," I heard him say; a mundane going into the city looked over and saw just a drunk carrying on, shook his head and hurried away, and the demon came like a black light, a freezing blanket, a thickness in the air.

It was man-sized, with great black wings that met the ground. Bird wings, not batwings. Their long feathers rattled against one another like something made to chime, not fly; its body was thick in some places and thin in others like something made for art, not living, and its face wore the look a man's face wears when he's so lost in planning he forgets he ever had a body. Its face was like a flame just starting to burn, like that first instant when fire leaps up the side of a building.

It looked at Rho like he was all it had ever dreamed of. It leaned over him, put its arms around him, he was hidden in those glorious wings, and I heard it murmur in the voice they told us all to wait for—the true-love voice, the voice the prince uses when he's crossed the seven oceans and climbed the seven mountains and fought his way into the hidden castle—that voice let me move again.

I wasn't sure what I wanted. One second it was Rho, one second it was the demon; maybe some seconds it was what Cleo said. I walked across the street without looking for traffic—that face, that laugh getting closer and closer—until someone's hand on my shoulder pulled me aside and someone stepped in front of me.

They were all still for a moment, and then they all moved, Rho lunging away from the demon and Cleo toward it. I couldn't tell if he meant to kill or embrace it, and its face said there wasn't a difference as long as whatever he did fed that flame. His hands were in those feathers, sunk so deep in them that just watching I could imagine how they felt, crisp and dry, the hard hot bones and skin underneath. The demon laughed and bent over him, and Rho gaped at them.

"Stop!" he yelled, gasping. "You can't bind it—you don't know its name!" The demon raised its head and looked at him, and then it bent back to Cleo and it spoke, in that voice that all the stories are written about.

"Cleo," it said. "Your name is Cleo." It folded the great wings around him and it was a shimmer in the air again, a thick heavy patch of darkness, and they both were gone. Rho fell through the place they'd left, grabbing at the air.

"It took him away!" I said. My voice didn't want to come out. "Where—where did it take him? What'll it do to him?"

"I don't know," said Rho, on his hands and knees. "It never asked me to go anywhere."

"This isn't about who it likes better! This is about Cleo! Where did it take him?"

"I said I don't know," said Rho. He got up as if his stomach hurt. "It's a demon. It lives in Hell. But it could go anywhere. Are you all right?"

"No." I was full of the grue, shivering as if I would never be warm again. "Nothing looks real," I said. My knees were wobbly; I sat down by the wall. Rho squatted down beside me and he didn't look real either, he looked like a picture of himself made by someone with a different taste in art, someone who liked dry things and bright things, and bristly textures. He was all eyes and hair.

"That happens, when you get too close to a demon," he said. "You start seeing things the way it sees them." His voice was hard to hear.

"I think I need to kill something," I said. Rho went away and then came back down the street, with his handkerchief full of cockroaches, but he looked better to me than they did. I could take him, I thought. Rho crouched down beside me and I couldn't think of a thing to say.

"Elaine? Are you all right?"

"No," I said. He reached out to me and I raised my hands toward his face. I knew just where to hit, how to smash his nose up into the brain, and how it would feel. The rush, the sparkle that would turn the whole night into a moment's glory. And after, how warm and strong I'd be; how easy I'd get up, and walk away—but Rho pushed the handkerchief into my hands and closed them hard around it. Then I felt the little cockroach lives go out, each one like a sharp clean spark of light, and that horrible hunger started to fade away. I sat for a minute with my eyes closed, trying to shut out what had almost happened.

"Are you all right?" Rho asked again.

"I think so. What'll it do to Cleo?"

"I don't know," said Rho. His voice cracked. "It never hurt me, not really. Demons aren't as bad as everybody says. When you look at it from their point of view, they're just trying to get along. Like all of us."

"You're crazy," I said. "Or you need some power."

"I'll have to wait till morning," Rho said. He sat down beside me and put his head on his knees.

"You'll be all right," I said. I leaned against him. His side was warm and hard, all bones. The streets were bright under lights, black between them. A big wind blew rubbish in circles and unsettled everything.

"I wish I could just shut my mind off," said Rho. "This poor body hasn't done anything to deserve it." I didn't really listen. I was trying to push everything out of my mind except the feel of the night, the pavement, the big wind; and even though I could tell Rho was crying, beside me, after a while I was able to ignore it and fall asleep.

It was getting light when I woke up. The wind was still there and it was going to be a clear, frisky day. Rho was asleep, washed out. I didn't see any point in waking him up before the sunrise, so I sat still and watched the edge of the wooded Academy grounds across the street. I saw a family of raccoons, with the young ones almost as big as the parents, and a lot of birds. There were different kinds of birds, which I guess I had known about. That made me look at the trees, and there were different kinds of those too—not just pine trees and regular trees, but different kinds of pine trees over there along the ley-line. I wondered if the ley-line made them all look different from one another, or if they were really different types. Then the sunlight darted through them and made speckles on my dress-front.

Rho turned toward the sun and opened his eyes.

"Are you feeling better?"

"Not yet," he said. "I need to get on the other side of the hedgerow."

"What's that?"

"The row of trees," said Rho. "I need to get into the sun on the other side of it, over by the ley-line."

"All right," I said. We stepped on all kinds of little live things on our way through the trees into a mowed meadow full of sunlight. It felt wonderful. I could have kicked my shoes off and run around that meadow all day, but since Rho had to lie down I threw myself down beside him. I'd never seen a daytime magician recharge; I was curious.

"Help me get this off," said Rho, picking at his necklace. I undid it at the back and pulled it out. It had twelve gray crystals about the size of poker chips, in those plastic rings people slip around keyheads to mark them, far too heavy for their size. "It's drained," he said. "That's why it weighs so much. I was living off it all night. You better not hold it or it'll fill up from you."

"Maybe you won't need it any more, now the demon's gone."

"I don't wear it for the demon," he said. "I use the crystals in my instruments." He put his head down as if talking was too much work, and I sat and watched things get up around us and start moving. When I looked back at Rho he was more filled-out looking, with some color in his face. He was shivering a little bit, but it was the way someone shivers when you touch just the right spot, and he relaxed after every shiver and sighed. I lay back on top of an anthill and felt pretty good myself. After a while the birds got brave and came down around us, eating bugs.

When I woke up again, Rho had the necklace draped across his chest. He looked fine. The necklace sparkled all colors; I could tell from the way he handled it when he sat up that it was light again.

"How do you feel?" he asked.

"Great," I said. "This place is wonderful! Every time I move, I kill something." Rho looked a little shocked. "There's things dying all around us," I said, trying to make him understand. "Everything's killing things. It's normal, here." It was like the feeling I'd had when I looked out his window and thought about animals seeing the world the way it really was, the night he'd told me about the demon—the demon, I thought. Cleo. It was like they were from a whole other world, the world I'd belonged in until last night. How could I have forgotten about them?

"What about Cleo and your demon? We can't just leave him with it," I said. "Demons kill people."

"I can't conjure the demon," said Rho. "I don't know its name. But we know Cleo's name. Why don't we go down to the pentarium, and ask someone to try conjuring him back? It opens at nine."

"That's two hours," I said.

"It can't be helped. It takes all of us to run the thing. Besides, he's been with it all night. What's two more hours?" Rho said it like he didn't care at all, but it wiped the whole meadow, the whole morning, out of my thoughts. All I could think of was Cleo, ripped apart by some demon. He didn't deserve that.

"Do you need a focus? Something he owned?"

"I don't know," said Rho. "That never comes up with demons."

"Well, it helps with bodies," I said. "Something they owned when they were alive—I can get something of Cleo's from my apartment, and meet you at your office."

Walking out of the meadow was tough. It felt like I was giving something up, every step I took on the grass. When I got onto the pavement, though, my mood changed. My shoes clicked on the concrete. I walked faster, businesslike, back in the human world where death had been fought back so it was an event, not a background, and I thought I'd been pretty stupid. Pretending there was a place where killing was pretty. Telling myself sweet little stories. None of that sunny-morning-with-trees crap was real, I saw now. This was the real sunny morning, hard edges of light coming between tall buildings. But then I thought no, this was the crap. Crap people had built out of their dreams. What made it more real than the world around it?

It was the same thing when I got into my apartment. I could look at something—anything—and make it change under my eyes. Jewelry Cleo'd given me was a friendly gift. No, it was payback. No, it was a claim; no, a tax write-off. Who knew?

"I hate this!" I said. I stopped looking, shoved the nearest stuff into my purse, and headed out, past my cage of crickets. And what were they, I asked myself. Pets, yeah, sure. Food? Decorations for an apartment with nothing alive in it?

"They're the only things in here that can see the real world," I said. The crickets didn't belong here. They belonged in the sun-and-trees world over on the ley-line. I leaned over them, looking at their big dull eyes, and I was leaning that way when I felt the grue from behind me. I turned around and saw Cleo, half-transparent, pulling a body for himself out of the air and smoothing it into place. I sat down, breathless.

He didn't look like he'd been in Hell. He must have killed the demon, I thought, and now he had the power he'd wanted—over oil, and air, and water. He looked around the room. I could see him shifting, making a better body as he thought about it. It was very nice indeed, a work of art, and then he ran his hands down its smoky surface and made an evening suit, as perfect as a suit could be. He looked at me in my wrinkled dress and smiled.

"You look half-dead," he said. "I hope you like it."

"Cleo! Where are you? Did you kill it?"

"I don't need to kill it," said Cleo. "It needs me. Being able to remake your world is nothing, if you don't have imagination; I dream things up, and it makes them happen. I can share it all with you, Elaine—everything you've ever wanted. Unlimited power."

I only stared at him, and he frowned. "Do you understand me? Take it now or leave it forever. If you send me away, I won't come again."

"Send you where? Are you staying in Hell?"

"That's a laugh! The magicians just call it Hell to scare common folks out of it. The world can be whatever you want, there," said Cleo. "The past, as well. You can remake the past—or kill it, if you want to. All you need are dreams. All you have to do is want it." He sat down beside me, in the plastic-covered chair I'd never wanted to see him in, but of course it turned to leather and mahogany as soon as he touched it. He was still Cleo. He had the same face and build and hands, but there was that look like a flame behind it. And his voice was like the demon's voice, the voice of everybody's dream.

"Are you happy?"

"We could be happier than you ever imagined," said Cleo. In that voice. "You can be whatever you want, Elaine. You can make a world where you belong. It's your choice." The whole room held its breath, and then a cricket chirped. A miserable black bug, hopping away from the others in the cage, jerking its feelers away from their nasty jaws before they could eat it alive.

"Could I have a cricket?" I asked. "Not what I think a cricket is, but really a cricket? Or a tree? Or a pigeon?" I could breathe again. I felt the whole world big and full of living things around me, and Cleo was small in the middle of it, like a man locked in a cell just the size of one body, one mind. "It's a big world," I said. "There's more room for me here than in any dream."

The edge of the wind came through the window and Cleo looked at me one last time, but already I could see his mind turning away from me and the breeze to something inside himself, full of nobleness and fire. He raised his head, looked into a future I wasn't part of and a past I was being wiped out of, and he thinned out into a shimmer, a black space, gone. I looked through the place he had stood, and then I carried the cage of crickets through that space and walked out the door, back toward the ley-line and the rest of the sunlit morning.

SF MINNESOTA (founded February 1992) is a multicultural, multimedia organization dedicated to improving contacts among groups and individuals interested in speculative fiction, in and out of the traditional SF community. We have a special commitment to making our state's SF community more representative of the cultural diversity of Minnesota in the third millennium.

Our biggest project is **DIVERSICON**, an August convention celebrating and exploring diversity in speculative fiction, including diversity of fan groups, diversity in media, and especially cultural diversity. Past Guests have included authors Eleanor Arnason, Ruth Berman, Paul Park, Joan Slonczewski, Maureen F. McHugh, Karen Joy Fowler, Pat Murphy, Lois McMaster Bujold, Suzy McKee Charnas, Laurel Winter, Steven Barnes, Tananarive Due, Melissa Scott, Martha A. Hood, S.P. Somtow, Mark Rich, and Minister Faust; editor/authors Pam Keesey, Nalo Hopkinson, and Sheree R. Thomas; editor Stephen Pagel; actor Bruce Hyde; futurist Earl C. Joseph; and artist Rodger Gerberding. Through our Posthumous GOH's we explore the history of speculative fiction, from Shakespeare to Mary Shelley to Verne, Wells, Kubrick, Roddenberry, and Dr. Seuss, and of science, from Lucy the hominid to Einstein.

The **SPECULATIONS READINGS SERIES**, the science fiction/fantasy edition of SASE—the Write Place's Carol Connolly Readings, are held monthly at DreamHaven Books, and include a reception with free soda pop and cookies. The readings have come to provide a major source of camaraderie among readers and aspiring and professional writers, who often hang out together at Dulono's pizza after the readings.

The **CLASSIC HORROR FILMS** video party in the fall surveys the history of the classic horror film, including liner notes on the films viewed.

We also host **DIVERSICON PARTIES** at MarsCon, Minicon, and CONvergence in the Twin Cities and OdysseyCon and WisCon in Madison, in Krushenko's, the floating SF salon. Other projects to which we make contributions are the Gordon R. Dickson Scholarship Fund for Clarion West students; *Tales of the Unanticipated*; and the Carl Brandon Society website promoting writers of color.

UPCOMING SF MINNESOTA EVENTS:

Thursday, August 10: **The Speculations Readings Series** featuring **KELLY LINK and BRYAN THAO WORRA**. 6:30-8:00 p.m., DreamHaven Books, 912 W Lake St, Minneapolis. Free soda pop and cookies.

August 11-13: **Diversicon 14**, Holiday Inn Select International Airport—Mall of America, Bloomington MN, with Guest of Honor **KELLY LINK**, Special Guest **BRYAN THAO WORRA**, Posthumous GOH's **Benjamin Franklin, Mark Twain,** and **Robert Wise**, and featuring a *Tales of the Unanticipated* Publication Party Saturday.

Thursday, september 26: **Speculations** featuring a *Tales of the Unanticipated* 20th anniversary reading by **ERIC M. HEIDEMAN**. 6:30-8:00 p.m., DreamHaven Books.

Thursday, October 24: **Speculations** featuring **CATHERINE LUNDOFF**, 6:30-8:00 p.m., DreamHaven Books.

Check the SF Minnesota website for quarterly updates on Speculations Readings.

Saturday, November 4: The **CLASSIC HORROR FILMS**, Part 15: "Fava Beans," 1988-1991, featuring six or seven films from the period. Free. Noon to midnight. RSVP Eric for directions: 612-721-5959, eheideman@dhzone.com

August 3-5, 2007: **DIVERSICON 15**

SF Minnesota Board of Directors:
Arthur C. Johnson David Christenson Eric M. Heideman
SF Minnesota President rekal@prodigy.net Membership/Corresponding Secretary
952-432-9014 612-721-5959
art_johnson@frontiernet.net eheideman@dhzone.com

www.diversicon.org

DIVERSICON 15

"When Cons Collide"
(a one-time co-sponsorhip with ConSume Relaxacon)

August 3–5, 2007
Holiday Inn Select International Airport—Mall of America
3 Appleton Sq, Bloomington, MN; 1-800-45-HOTELS or 952-854-9000

Guest of Honor: ANDREA HAIRSTON

Andrea Hairston is the author of the novel *Mindscape* (Aqueduct Press, 2006) and fiction in *Dark Matter: Reading the Bones* (Sheree R. Thomas, ed.) and *So Long Dreaming: Postcolonial Visions of the Future* (Nalo Hopkinson and Uppinder Mehan, eds.). She is a professor of theatre and Afro-American studies at Smith College in Massachusetts and artistic director of the Chrysalis Theatre, which has produced her science fiction plays *Soul Repairs*, *Lonely Stardust*, and *Hummingbird Flying Backward*.

Posthumous Guests of Honor:

ROBERT A. HEINLEIN (1907–1988): author of *Double Star*; *The Door into Summer*; *Have Spacesuit, Will Travel*; *Stranger in a Strange Land*; *The Moon Is a Harsh Mistress*; and *Job*.

GEORGE PAL (1908–1980): producer of *Destination Moon*, *When Worlds Collide*, *The War of the Worlds*, *The Naked Jungle*, *The Time Machine*, and *7 Faces of Dr. Lao*.

OCTAVIA E. BUTLER (1947–2006): author of *Mind of My Mind*, *Kindred*, *Dawn*, *Imago*, *Adulthood Rites*, *Parable of the Sower*, and *Bloodchild and Other Stories*.

R A T E S	
	NOW: Through the Ides of March (15 March) 2007: Adult $25, Student (ages 5-17) $15
	Through Bastille Day (14 July) 2007: Adult $30, Student $20
	At the Door: Adult $40, Student $30
	Supporting: $5/Converting $25
	Mail check or money order to: Diversicon 15, PO Box 8036, Lake Street Station, Minneapolis, MN 55408

For Further Information:
www.diversicon.org
Chair: Rick Gellman, sf@visi.com, 651-483-6290
Programming: Eric M. Heideman, eheideman@dhzone.com

Laurel Winter is an accomplished reader of both poetry and prose. This chronicle of lovedeath is a bit of both.

Flo & Eb

by Laurel Winter

It was one of the more-recent-ish of the times they didn't get together. She reminded him of milk & cookies. He was into tits & ass.

You have to understand about the conservation of knowledge, even though they didn't/don't/won't understand it themselves. There always was/is/will be only a certain amount available to the two of them, regarding the nature of their relationship. It can be divided up however—a little for one, a lot for the other; vice-versa; equally dispersed into not enough for each—but there's never enough for both of them to know all that is necessary. Never.

In this case, she had it all. "Sorry kid," he said, when she rang his doorbell at 7:22 a.m., interrupting his coitus. "Not interested."

He was way into sex, but he wasn't a perv, so a little girl in a green dress didn't do it for him.

"Cookies," she said. "The peanut butter ones are really good. The Peanut Butter Patties, not the sandwich ones. You'll like them. I know you will."

"Don't need any," he said.

She tried to thrust the clipboard into the closing doorway. "Please." He was thirty-something and maybe cute, but in a scary grown-up-man sort of way. She was in sixth grade and about to move to Texas. Some other member of her troop would end up doing the delivering. But he was why she'd become a Girl Scout, knowing, somehow, that selling him three boxes of Peanut Butter Patties the year she turned twelve would be all the contact allowed in this lifetime.

"No, thank you," he said, firmly, not wanting to encourage her desperation and being rather an expert in the art of the brush-off. He closed the door and went back to his current lover, who'd come from Canada to see him and had plenty in the way of T & A. "An early Girl Scout," he said, slipping out of his robe and back into bed. "I told her we didn't need cookies for breakfast." They laughed and got back to sex.

They finished to both their satisfactions, more or less. At a certain point he couldn't put off work any longer, so he showered and shaved and donned his office GQ.

When he opened the garage door she was standing in the middle of the driveway, behind his car, obviously late for school. "I won't go until you buy some cookies."

She was skinny and lightly freckled and something about the way she looked at him made him want to cry for a second. Instead, he bought three boxes of milk chocolate-covered peanut buttery cookies and some other girl, rounder and less intense and accompanied by her mother, delivered them some weeks later. And that was that, except that the cookies almost reminded him of something that would have made him cry. He was grateful they were over-packaged and short on actual cookies.

One or the other of them got hit by a bus before she could grow up enough to make it remotely legal.

Most of the times they didn't share location or language, just a vague or specific sense of something missing.

Only rarely did their names actually have anything to do with ebb, or flow. She was Florence Nightingale and he died before she arrived at the battlefield. Maybe that's why she went in the first place, looking to heal that wound.

Another time his name was Ebony and he cooled her with a peacock fan in the big house. She called him boy and sold him to a friend of hers when he was four years old. He clung to her leg and cried. She had to beat him with a wooden serving spoon to detach him.

Once he was a barnstormer appearing near her town. Her friends were so surprised she actually went, since she'd gone from child suffragette to teenage intellectual to college professor, with no time for such foolishness. But, she was bored and it was sunny but not hot. She dragged her stuffiest friend to the field.

He knew she was there. He could sense it. He'd never flown so well, so daringly. He picked out her straw hat amongst all the others—then the biplane went into a spin and not even his parents would have recognized the blackened bits of him after the volunteer fire department put the flames out.

She didn't understand why she cried so hard she fainted. The doctor who pronounced him dead had to be called over to administer smelling salts to her.

He came back to her that lifetime, when she was two steps shy of the grave. Her friends teased her about the handsome young handyman who mooned around her all the time. When she'd taken those two steps, they wondered who left wildflowers on her grave nearly every day.

Fifty-some years of wildflowers—no one else in that cemetery was ever so cherished.

Once she was almost his child, if his ex-girlfriend hadn't slit her wrists when the rabbit died. It was more than a 17-year-old Catholic sweater girl could handle. He was in Colorado when she did it, whitewater rafting with a couple of frat buddies who weren't as smart as he was and drank their weight in Budweiser every day. No one could reach him, but he knew anyway. He ditched the frat boys and got back just in time for her funeral.

Her parents blamed him because of the autopsy report. He blamed himself. They'd broken up before either of them knew and there was no future in it and he hadn't even wanted children—ever—but the loss of that unknown daughter bit him harder than he thought possible. No one really believed it was an accident when his Chevy went off the bridge.

It wasn't.

Maybe it was the gods and goddesses keeping them apart. Maybe it was physics—the certainty that it was too early for the heat-death of the universe.

Before any alphabet was invented, she put her hand over his ochre handprint on a wall in a cave in France and shuddered. She wanted to turn to stone. The closest

she got to that was bone, before he came back through. He drew spears through his own handprint without knowing why.

If you knew it would be the end of everything, would you introduce them at a party, being a good hostess and incipient matchmaker and friend of a friend of each of them? Knowing how long they'd longed for each other? Knowing that this was their only chance to couple, in any real sense of the word, while they both still had anything resembling bodies?

Please say yes. Your hair will never be shinier than it is today, more manageable or buoyant. Your figure will only sag and pooch from here on out. You won't save the rainforests or the whales or the children. Why not let Flo & Eb have their electric transcendent passion?

They will put their longings to bed on the futon couch in the upstairs study. One of them will surely be able to operate a futon. Or they could do it on the floor—they won't care. Anywhere. Anywhere.

Anywhen.

SONG THE CITY SANG OFF-KEY
(Greg's Remix)

Greg couldn't taste the morning coffee, but he could see his
reflection in it, and a piece of paper floating on top.
He extracted it and read the words out loud:

*"Lips tasting of women's purses and
cannibalized lies, or worn theater seats rejected....
The wart on her thigh enlarged and laminated;
my alligator lover comes in different shapes and
sizes.... Today the city sings off-key and rises."*

Greg tossed the paper in the trash
and went out into the buzzing street

(The city groaned, took a deep breath and
sang a note: a strained note of imperfection.)

At the corner, he hails a taxi.
The driver's got a bullet in his head,
and dabs at the raw hole with a red Kleenex.
"That's alright, I'll take another," said Greg.
"You sure?" said the taxi driver. "The city's in
a piss mood. You might get lost."

Greg got in anyway.

(Reptilian eyes stare at him from the rearview mirror.)

High above, broadcasting on a building were the words:
SEXY SOMETIMES FORGETS TO MENTION
HER ENDORSEMENTS:

**Vagabond. For the lonely traveler.
The cologne that can't stay in one place.**

A rugged man with cowboy hat and alligator teeth
fills the advertisement, and takes a bite out of
a horse's ass.   *Saturation. Excess. Product displacement.*

Greg picks up the newspaper on
the seat, skimming the headline:

TODAY THE CITY SINGS OFF-KEY

"That's not news," he said.   *But what is anymore?*

Air conditioner's going sour, so he rolls
the window down, and the sound pours in...

The streets are automated, children drift by
with cotton candy sticking to their lips,
and alligators on leashes rest by fire hydrants
and contemplate the city's voice
        rituals   are
                      performed everywhere,
for all   to see
                             and   hear
A woman in an enormous pink hat saunters by.
Greg wants to love her. He tells her so, and
she gets in the taxi with her alligator.
"Hope you don't mind," she said, "he hasn't
eaten yet."

The alligator eats the taxi driver.
"Where to?" said the alligator, resetting the meter.

(Greg tells him where to go.)

He can't see the woman's eyes—
only her smooth jaw and scarlet lips, parted
for a kiss; he tries not to look upon her before the ritual.
Starts. To. See. Lampposts and street signs, recklessly
dance about; the city has come alive in song and dance.
The alligator driver joins the ceremony on all fours,
tail thrashing in 5/4 time.

Greg takes the woman's hand, and leads her to his
bed where they tear each other's
clothes off…the window shatters as words are
projected across their skin from the waning sunlight
spilling letters into the sheets.
                He feels a strange sensation of falling…
the words cut through him (as words often do)
…the sheets, bloody…the lyrics remixed in Hi Def…

orgasms out of focus; hazy conclusions drawn from a
televised assassination; wakeful gesture; mournful Jester;
she sheds skin like raiment (her lips tasting of women's
purses), padding around in bare feet, slapping at the tiles,
scales peeling from her heels

Alligators atop skyscrapers, dissolving—

she shivers beneath him,
and night knows not its
name

—CORNELIUS A. FORTUNE

The publication that ran the first published stories of Carolyn Ives Gilman (#1), Peg Kerr (#2), Kij Johnson (#3), and Nathan Walpow (#13) is proud to serve up the remarkably assured—and creepy—fiction debut of Douglas J. Lane.

Mister Eddie
by Douglas J. Lane

I hate the muthafuggin dark.

It wasn't always that way. I never used to mind night time, used to prowl, to shake down suckers who didn't know I was in the shadows. The night was kickin, and me and the other Dry Bones owned it, from Butcher's Hill to Eastwood to where Fells Point dipped its toes in the harbor. Wasn't nobody could take it from us, neither. At least not until that night with the Hat Man. That changed all the rules, gave the night back to Mister Eddie.

I don't expect you to believe the shit that gone down. You'll be sayin that I been busted in the head one too many times. "Ty," you'll tell me, "that's a lot of bullshit, even for you." But I'm the one in the muthafuggin dark, not you, and I'm the one who peeped what's in it and run away from it. But that changes tonight. I got the booze and roses and I know the words, branded them into my brain so they's like a neon light, and I can put it all to rest. But for now I need to stay on the down low, 'cause maybe he's not done yet, 'cause I'm the last bitch that Mister Eddie needs to take out of the box so he can go on killin, ghostin fools forever.

We never shoulda jacked up the Hat Man. I was different then. I thought I was hard—all bangers do, like we was poured out of steel and anger and couldn't be stopped. I was a player. I copped what I wanted when opportunity knocked, threw down with my set when other bangers tried to muscle our turf. I never smoked nobody, even though I said I did. I claimed three because that's what bein hard is, the boast about how you're badder than Camden, even if you're not. But I never took nobody's life by my own hand. I just liked the bangin. That's the only reason I was with Jojo and Rondu the night the Hat Man got knocked.

He'll always be the Hat Man, 'cause of the lid he was wearin. Two-thirty in the mornin, middle of January, nothin movin on the streets but the cops and the crooks and so damn cold that standin still was like askin to die. We was rippin off shit from cars parked on the street when we spotted him. He was a queer sight, creepin in the shadows but still steppin fast, a man with a mission. His suit was so dark he woulda disappeared, 'cept for the white scarf. Even in the shadows of doorways, of overhangs and the dark mouths of alleys, my eyes could pick him out.

On top of his head was a hat that matched his suit, the same dark color. When he slipped into the light, I could see the sharp lines. It reminded me of the movies Hollywood J liked to watch, old black and whites about mobsters and tommy guns and turf wars, shit that shoulda seemed like comedy to a Roller like Hollywood J, but they was phat, you know? They was the first gangstas, hard boys with scars and bad attitudes and the loudest guns you ever heard, even if they talked a lot of smack and always sneered before they started bustin caps. The Hat Man looked like one of those gangstas, but instead of a semi-auto, he had a bag under his arm, a brown paper sack rolled at the top. He clutched it like it was his baby.

When Jojo saw that, he said it had to be either drugs or money, and either way, we was gonna get it. We bolted down a side street, footsteps echoin off the empty buildings, and got a block ahead of the Hat Man. We waited at the end of the alley until Jojo gave the sign, a hand signal that he copied from some crew cut he sold crank to. We jammed the Hat Man and pulled him into the alley.

That should have been the end of the story, like any good snatch and grab—a shove, a grip, a yank and jet down the sidewalk until you're somewhere you can see what you scored. But when Jojo looked in that bag after he took it from the Hat Man, when he unrolled it

and peered down its neck, he got all worked up, like he been cheated. He threw the bag against the wall and it sounded like a domestic, all broken glass and bad news. The bag landed with a plop and three of the reddest roses I ever seen slid out the open end. They laid there in the cold, in a dark puddle that smelled like booze. I think about those roses all the time. I think about them so hard, the color hurts my head.

You could tell by eyeball Hat Man was educated, a college boy once, but way past the point of chasin booty and suckin up to professors. His face had gone craggy, but the eyes—if they'd been knives, they'd have taken a little slice of each of us. Those eyes saw everything, straight down through my soul and out my kicks. They shoulda been the eyes of a dead man waitin on angels, but they was nothin but chill. I seen that look once before, on the face of an old timer lived over in Saint Helena. He'd done a stretch in Da Projects for accidentally smokin the homie of some PoPo up in the Bronx. I gave him two dollars once to buy crank with so he'd tell me the story. He said The Man don't like to see one of his own bleed, even if it's just family or a homeboy, so they beat him every day in lock up 'til poppin wheelies became his only way of gettin around. Crippled him so proper, the state turned him loose with nothin but spokes and rubber for legs and empty years ahead of him. The whole time tellin what they done to him, he had that same expression—somebody who already known deeper shit than anything he'd ever face again.

That was the Hat Man's face, starin down Jojo. But Jojo was expectin drugs or money, 'cause he was one-track, so when the Hat Man smarted off to him about not even havin a wallet, it pushed all the wrong buttons. Hollywood J didn't let Jojo throw fists during jump-ins no more because when he tasted it, when his blood got angry, Jojo was a machine, worse than a rotty trained for the throat or the nuts.

We never saw how it started, me and Rondu. We was leavin. I mean, it was a big zero. Hat Man had nothin but his clothes, and he was stick-skinny at that, and there was no sense freezin for nothin. But we heard it, the sounds, fast like an uncorked Mac 10 mowin a row—the wet smack, the grunt, the body fallin, bone on stone. Jojo carried a piece of rebar, ragged at the ends, with black electrical tape wrapped around it. He liked the feel of it when he punched, the way he could break and rip in the same stroke. When we turned around, me and Rondu saw Jojo was already on top of the Hat Man, knee in his chest, beatin him down with a rebar left, his right hand on Hat Man's windpipe. The man's face was already a mash of blood and twist. Rondu tried to pull Jojo off. I stood back and kept eyes on the street.

It didn't pay to mix with Jojo when he was wide-eyed, four-alarm freestylin, kickin up a red mist. Hat Man may not have earned it, but I wasn't gettin scars for him, neither. Rondu found out the hard way when Jojo gave him a taste. I waited until Jojo was done punchin and cursin, until he'd gone through every pocket and found nothin, and by then it was too late.

He even tried on the dead man's shoes, and swore harder when they was too small for his big ass clown feet.

Rondu shook his head when it was over and tore ass out of there. Jojo spit on the body before meltin into the dark. I lingered. I didn't want them to see what I was gonna do, 'cause it would have brought Jojo down on me, too. When they was gone, I stepped over to the Hat Man, limp on the frosty ground. His face was like chopped meat, one side tore up and crushed in. Blood oozed from everywhere. I could smell that he'd pissed himself, but I still went over. See, Moms always said that death and dignity should walk hand in hand, so coverin his face seemed the right thing to do. I picked up his hat, turned it in my hand, and brushed dirt off the brim.

I was lowerin the hat onto his face when he sucked wind. His unruined eye snapped open, and I could see a milky film gatherin over it, but it was still sharp, still tore through me. Ocean blue in that hazy cloud.

"You're all going to die," he wheezed. It was immediate and certain to him, the way a banger talks when he's got the world's biggest piece in his left pocket to back up his trash talk. Then he made a stranglin sound and the good eye closed again as he exhaled a final time. I dropped the hat over his face and ran out of that alley. I didn't stop or look back until I'd caught up to Rondu.

I never saw Jojo again. None of us did, because before the sun came up, he'd already split to join the Hat Man.

I didn't give the Hat Man a second thought the next day until the limo. Done is done, and there ain't no time machine can take it back, even if I wanted to. I had other tricks up my sleeve, like a DB girl named Shawna—tasted like honey and hooch, with a booty to make the full moon jealous. She was on fire that day, all but begged a player to swing by her crib. I was on my way to break off a piece when the black stretch limo rolled up on me. Three homeboys with the same wrinkled faces and college-boy look as the Hat Man piled out and hustled me off Pratt Street in broad daylight. Not one passerby twitched when it happened, even when I shouted. I never understood how kids could just go missin, could wind up on the sides of milk cartons as if they was ghosts, until that day.

I could tell they was a gang of some kind—the black suits, matched down to phat silver cufflinks with the letter "F" on them, to the black leather shoes that was so glossy they always looked wet. Two of them flanked me, blockin me into the center of the limo. The third sat opposite me. That one had a piece in a holster under his jacket, a 9 mil from the look, the butt bobbin into view whenever he shifted in the seat. The old guy next to him was their High Roller. You could see it in the way he did the talkin.

He was the oldest man I ever seen. His face was nothin more than a skull with skin, his head crowned in thin, white hair that reminded me of snow. A tube hooked into his nose from a tank at his feet. His eyes was the yellow of old paper, sick, dyin slow. His suit was rumpled, but it made no difference. He was their power, and they all knew it.

He told me his name was Reynolds, said he and his peeps was an outfit called "the Folio Club." Then he handed me a picture. It was grainy, black and white, but that didn't stop me from recognizin myself, standin in the mouth of the alley where we'd wasted the Hat Man. Rondu was almost out of the picture, and Jojo was pushin past me. Two feet in socks stretched out behind me on the ground.

"From a security camera across the street," Reynolds said, his voice thin as his hair. He took the picture back, and I was sure they was gonna kill me. I realized I had no idea where the limo was. We were rollin hard, circlin the city. I felt helpless, no one to get my back, no gun, not even the switchblade Big Johnny gave me last Christmas. I expected the one with the piece to draw on me.

Instead, Reynolds asked, "Have you seen the papers today?"

I shook my head. I didn't listen to the news, didn't read even one word of the *Sun*. Wasn't even worth it for the ball scores. "Why? Was I in 'em?"

"I want to share a particular news item," he told me, and held out a clipping. It rustled in his wrinkled fingers, flutterin like a bat tryin to escape his tremors. I took it, glad he hadn't shook my hand.

MAN FOUND BEATEN TO DEATH IN ALLEY
Body Believed to Be 'Poe Toaster'

Fans of author Edgar Allan Poe, who were disappointed early today when the mysterious figure known as the 'Poe Toaster' failed to appear at the author's grave, got a second shock when the body of an unidentified man believed to be the anonymous visitor was found beaten to death several blocks from the church cemetery.

"Based on the victim's attire and items found at the scene, we believe that he was the individual known as the Poe Toaster," the Baltimore City Police disclosed in a written statement issued this morning. Police sources cited the discovery of a broken bottle of cognac and three red roses in a bag near the body. Police estimate the time of death at approximately 3 am, consistent with times in the past at which the unidentified visitor has made his appearance.

Dressed to hide his identity, the Toaster has attained the status of a modern folk legend over the years, with an annual visit to the author's grave on the anniversary of Poe's birth in order to leave a memorial. This is the first time since the original sighting of the figure in 1949 that he has failed to call at Poe's grave site at the Old Western Burying Ground.

I handed the article back. "Are you guys cops?"

Reynolds took a long, slow drag on his oxygen hose. "No. We're here to get you on your way."

They wanted me to run. Reynolds tried to lay this trip on me that we'd pissed the wrong person off when we whacked the Hat Man, and he was gonna come after all us Dry Bones now, especially me and Jojo and Rondu. It didn't make no damn sense. As Hat Man's Roller, Reynolds would be gunnin for us if anybody was. But Reynolds said the same guy would be comin after the Folios too, 'cause they hadn't made their tribute like they was s'posed to. This guy would be up in our grill first 'cause we was directly responsible for breakin the chain. Then Reynolds had the nine-hundred pound brass balls to tell me that so long as I was runnin, the guy with the axe to grind wouldn't be chasin *them*.

I ain't nobody's nigger. Especially if you're suggestin I red flag the bull so he forgets about carvin himself up some rich old suckers. I told Reynolds I wasn't afraid of nobody who wanted to mix, that this boy who was so pissed off was welcome to bring it, but he better come packed for bear. Otherwise I was gonna take his picnic basket. I asked him who the little bitch with hoop dreams was.

He told me it was Mister Eddie.

When Reynolds started to go on about Mister Eddie, I turned on what Hollywood J calls the Autopilot—a nod here and there, eye contact, the kind of shit that'll save your ass when the PoPos come askin about somethin they think you done. There was no need to listen. Mister Eddie was bullshit kiddie talk.

We'd all teethed on the stories. Our parents started us young, like they do with any bogeyman, but Mister Eddie was different. He was homegrown, right in our own hood. Mister Eddie was messed up, too. You could see it in the stuff he wrote about, men going crazy and killin people, cuttin out their hearts or brickin them up in the walls. Moms told me and my cousin Maurice when we was both five that if we was good all year, Santa would come at Christmas. But if we was bad, if we lied or stole or talked back, Mister Eddie would come earlier, at Halloween, and he would eat us down to the bones, because Mister Eddie loved bad kids to death. They said his ghost haunted his old crib, right near the projects, so he was always close by, waitin to pounce if we strayed.

We all believed it to a point—dumb kids will believe anything—but when you live in the projects and you get older, and every week someone gets stabbed or popped in a drive-by or busted, the bogeyman is the hard-core banger in different colors who wants to slice you up for somethin one of your set done, not some old writer with a thing for ravens. Reynolds went on, but I was tuned into two other things instead: the motion of that limo, and how the fool across from me swayed with it.

I wanted his piece.

Reynolds finished. He sat back in the seat and eyeballed me, waitin for a reaction. I sweated him a little before I told him his story was a real chiller, but I had a better one about three kids with a father so out of his mind on blow that he grabbed an axe 'cause he thought they was a wood pile.

Reynolds wasn't down with it.

"Don't you get it, you little bastard? You killed the Bearer of the Ritual! You disturbed Poe's fucking sleep!"

His bony fingers grabbed for my throat, but he was old man slow. When he pivoted, I ducked forward and dropped my itchy right hand inside the Folio's jacket. Damn, it was a sweet move. I wish Rondu had been there to see it, on account of he always said I was clumsy. I dipped and came out with the piece, not a 9 mil at all, but a Glock 40. Before Reynolds could get his claw on me, I had the mouth of the pistol reinforcin the air hose crammed in his nose.

"I didn't do a damn thing," I said. "Never touched your homie." Nobody in the limo moved. Reynolds was chill, even starin down the barrel.

"No. You stood by and let him die. His blood on your hands. His and the rest who will die. One careless act and you've killed more people than an airline crash. But you're not going to get *us* killed. You're going to run for your pitiful, worthless life."

I thumbed the hammer back until it clicked and told him I wasn't doin anythin except gettin out of the limo, and if I had to do it wearin his brains for a hat, I would.

He weighed my words. I could see they was a ton on his mind. He nodded to the homeboy who lost the Glock, who tapped on the glass between us and the driver. I felt the limo wheel over to the shoulder. Beyond the windows, the Inner Harbor was flowin with tourists.

I slipped my free hand inside Reynolds' jacket, found his wallet. It was fat with my favorite things, money and plastic. I stuffed it down the waistband of my jeans. "This is insurance. You keep your set on a leash, Skeletor, or the Dry Bones will be payin you a visit, and all the canned air on Earth won't help you breathe any easier." I reinforced it with a poke of the gun.

Reynolds didn't say nothin.

I gave them all the once-over and stepped from the limo. I tucked the Glock away. It was five hundred easy to the right banger, if one of the DBs didn't pony up for it first. They was about to close up when I grabbed the door. I peered in at Reynolds and told him I thought he was crazy, all his whack talk about ghosts killin and some ritual to keep them in their graves. "You wanna know about killin, let me see your face around here again, bitch."

Reynolds stared a moment. "You won't. But if you remember one thing, remember this: keep moving."

I slammed the door. The limo pulled into traffic. The breeze off the water was bitter cold. I walked six blocks in the fadin day to Shawna's crib. We got sweaty and sex-funky in her parents' bed, and I just made it out the window ahead of her daddy's meaty fists, her shoutin at him to leave me alone.

It was the last normal night of my life.

Jojo died scared, his eyes so wide they looked like they'd been broken open by what he saw. Cops found him in a parking garage about four blocks from where he'd rearranged the Hat Man so bad that even Jesus wouldn't know him. The DBs was buzzin with the news when I arrived, still full of Shawna. Our crib was a empty warehouse in Holabird, a lost place waitin to be tore down or to fall down. Weeds grew clumpy along the base of the building and through cracks in the asphalt. It was after midnight when I went under the fence into the yard. I slipped in through the side door, the one with the secret latch we'd installed to keep wanna-be's out. There was a dozen small lights on, flashlights mostly, though there was a couple lanterns too, enough light to see by, not enough to attract PoPos prowlin around.

Half of gang life is drinkin and bullshittin. A few

members was doin both, Jojo and 40s mixed on their lips. He could go buck wild, even bring the heat down when he went mental, but Jojo was still blood, and when a fellow banger gets burned down, it makes us all a little jumpy. Guns get loaded, fingers begin to point. I suspected Reynolds or one of his peeps, but I didn't want to talk about it with nobody but Rondu. He needed to know about the Folios, their picture of us and their malfunction.

First DB I ran into was a pee-wee named Goldie, who sucked up to Hollywood J like he was made of candy. Hollywood J kept him around for small jobs, errands, messages. I thought he was annoying as hell, but I wasn't the Roller. He told me Rondu was in the office, tryin to catch some winks on account of the long day with Jojo and all. He said Rondu's cage been rattled bad.

I was half-way there when a scream tore through the warehouse, off bare walls and high metal ceilings, comin from everywhere and still from straight ahead.

I ran, kept runnin even when the scream stopped. I was the first one through the office door. I saw Rondu and wished I hadn't. Propped in the corner, back to the wall, his dark hair had faded pepper gray, his mouth fixed open in a scream that had run out. Blood seeped from behind crazy wide eyes. I followed their dead gaze across the room. Before Reynolds, I might have dissed what I seen as a trick of the light, or that chill you get when your eyes peep a shadow as a thug with a hand cannon. But what I saw standin there, what walked away through the solid wall, was real.

It was Mister Eddie, snatched right out of an old picture, so pale he might have been standin in the moonlight. His cheeks was sunk inward, a mop of dark, wild hair clung to his head, with more drooped under his nose. His suit was dark but dusty, like someone who'd been hidin in an attic. His glance was a cold blast at me, his brow narrowed in rage, his eyes a silent accusation. He looked like the baddest roller who ever lived. Maybe he was.

I heard him in my head

Lord help my poor soul

before he was gone, stridin across the room and through the wall, and his gaze never left me 'til he was out of sight. There was promises and threats in that stare. Then I felt Goldie at my shoulder and a bunch more of the Dry Bones at my back. I read on Goldie's face that he'd seen Mister Eddie too, but before it came up, Goldie caught a peek at Rondu. He whistled low as he crossed himself.

You'd have thought a swarm with the Northside Irregulars had broken out, people runnin everywhere. A bunch of bangers gathered Rondu's body up and took it out of the warehouse. Goldie jetted to wait for Hollywood J outside the police substation where they'd made him cozy to talk about Jojo. I stayed off to the side. By the light of a lantern, I pulled out Reynolds' wallet.

I wished I'd listened to him. I realize now it wouldn't have saved Rondu even if I had, but it would have made things a hell of a lot easier later. From the wallet, Reynolds' driver's license gave me an address, but when I checked it out the next mornin, I found a house that was empty with a fresh "For Sale" sign on it. Big, bare windows that opened on fancy, empty rooms told me everythin I needed to know about whether Reynolds was home.

Most of what was left in the wallet was for shit, except for the $300 in cash—business cards that led to disconnected numbers, credit cards that came back canceled. Skullface even had a gym membership ID card that wouldn't expire for four years. The thought of him wheezin his grizzly ass along on a treadmill might have been buggin in a different situation. There was a magnetic stripe card like you see in movies, the kind those smooth pimp spies like James Bond use to go through doors to where the secret shit is kept. I knew it was the key to the Folio's crib, but there was nothin to point to the door.

I took it all in, over and over until I thought I'd go gangsta on someone, until the answer leapt up at me. The address on the gym membership card was the color of the Hat Man's roses.

The name of the place was Eddie's Gym.

From the street, the Folio Club looked like every other beat down building on the block. I'd have never found it without the address. The swipe box was hidden behind the mailbox on the front porch. The little light on it blinked green on the first go. Inside the door, things rattled and clunked, and the door buzzed. It swung in easy, like I'd been invited.

The Folio Club was the phattest place I ever broke into. It smacked of places like the White House, maybe fancy hotels—wood floors, wide staircases, furniture what looked like it came from an antique store. Daylight sneaked in around the drapes that blocked the windows.

It was obvious the Folios had ditched their club on Red Alert. Half a pot of cold coffee was still in the kitchen, dishes in the sink, and a desk in one room had been looted. Papers was everywhere. It was more of the same upstairs. Squatters in a couple of bedrooms had packed quick, drawers out of dressers, stray clothes layin around. Three floors of echoes was all that was left.

I was about to clear out, thinkin it would be an upscale new crib for my set, and let the Folios just try to take it back, when I saw light through one of the walls. Turns out it was a door set in the wall, very sly. I'd have never seen it if the sun wasn't out. It took some doin, but I finally figured out how it latched. When it popped open, light poured out of the secret room.

It was a library. Monster wooden bookcases with glass doors lined the walls, floor to ceiling except where there was windows. Those shelves was crowded with more books than I'd ever seen in one place. Old books, too. Not a paperback or booty magazine in the bunch. There was a dozen leather chairs, old school sticks that was fresh again, each with its own lamp. In the middle of it all, a long table stretched. A single book sat on the table, fat and stinkin like old dirt. Parts of the cover flaked off when I picked it up. The title was in gold, some of it wore away.

BEING AN ACCOUNT OF THE FINAL DAYS OF
EDGAR ALLAN POE, THE AUTHOR, 1849

The book was written longhand. Teachers musta had mad skills back then, 'cause I could read most of the scribbles. First page said the whole thing was jotted on the down low, while Mister Eddie was dyin in the hospital. The author snuck in around the doctors to get the truth. This was the Folios' secret book of knowledge, the whole reason they was who they was. Hollywood J always said "Know the enemy." I sat in a chair near the window and began to read.

If I hadn't peeped Mister Eddie in our crib, I'd have thought the whole story was the tripped out blow nightmare of a jacket-wrapped junkie.

Sez the book, a few days before he died, Mister Eddie jumped a train to Philly. It stopped along the way, and while they was waitin for God knows what, Mister Eddie saw this queer little thing crawlin through the grass. It looked like a rotty with needles for teeth. He followed it into the woods, but the bitch got lost. Hours later, sun traded out for the moon, he blundered up into the crib of some kind of monster.

Mister Eddie called it the Prince of Wonders, which is mega-double-whack with a fuggin cherry—if I saw what he claimed, I sure as shit ain't gonna stop to name it. I mean, tall as an oak tree, the color of ink, and blades comin out of its jaws and paws? I'd be jettin. But Mister Eddie musta had stones made outta diamonds. In its crib, Mister Eddie said there was a pile of bones as tall as the monster was. Realizin he was in up to his lobes, Mister Eddie tried to creep without being seen, but one of the needle tooth rotty things took a bite out of his ankle, and sucked out his soul. That's what he told the fool what wrote it out—he knew his soul had been ghosted. Mister Eddie wandered around the woods for a few days before he found the rails again, and hopped a train goin back to Baltimore, where he died. That's where he said what I'd heard full blast in my head: "Lord help my poor soul."

That was all there was of the book. There had been more pages, but they was gone, ragged strings hangin in the binding where they'd been tore out. In their place was an envelope, taped inside the back cover, crooked, done fast. My name was on it. I pulled the envelope out, looked inside. My eyes nearly dropped out of my head. Benjamins stared up at me, more than I'd ever seen before. Tucked in next to them was a slip of paper. Two things was written on it:
BEAUCHAMPS FOUTREAUX, NEW ORLEANS.
and below that in neat letters was the words
Keep moving.

Reynolds had planned on me at his crib. He even knew my name. I felt like I'd been played.

I tucked the envelope in the band of my jeans, their money for my trouble, and the Folio crib was abandoned for the second time. They wanted me to keep movin, so fuggit. I went to the rail station and bought me a ticket to DC. Shit, if crazy old men wanted to line my pockets to move, I could dance. I decided to live large for a couple of days, let all this shit with the Hat Man blow over, and life could fill up with honeys and all the trimmings again. Reynolds, and the Hat Man and the fool in New Orleans could all suck it blue.

I came back to a defcon 1 shit storm. Night I left, Goldie died hard in the warehouse, instant replay of Rondu, bloody eyes and all. Foot soldier named Tommy followed him the next night. Tommy was a good guy, had the hook-up at the Yards so we could watch baseball in the summer. It happened down near the harbor, while he was waitin for a water taxi to carry his ass home. Third night, while I was groovin on a cut of Grade A named Danni at a club on E Street in the District, Hollywood J went off to Roller Heaven. PoPos found him in the church yard where Mister Eddie was supposed to be dirt nappin. Hollywood was laid back against Mister Eddie's tombstone, pointin up at the author's name. He knew. He'd seen. I wondered if Reynolds got to him somehow.

Five dead Dry Bones in five days. It didn't take a diploma to puzzle out the math. Wasn't any of the DBs could see beyond the usual suspects—Irregulars, one of the local Crips sets, another gangsta group what had a big breakfast. The fools were preppin for war without even knowin who to fight.

I did a ghost on them that same night. What else could I do? They'd have only dissed the notion of a killer Casper. I left out of the warehouse, tossed a bag together while Moms was at work, left her a note tellin her I'd be back. Hollywood J and Rondu and the rest buzzin in my brain, Mister Eddie's cold glare a fresh shiver, I snagged the first plane I could to New Orleans.

It took a phone book, two streetcars and an hour of wanderin around quiet neighborhoods before I found Beauchamps Foutreaux. He was stashed in a lime green rat hole, two stories worth of beat down, hidden off an alley across the street from one of those crazy bone yards they got down there, with all the people stacked in little buildings instead of the ground. Standin on the porch, I heard rustlin inside, before I rang the bell. They was draggin sounds, like lazy people who couldn't hoist feet to step. It stopped when Foutreaux came to the door.

Foutreaux was a Cajun. He looked forty, but claimed three times that. He was three large, pimped out in a blue sheet and sweatpants that never came close to coverin his roll, sunglasses hidin his eyes. He called me by name when he came to the door, said he knew I was comin. It smelled like more of Reynolds yankin strings.

I never put no stock in hoodoo, for the same reason I wasn't down with ghost stories. Zombies are for X-Box games and bad Mekhi Phifer movies. But Foutreaux claimed he was a Hoodoo Man, said he knew I was there for the same reason the Folios had come years before: to throw a wrench into Mister Eddie's works.

The Folios rung Foutreaux up back in 1948, on the run, scared, hunted by Mister Eddie, who was bringin it old school to their door. They'd caught themselves in their own drive by. Foutreaux said they stumbled across the story Mister Eddie told on his way to the grave. Reynolds led his set into the woods to get Mister Eddie's soul back, 'cause the Folios worshipped him and his messed up stories.

They found Mister Eddie's monster. It was tits up by then, half buried under its pile of bones, the needle rottys long gone. Mister Eddie's soul was swirlin around inside a glass ball like a storm cloud, sittin in a groove on a rock, on display for nobody. Reynolds busted the ball open, figurin they'd set the soul free, 'cept they didn't understand: Mister Eddie's soul had nowhere to go. He was trapped here 'cause of how his soul was ripped out while he was alive. It was like he missed the last bus to Hell when his body died.

Mister Eddie was as much a machine as Jojo was on blood and bad feelings. He kept comin after them, killin one a day, every day. When he couldn't get a Folio, he snuffed someone else, anydamnbody, all the while bloodhoundin Reynolds and his posse.

The Folios paid Foutreaux big coin for some hoodoo to keep Mister Eddie from makin the world his personal slaughterhouse. The Cajun cooked up a ritual for them, a toast with some fancy French hooch, said in private, and then three blood red roses for leaving in public, on Mister Eddie's grave. He explained them roses as "one for the land of the living, one for the land of the dead, and one to draw the veil between the two." He said the only catch was that his hoodoo only worked at Mister Eddie's grave. Only on his birthday.

It might as well have been a sentence for dealin. Three hundred fifty plus days on the run, only to go back to Mister Eddie's grave, where Hollywood J cashed out. My lunch tried to come callin again.

Foutreaux dissed me when I asked for a copy of the ritual. Wouldn't take my Benjamins. Instead, he wanted blood in exchange. In that funked-up accent, he said "Nothing's free, but blood guarantees." I saw in his smile he was tricky, and I could hear Moms curse a blue streak at me while crossin herself over her boo gettin in deep with a Hoodoo Man. I let him take it anyway. Pricked me with a thorn and squeezed seven drops into a small bottle, his hands rough and cold.

I figured it like this: I ain't ever smoked nobody. More then three hundred suckers who never did nothin to me was gonna miss their next birthdays, 'cause I didn't try to stop Jojo from perpetratin. It was Mister Eddie's black heart, but it's me what let it happen, and that makes me a hardcore gangsta killer, whether I cap 'em or not. On that score, we was all marked—me, Rondu, Jojo, the DBs, the Folios—we was all damned already. The Hoodoo Man deserved to have my blood to play with.

The sky started to cloud up. Foutreaux disappeared into the house, hummin a tune, and I thought he was gonna play me. I was ready to lay the beat down on him, hoodoo or not, but he came back with a copy of the ritual. I skimmed it and tucked it away in my pack. Foutreaux was gone before I could say anythin else, went inside and locked the door behind him. In an upstairs window, I saw someone move behind a window, pale and stiff. I thought of the shufflin, the cemetery next door. I beat feet out of that yard.

I stayed the night in New Orleans, but I could feel Mister Eddie rollin in with the fog, and I was happy to kiss hoodoo town goodbye the next mornin.

The money held out a whole year, but damn, I'm skinny now. I been just about everywhere, but I still only seen the inside of my heart. It's chill in there.

I started readin the newspaper everywhere I went, tryin to spot Mister Eddie's victims along my path, evidence he was creepin. I could for a while, saw them starin at me from the obits, but the guilt over dead peeps I never wished no ill on, women and kids whose only sin was standin between me and what I had comin, got to be too much. I took it on faith he was still creepin closer, everywhere I went.

I'm in the warehouse tonight. All the Dry Bones are gone, and I ain't tried to find them. I wanna believe one of my homies got away while Mister Eddie was on my ass, but I doubt it.

The Folios all been slabbed too. Heard on the radio that Reynolds' card got punched just after midnight tonight, a few blocks from here. Guess Reynolds bit it hard on the whole decoy theory of rich white survival, and came back a day too soon. The radio said he was the last livin banger of Baltimore's oldest book club. They didn't name it, but they didn't have to. I knew, 'cause there was still one member, even if I never was jumped-in proper. In this shit, we was all one fat hairy dysfunction at the junction.

One way or the other, it will be over tonight. I been readin the ritual every day since Foutreaux vamped me for it. I only got to hold out another hour or so with the rats and with what I done. Then I get dressed in the suit, make the toast, speak the words and drink the booze, and head off to the cemetery with the roses.

Like I said, he's already smoked Reynolds tonight. One a night, that's the way it works. But I'm close, too close here in the warehouse, and Mister Eddie is still out there. Who knows if he'll play by the rules when he's so close to bangin forever?

Shit. He could already be here in the muthafuggin dark.

The Memory of Vermouth

When wonder has been officially measured and
filed away with the answers to
every question ever possibly asked,
the official will close the drawer
and rub his collarbone
and make himself a martini with no olives because
those are gone the way of admiration and insult both.
There will be only just enough vodka
and the memory of vermouth
and he will drink it down
and swallow himself
and the glass will fall to the floor
and shatter into pieces that no one
—should there be anyone—
could ever assemble into a martini glass.
And no wonder.

—Laurel Winter

Can Art And Politics Peacefully Coexist?

In These Times We Live In, Can We Afford The Alternative?

Mobius: The Journal Of Social Change Has The Answer

Mobius Features Fiction, Poetry And Commentary All About Social Change That Seeks A Better World And A Better Tomorrow.

Check Us Out At:

WWW.MOBIUSMAGAZINE.COM

Or Subscribe To Our Print Version. Ten Bucks Gets You One Year And Four Exciting Issues. Mail Checks To:

> Mobius
> 505 Christianson
> Madison, WI 53714

We're Always Looking For Good Speculative Fiction. Feel Free To Share Your Work. Guidelines Available From Above Address Or E-Mail At fmschep@charter.net.

Brandon Sigrist, come aboard the good ship TOTU. *Our interstellar readers should find this article particularly vital.*

Tips on Moving to Earth

by Brandon Sigrist

Just some Do's and Don'ts: helpful advice for anyone considering a move here. It's good to do something nice for others when you are feeling blue.

Do not become dazzled with the glory of claiming a rare double planet. Keep your thinking liquid and smooth. The gentle gravity and mild temperatures of Luna will indeed make it an ideal home, but only after years of difficult hydraforming. And to begin that process, you must first master the only source of useable bodies in the system, the blue companion called Earth. It won't be easy. You can't float here in person; the ferocious atmosphere would whip you to froth and boil your mind away. Be prepared to live in remote tendril gear.

Do not entangle an Earth body with skinny arms and large hindquarters. You wouldn't think it considering the intense gravity, but top-heavy females have the most influence, followed closely by top-heavy males.

That last bit of advice needs some explanation. It's easy to forget the strangeness of this place after having been here so long. Earth life is comprised of two distinct types, male and female. These are called sexes, one of each required for reproduction. Very unusual, but that is not all. Their brains are also quite advanced, circumstances having left them to evolve alone. They possess intellect, language, and a fledgling technology. They are almost like entangled Ril on their own - mind and body in the same individual.

Start out in a settlement well away from the equator. It's almost pleasant there for part of the year. The rest of the time, it gets so warm that the snow melts and liquid water drips from the sky. The local bodies seem to enjoy the heat, but it's still depressing. You could move north to the poles, but there are few useful bodies there. It's not like home.

Select an Earth body with a nice car. That's a clever type of ground transportation device they've developed here. It's exciting to drive them fast and spin around in the snow. Good for morale. Avoid entangling stupid Earth bodies who think cars are fiendish inventions from Hell, designed to impoverish the masses and destroy communities. The machines they drive are crap. In fact, cars are effective at killing small mammals, an under-utilized food source that would surely benefit many.

Operating an Earth body is heady and dangerous. Give yourself at least a full season to entangle one properly. Don't rush the process. Their large brains do provide spectacular handling, but they are more subject to malfunction: delusions, paranoia and other disturbing conditions. You really have to watch out for that kind of thing. It's also impossible to handle more than one at a time. That's why it is such slow going here – no leverage. You have to hide among the wild bodies, working from within.

Don't get a dwelling on a corner lot. Pathway maintenance is important here, and a corner lot is three times as much work when the snow falls. Don't live where the pathways are right next to the street. The plowing machines wait until you finish, then they push dirty snow back onto your paths and you have to shovel all over again. You want what is called a boulevard, a little grassy space to pile the snow.

Observe your prospective neighbors before making a final decision on a dwelling. Lie on the seats of your car and watch them with a small mirror or other discreet reflective object. Hire a specialist called a private detective if you can't be there, to photograph them after a snowfall. It's the only way to be sure what you are up against. It might save you from a neighbor who gets up at 5:00 a.m. and uses a noisy device to throw extra snow on your walks.

Do not take a swing at the back of your neighbor's head with a snow shovel. The blades are just plastic, and the best you can hope for is a flesh wound. Keep a first aid kit close at hand, for nose bleeds and fat lips.

Be very careful with the tendril signals from your Earth body, especially if you have come here by yourself. Keep the feedback shields in good order. It's a far, lonely way from Hydra, and there are no other Ril nearby to save you if your tendril calibrations go native.

If you are considering recreational relations with the wild Earth bodies, don't. Reproduction by cell division does not prepare you for this. Go for a drive instead. If the loneliness and boredom force you to proceed anyway, avoid dating the type with cartoon tattoos peeking out of her clothing. At first, the titillation experienced by your Earth body may seem enjoyable, but she could be obsessed with the fading effects of the sun, even in wintertime. She might wear a time band, buried amongst a hundred bracelets, set to beep on the hour as a reminder to rub suntan oil on the brightly colored tattoos. The sight of her doing this in your very own Earth vehicle could distract your attention from the road, and cause what is known on this planet as negligent property damage.

She might also invite you up to her apartment, despite the bumps and contusions caused by the garage demolition incident, and give you a tour of the place, with particular emphasis on the bedroom. Do not, in this situation, fall back on typical Ril reserve and flee the premises. All you will have is an oddly increased respect shown your Earth vehicle in parking lots, and a lingering desire to make a shrine featuring the impression of her buttocks on the front seat cover.

Don't let your Earth body's personality surface to give dating advice. His research on winter survival, especially the photos of hypothermia victims, won't impress her. Earth minds are no match for the Ril, but don't let this fool you into complacency. Make sure to keep their thoughts down in the subconscious, where

their libido and strange passions belong. You can dissolve in that monkey sea.

Don't engage in pathetic attempts to get her back. Don't put bars of rubber in the fuel tubes of your starship, and use the exhaust to sky write, 'Heartsick alien laments loss of Earth girl!' in the style of local tabloid journalists. This will not get you anywhere with her. It will only attract unwanted attention from real journalists, and cause irreparable damage to the ship - your only means of escape from this grief-stricken hole.

Don't let your Earth body seek counseling. Positive self-talk makes it want to vomit. Don't stop your Earth body from taking its medication. The dull haze in the mind, the constant dry mouth and nausea, are not such a bad trade for the will to live.

Don't remember the black plains and quiet, snow-covered seas of Hydra, or the cheerful minds of the scaly First bodies. It will only bring water to the eyes of your Earth body. Don't mope around in the crippled starship, riding its hidden orbit as the power fades. Don't try to retreat into your Tool bodies inside the ship. They have already been infected. There is nothing but Earth blues there.

Return to your Earth body one last time as the starship drops into its final trajectory. Go stand naked outside her window at night. Let the sharp crystals of ice pull away the warmth in your bare feet. Find the snow angel she made in the back yard, and lay your Earth body down in her divine impression. Listen to the muted rumble as the snow crust breaks under your weight.

In a few minutes, you will be able to watch yourself burn across the sky as your ship hits the atmosphere. Keep blinking, or else ice will form on the Earth body's lenses and blur your vision. Talk to your Earth body quietly. Be soothing: Hush now, Earth body, the madness is going. No more sadness. Time to sleep.

Send the message buoy, with its cargo of advice, before it is too late. Maybe it will help someone out. It's good to do something nice when you are feeling blue.

We Gave Them to the Aliens

We gave them to the aliens who came
in ships of crystal fear to sample minds
of spiciness, uniqueness. Nothing tame.
Our leaders smiled & said they knew that kind
for trouble…claimed our prisons could provide
seditious succulence beyond their dreams
if, in exchange for being satisfied,
they told the state their victims' secret schemes.

For long years now, our land has been secure.
Yet prisons empty faster than they fill
these days, while searchlights of no earthly hue
haunt our horizons. Only one thing's sure:
our leaders have a heavy butcher's bill
to pay—& all of us hold secrets, too.

—Ann K. Schwader

Bryan Thao Worra makes a strong TOTU *premiere with both poetry and this evocative historical tale.*

The Dog At The Camp
by Bryan Thao Worra

Npua ua rau dev noj
Pigs do and dogs eat.
—Hmong aphorism

Adapted from an interview with Corporal Kou Her, 62 years old, Saint Paul, Minnesota, September 2000 for the Hmong History Collection Project.

Captain Yee thought he was some kind of tough guy.

During the war, he, like many of us, watched a certain royalist colonel stationed in Xieng Khouang province make his points by shooting a stray dog in front of the troops every day. It was some sort of an object lesson. I never saw much sense in it, but that may be why I never became an officer.

As for Captain Yee, he'd seen the good life officers lived, and that's why he pestered his father until he got his way. They made "donations" to enough of the right people in the army to get him a small command a few months earlier. My sister-in-law, who now lives in Merced, used to baby-sit him and his brothers before the war. She says they were always like that.

After the colonel arrived to motivate us, Captain Yee thought to himself, "That's the lifestyle I deserve to be living." So he began following the colonel about, emulating everything he did like some puppy in a uniform. Captain Yee even started shooting stray dogs too.

Now, I'm not a dog lover. The beasts aren't good for much more than eating poop and licking babies clean, as far as I'm concerned. But there was enough death going on in our country that I didn't see why we had to kill dogs so senselessly.

Whether the colonel knew and was flattered or insulted by this ridiculous behavior was anyone's guess. We for the most part just tried to keep our heads down and stay alive. That task alone was damn harder for us than most people would think.

It's no secret I didn't care for Captain Yee. The feeling was reciprocal. I doubt he really had our unit's best interests at heart as he sent us out on patrol after patrol and his "special missions." He thought it made him a better officer if he volunteered us for the suicide runs no one else wanted.

He became predictable that way. Some people mistake that for dependability.

He was always losing men and saying idiotic remarks like, "The greater the glory, the higher the costs," while he stayed back with the other officers planning our next day.

I suppose many of the Americans were impressed with him and his ability to motivate his troops. There was talk of promoting him to major in a few months, and giving him more men to manage.

It was my lousy luck to be assigned to him. And it was my lousy luck he got us assigned one of the most hazardous sectors to patrol, one that most of the locals considered haunted, just west of Sam Neua. This kind of luck of mine is why I don't play cards today.

Back then, anyone who saw those old gnarled trees and the blasted landscape charred by our constant shelling would know why it was rightfully thought accursed. Sensible men wouldn't set foot near that hellhole.

But this was the Army, and we don't have the luxury to steer clear of such places, because the Americans, from their relative safety at Long Cheng, were determined to cut the enemy off at any cost.

There were dogs here, but they didn't look right. Don't ask me to put it into words. You just sense this sort of thing.

One day at our firebase, my platoon clustered by an ammo depot, gambling over lunch to pass the time. The depot was an out of the way corner, and with Captain Yee, "out of sight, out of mind" was where we wanted to be. He was always nervous about being near so many bullets and explosives, and we used that to our advantage.

Captain Yee's commitment to his personal preservation was an inspiring example for us all.

Most of my platoon and I went through training together at Muang Cha two years back, so we knew each other well, although Captain Yee was never interested in being friends with us. "Not until you've proven yourselves," he barked authoritatively. There are always officers who consider this an effective incentive.

We had seen a lot of firefights that month, mostly with lightly armed scouts. It was near the dry season and the Vietnamese were busy probing our positions, trying to find our soft spots to focus their annual offensive against us. We were losing men daily. Playing games took our minds off things, even if we lost.

Some of the newer men in my unit were grumbling that day about what a bully Captain Yee was being to them.

He constantly had them washing his bowls and clothes, running his personal errands like they were his personal slaves. He even borrowed money from them to play cards with the other officers. "He's treating us like dogs," they cried. "Like dogs!" They cursed him like children.

I tried to be sympathetic, but they weren't saying anything new. And by now, I doubted how worthwhile it was to get to know the newer men in my platoon. I idly wondered who'd bury these poor fools, if there was enough left to bury when their time came.

It was too hard to feel sorry for so many different people who wanted pity, whether they deserved it or not. I'd already lost several cousins and an uncle who were fighting on the other edge of this Hell of ours.

While I expelled those terrible thoughts from my fatigued mind, the biggest black dog I ever saw, before or since, appeared from nowhere. The hairy shadow embodied silence and power, unsettling every soul in his bestial view.

Other mangy dogs here were skin and bones. This canine was akin to a well-fed tiger, accustomed to absolute dominion over all he surveyed. None of us dared lift a hand against him. The hulking cur could easily bite your head or a careless hand off.

Moua Sue, who was always really the crazy one among us, actually gave him a few scraps from lunch. As I said, this dog wasn't like any I'd ever seen before or since. When he ate, he ate with a deliberate, calm dignity rather than the usual slobbering of your ordinary jungle mutt frenzied at the sight of food.

We didn't dare make any remarks about him in his presence. The hound stayed out of our way for most of the afternoon, slipping in and out of sight between the crates and barrels surrounding us. Now when I think about it, we never even heard him pant or breathe.

Around 1500 hours, I heard some cursing and the sound of buckets being kicked and the usual snarls that alerted us that Captain Yee was on his way, no doubt with some new assignment. I felt sorry for the doomed dogs nearby.

As he walked towards us, I could see officer life *was* treating Captain Yee well. He was getting heavy around the gut, moving like a bloated slug.

He began barking his usual epithets about how we weren't motivated, and that we should be volunteering for these missions, not waiting for them to be assigned. That we'd never become officers like him unless we took heroic initiative, the kind that our commanders would notice. We were so lucky that he was going to take us with him, he told us, but we'd better start doing our share to beat the Vietnamese, who weren't any better than dogs.

That's when Captain Yee pulled out his pistol, and the rest of my story turns into a blur.

Captain Yee predictably put a bullet into the head of a harmless little brown dog, who five seconds earlier had been doing nothing more offensive than yapping at some beetles in the weeds nearby. It took nearly a minute for the pup to stop twitching in his own blood.

All of us whirled around when we heard a ferocious growling behind us. At first we thought it was an angry tiger, but quickly realized it was the black dog, barking fiercely as if dispatched from the darkest pits of Hell, his eyes red as blood. Moua Sue screamed, and hid behind a crate in terror. Several other men followed suit.

"Oh, do you want some of this too?" Captain Yee said snidely, recovering from the initial shock. "No dog dares to bark at me!" He fired. And missed, from six feet away. The dog didn't even flinch, and kept barking. Were he not so terrifying, many of us would have probably laughed.

Captain Yee fired again. And still missed. My friend Pao finally snickered, and I was sure Captain Yee was going to shoot him for insubordination.

A man of his ego can't lose face to a dog, and Captain Yee began walking angrily towards the big black beast, who loped into the afternoon jungle.

Of course, Captain Yee followed, chasing after the hound until they both were out of sight.

Then we heard a scream, the terrible kind you aren't supposed to hear, even during a war. I admit, we were too afraid to follow. There was a silence throughout the entire camp. Not even the birds talked. In fact, one may have even dropped dead out of the sky at that moment, but I'm getting old. My memory could be playing tricks on me, and that could have happened another time.

Captain Yee staggered back out of the jungle, his hair completely white as an old corpse, with a look of sheer terror on his face. What he saw must have been so terrible, a thing of nightmares. We tried to get him to talk, to tell us what happened, but he had gone mute.

We took him to the medics, who said there was nothing physically wrong with him. They didn't understand it, but told us to take Captain Yee back to his tent before he spooked the rest of the troops.

Lieutenant Tou Chang took over duties for Captain Yee temporarily, and we went on patrol as if nothing happened. We lost Tzia Neng Vue on that one. He'd just won big at cards that day, too, was the pity. His widow is out in Wausau, Wisconsin, now.

When we got back, I learned that at some point, Captain Yee caught a violent fever and died with that same, wild-eyed look of terror on his face, twisting like a madman on his pathetic cot. He never spoke another word before he died.

We never saw that dog again. I'll never know what he saw. I'm not sure I want to know, anyway. But I do make sure that whenever I see a dog, I treat it nicely.

I hear that colonel who started the whole thing of shooting dogs in front of the troops also met a bad fate in the end, but everyone tells me there was nothing mysterious about that death at all. It was just the hazards of our war.

THE MONSTER UNREASON

With Captain Rage under one arm
and a fifth of mud whiskey
under the other fat arm,
he comes lumbering into our circle
and plops himself down,
a slabby sort of encrusted creature,
goat grey and of enormous girth.
His features are a puffy affair,
the eyes lost in folds of flesh.

As he sits down among us
we try to ignore his churlish ways
and the faint odor of ozone
that emanates from his being.
Then he passes the whiskey around
and digs into one wide pocket,
wide as the shoes of Asia,
deep as your mother's womb,
and comes up with a fist of cards.

"Take a card," he bellows, "any card,"
and we discover the monster can fly:
there is no subtlety to his performance,
no sane geometry to his progressions,
yet he flies nonetheless.
Like the white noise of space,
like the thin man,
he has been here from the beginning,
he is everywhere at once.

—BRUCE BOSTON

"Monster" is in the eye of the beholder.

Nosmo Girl

by Judy Klass

A visit to Nosmo grates on me, scrapes my nerves raw. I feel angry and irritated the whole time I'm there, and not for what they would consider the obvious reason. I'm patched during my trip; I'm chemically fine. No, it's them, it's their sanctimonious careful planning, their radiant health and the sweet air of righteousness they make me breathe that get to me.

The thing is, though, I metabolize the Nosmo lace-ups better than most of the guys I know. I stay polite when I talk to them. I've never taken a swing at one, like my office mate Frank. So, when the company has business they want done face to face over there, it's me they always send.

I was sitting at a conference table with Grover Metcalf, the deputy governor, and Myra Danning, who owns their supermarket chain Cornucopia. She's an old granola lace-up; it figures that she'd give her corporation a hippie name. I bet if she visited us sometime over in Freeville, in a fun back parlor and we eased her into the right mood, we could get her to smoke a doobie with us.

"I'm afraid your bosses simply don't understand," Grover purred, with that patronizing warmth of his, like I'm his favorite menial laborer, "just how important this issue is to us."

"Oh, yeah, sure we do," I told him, all upbeat and friendly. "We really took your studies to heart. We've halved what goes into the animals we send to Nosmo. We've got scientists and inspectors going through the plant—"

"Not *our* scientists and inspectors," Myra broke in. She had her inner hippie masked; she was in her severe, corporate mode. She looks around eighty; sometimes I think they wheel out their most geriatric lace-ups to interface with us, to rub in our faces, imagining we've never seen geezers that old before. "Random tests we run on the meat have shown no change. Inspectors of our own in the plant would be the simplest solution to the problem," Myra went on, "and we'd be able to re-establish trust all around."

"The public would never even need to hear about it," Grover added. He always talks to me slowly and with emphasis; Nosmos think they have a monopoly on higher education.

The wind chimes near the door tinkled. Only in goddamn Nosmo would there be wind chimes in a conference room.

This meeting was about hormones in the meat, as usual. Lots of the lace-ups are hypocritical carnivores, but of course, they want us to run the battery farms and slaughterhouses over in Freeville. They buy our products, but we disgust them all the more by producing what they need. And of course they consider the meat they get from us suspect, so if one of them ever gets sick or bites his own tongue or whatever, they blame us.

"Outside inspectors would be insulting, bad for morale," I said firmly, but with a smile, wishing I had a cigarette to tap on the table, tapping my finger instead. "They'd slow things up, but if you'd be willing to pay more to compensate for the interference—"

"How could it possibly drive up production costs for you if we were to occasionally send in inspectors?" Myra seemed incredulous.

"—if, as I say, you agree to a three percent price increase, then I am authorized to make a deal," I concluded, going for Grover's warm, pleasant, full-of-it tone. Neither they nor their aides seemed pleased. "Wanna get back to me about it tomorrow?" I suggested. And the meeting was over.

What to do in Nosmo on a Thursday night? No Beat Poet dives, obviously. They do have clubs that serve al-

coholic drinks, and some of them are real drinks—the guys back home are stretching things when they call Nosmo martinis thirty variations on a Shirley Temple. But the drinks have all got that cloying sweetness and tropical fun wackiness to them, together with their umbrellas and hats and spyrotwirls; it seems to neutralize every drop of alcohol in them.

Nosmo music is too cute and well-adjusted/healthy also—except for their bratty little boys who listen to Freeville bands, who try to write "tough" and "demented" songs like us—and their music is the saddest and most embarrassing of all.

Might as well play to their strengths—I took a walk in the planetarium garden. It's nice, actually, with t-scopes of various strengths roundabout, at every bench and in every grove, with tastefully placed t-scripts teaching kids about the history of colonization here, terraforming and land grants, the decision to segregate the communities, our fight to break away and gain more autonomy since they wouldn't share medical costs and other community costs with us anyhow, and our name change to Freeville. The Nosmo version of history on the t-scripts is slanted pretty far their way. Surprise, surprise.

She was sitting on a bench ignoring the turbo-t-scope pointed at Earth, examining a fuzzy native plant instead. It's a free-standing vine-y thing only found way up high on the un-terraformed ridges, usually, but the lace-ups have tinkered with it enough genetically to where they've got a version of it growing in their gardens. The fur covering its tendrils is every shimmering shade of blue and green you could think of, and rustles like grass almost when you pet it. Which she was doing, as she inhaled the mossy, herbal smell of it.

Okay, so we don't have delicate, pretty little girls back home like they do here in Nosmo. Our girls are loud and fun, and look you in the eye, and crack their gum and laugh loud, even when they have degrees and three kids and a life-time of disappointment under their belts. This little laced-up hothouse girl belonged right there in the garden next to the bioengineered plant she was petting like a cat.

"What do you call that thing?" I sat down beside her.

"It's called a phytthi-lictelis-who-the-heck-knows," she said. Of course Nosmo girls don't swear, but her response had been quick and sardonic enough to please me. They're usually so earnest, so humorless, so plodding, so frigging positive!

"This one seems to know you," I remarked. Some of the native fauna are muscular and mobile, and this thing was creeping a slinky tendril around her shoulders like a boa. "Don't let it hug your neck too tight, now."

She laughed. "It's not out to get me. We're old friends." Her eyes were impossibly large and green. Her blouse was that pale shade of lemon yellow they go in for, and her hair kind of matched it. Me, I wear a lot of basic black, wear it almost defiantly when I'm in Nosmo.

They don't believe in tanning. They've got free-floating lens shields above their whole region, blocking the respective harmful rays of both suns. The twin stems that came down from her pert little skirt were as pale as the tofu she'd probably been nibbling her whole life. Just sitting next to her, I felt grubby, dirty.

"You from out of town?" she asked.

"Yeah," I said. I let her go ahead and assume I was from off-world. Tourists come to Freeville to party and gamble and buy a lapdance or two, wink wink, and to Nosmo for the gardens and restaurants and art galleries full of pastel pablum; they often take in both cities on the same trip.

"Do you like it here?" she pressed me.

"It's—different from what I'm used to. Very quiet," I said diplomatically.

"Yes," she beamed, taking this as a compliment to her fair city.

"Do you, uh, ever make it over to Freeville?" I asked casually.

"No!" She shuddered. "I've—never been there."

"Not even curious?"

"To visit a meat market?"

I was hurt by the contempt in her voice. I wasn't sure if she meant companies like mine, or entertainment palaces featuring girls plying variations on the galaxy's oldest profession…maybe she meant both.

"Yeah, but to share a planet with a whole autonomous region, a whole culture, and never visit it…doesn't that seem…a little narrow-minded to you?"

I thought I saw doubt cross her face. "There are places I'd be curious to visit," she admitted. "Very different from here. It can be, you know, kind of bland here, I think."

As if on cue, wind chimes hanging from a tree near our bench moved in the breeze and tinkled. Christ, nothing gets my back up like those goddamned wind chimes!

"I'd like to visit Old Earth," she went on, "all the continents. And see the sea life on the Omega Station. But—go to Smokeville…."

"Freeville," I corrected automatically, irritated. And that gave the game away. She stared hard at me, and her hand flew to her mouth.

"You're…."

"Yup," I told her sourly. "Why do you look so surprised?"

"You—you don't—"

"I don't smell?" I challenged her. And if she wasn't so pretty, if I didn't genuinely like her, if she wasn't the first lace-up besides that old geezer Myra that made me think she might actually be fun to hang with, I wouldn't have been so bitter and defensive. "I shower and wash my clothes before I come here. It's not worth it to be harassed by your gunless, clueless cops, to walk down the boulevard here smelling like I know how to enjoy tobacco."

She just stared at me like she was Little Red Riding Hood or something, so I went on. "And yes, I'm wearing a nico-patch right now. And besides going through a pack a day at home, I chew tobacco. I like big, stanky cigars at night, sitting on the balcony with my friends. Barbecuing burgers. Sometimes, when I see my family, I even dip snuff." I almost added: So kiss my ass. But I didn't.

She looked away from me, there on the bench. She didn't seem scared that I would attack her or anything; she looked like she might cry.

"Ever meet someone from Freeville before?" I asked.

"No."

Tinkle, tinkle went the happy little wind chimes. She snuggled down into the comforting embrace of her furry plant friend.

"What's your name?" I asked.

"Ariadne."

I wanted to snort at the pretentiousness of it. But it suited her. She turned to me.

"What's yours?"

"Leo."

She smiled a little smile, a smile I don't associate with Nosmo at all, one with humor and irony in it, and held out her pale little hand to shake. I picked it up in my big old mitt, pressed it, and let it go.

"Do you come here to Nosmokeville a lot?"

"Often enough."

"And you don't really like it, do you?"

"No."

She nodded. "So, why do you come?"

"Business."

"Who do you work for?"

"A meat market. Parker Foods," I clarified, so she wouldn't think I recruited dancing girls or something. When good girls from Nosmo decide to upset their parents and go bad, they can actually earn good money in Freeville for a time—that whole wide-eyed virgin routine. "What do you do?"

"I'm still in school," she admitted. "Getting my doctorate."

"In what?"

"Plant psychology."

Jesus. Leave it to Nosmo universities to come up with a field like that....

She continued: "So, I guess I really ought to know how to pronounce the bioengineered phylum of Flossie here, right?" She stroked the tip of the vine, and it curled lovingly around her finger. Maybe I should have told them to get a room.

"Has anyone you've ever known moved here?" she asked.

The question surprised me. "Yeah," I said. "Ex-girlfriend."

"Why did she move?"

"She said—she wanted a higher quality of life. To meet 'higher quality people.' Get married, have kids in a nice, sterilized, straight-laced environment, I guess. And it wasn't that hard, for her, to give up the substances that keep people out."

"Is that why you hate us so much?"

"What? No, I wasn't in love with her or anything. You have to understand—we all hate you. Most people I know wouldn't set foot over here!"

"Isn't that narrow-minded?" she asked, deliberately echoing me. I must have gotten to her, before.

"Depends on how you look at it. This whole place is about the absence of stuff. The wild, reckless, exciting parts of life. You've sealed it all off from yourselves. You condemn us for being addicted to it, addicted to life—"

"To death—"

"And you judge us and sneer at us—so, why the hell should we want to come here?"

She shrugged. "I don't know. To see if we're onto something? To see if the absence of those things is actually a gift, if it—makes room for a kind of quiet thought, and clarity—"

"I wish you'd come to a Beat Poet club with me sometime," I said, and I wanted it to come out like a sarcastic challenge, but it came out like a real invitation, like pleading, almost, "and hear those guys rapping their rapid-fire Bukowski and Howling their Ginsberg and burrowing into their Burroughs stories, and you'd hear more mind-singeing clarity, more painful, searing truth—"

"Truth doesn't have to be painful. Or searing. Or swaggering or self-destructive."

"It doesn't have to be passive and insipid and positive and affirmational and warm and snuggly, either," I shot back. "A lot of the time, it *can't* be."

We had squared off to our respective ends of the bench. We weren't going to convince each other. If I listened to her, if I gave her worldview a chance, if I conceded that okay, maybe there's something sane and nice and appealing about Nosmo families playing in the park, telling weak little jokes instead of worrying about crime and sickness and making ends meet, something enviable about lace-ups feeling better about themselves and learning more in school, if I were to turn my back on the whole ornery, two-fisted, white trash, proud and stubborn line of us, going back generations, taking rough, honest jobs, working hard, loving hard, playing hard, drinking, fighting and laughing until the tears come, if I were to spit on my parents' graves like that, renounce who I was—then I would lose myself in a pastel abyss. And that wasn't going to happen. "I guess I shouldn't expect you to visit any time soon," I said gruffly.

"I tried to read a book of your Beat poets...."

"It's not the same. You've got to see them live," I snapped.

"I know boys who—who try to talk and act like they're from your, uh—"

"I hate those wannabes. I hate them most of all. Even when they move to Freeville, you can still spot them five years later. They're trying too hard. They're the crudest and the stupidest guys you can possibly meet."

We were running out of things to say. But the attraction of the Other was there, between us, and maybe we were both too honest to hide it.

"I'm going back to my hotel," I told her, finally. "I got one more meeting tomorrow, and then I'm going home. I'd like to kiss you." It came out, bald and simple.

"I, uh—"

"Don't worry, my breath doesn't smell, either. I brushed my teeth." Jesus, I wanted a cigarette bad. "I'm sorry, I shouldn't try to guilt you into kissing me. That's a cheap move on my part."

She gave me that little smile again, deftly removed the fuzzy tendril from her shoulders, and scooted down to my end of the bench. Her own arms were like tendrils around my shoulders, and her mouth was soft and fluttering and light. It wasn't a goopy, go-for-it first kiss—it was nice. I liked her lack of perfume, the lack of a tobacco smell, the subtlety of everything about her. I liked how low-key and gentle it was. Maybe she's right, maybe with them, absence is a kind of presence, a kind of substance....

I got that quick, glancing smile once more. And then it was gone.

Our Monsters issue includes two very different takes on characters created by Bram Stoker, including this fascinating psychological study by one of our mainstay writers. "The Facts of Dr Van Helsing's Case" first appeared in Andromeda Spaceways Inflight Magazine *#11, February/March 2004.*

The Facts of Dr. Van Helsing's Case
by Stephen Dedman

"True!—Nervous—Very, very dreadfully nervous I had been and am; but why will *you say that I am mad*?" Abraham shudders in excitement as he reads the words aloud, and his young brother smiles back at him, desperate not to be the first to show fear, but secretly gripping the blanket in case he feels the need to hide.

Their father is a gifted linguist as well as a skilled bookbinder—fluent in English, Dutch, French, and Latin as well as Hebrew and his native Schweitzerdeutsch. To Abraham, his little shop is better even than a candy store, for it is filled with books and papers—and despite his mother's occasional protests, nothing is forbidden the precocious ten-year-old. Abraham has inherited his father's love of gruesome tales, the ghost stories and gothic novels that he translates as much for pleasure as for the few extra guilders they bring in. This new collection, by an American writer named Poe, promises to be even better than his beloved *Frankenstein*, and his eyes gleam as he continues to read 'The Tell-Tale Heart.'

From Dr Van Helsing's Memorandum
She lay in her Vampire sleep, so full of life and voluptuous beauty that I shudder as though I have come to do murder. Ah, I doubt not that in old time, when such things were, many a man who set forth to do such a task as mine, found at the last his heart fail him, and then his nerve. So he delay, and delay, and delay, till the mere beauty and fascination of the wanton Un-Dead have hypnotise him; and he remain on, and on, till sunset come, and the Vampire sleep be over.

Every night the same dream, like some foul monster on his chest, something dead but worse than dead. He is sure he will see the same faces every night until Judgement Day.

He is not yet twenty-one when he receives the first of his doctorates from the University of Wittenberg—though his receding hair and already furrowed forehead make him look older than his classmates, not younger. He is already known as a brilliant philosopher and natural historian as well as a medical man, but his appearance at the College of Lynxes is treated as something of a joke by the priests—not because of his youth, but because of doubts about his religion. It is no secret that his mother had wanted him to become a rabbi, while his father died an atheist. And the timing is suspicious. *The Origin of the Species by Means of Natural Selection* has recently been published, and every copy sold within a week. Has this young Jewish know-it-all come to plead Darwin's case, or perhaps that of Pouchet's *Heterogenie*, with its theories on the spontaneous generation of life from non-living matter?

Instead, Van Helsing delivers a lecture on Haiti. Its native religion, he tells them, is an abomination that the Church must work to destroy. Speaking haltingly but vehemently in Latin, he tells them of zombis, the Un-Dead summoned forth from their graves to work in the fields.

The Pope's advisors look at each other in amazement. The Vatican had severed ties with Haiti nearly sixty years before, during the rebellion which had ousted the French slave-owners from the island. One cardinal peers at the young scientist and asks haughtily, "Have you seen these…zombis, doctor?"

"No," Van Helsing replies. "I have spoken to eye-witnesses, and read many accounts, but I have not been able to travel to the island myself. If the church would provide me with funds for my passage, I could make a further study. I think it likely that the potions the

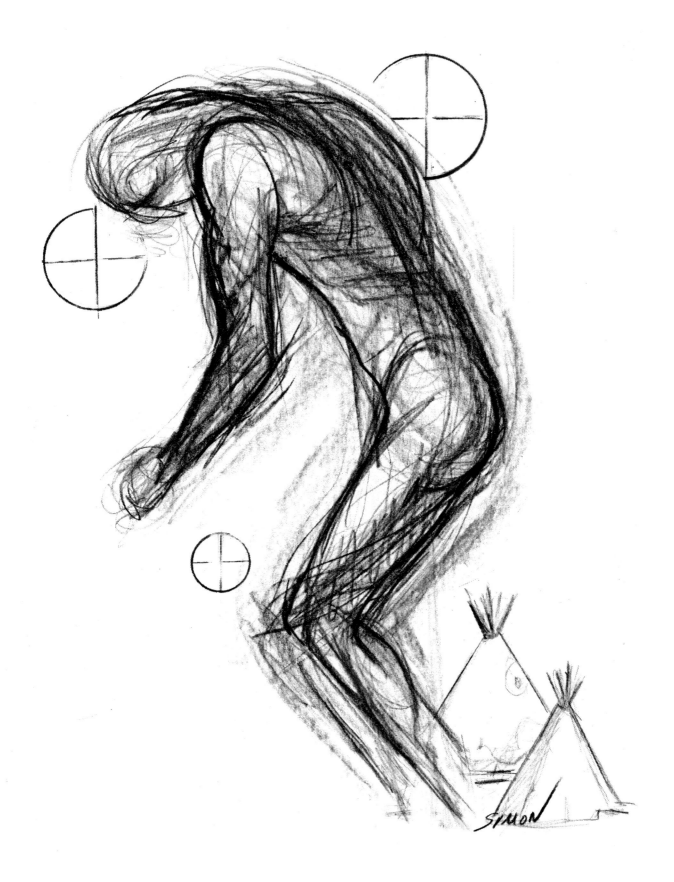

voodoos use to raise the dead are, in fact, mere poisons that slow the heart and mind, still the tongue and kill the soul, leaving only a...." He wracked his brain for the appropriate Latin words.

"A golem?" suggested one of the priests, lightly.

"A creature, like the one in Shelley's novel *Frankenstein*: something of human form, perhaps, but they are neither brute nor human; they are ghouls," he says, unconsciously quoting Poe. "The dead can not be raised."

The young priest strokes his beard, hiding a smile behind his hand. "Are you familiar with the resurrection of Lazarus, doctor? Or of that of Christ, after he was—" He sees a cardinal glaring at him, and the sentence ends with a cough.

"I have read the gospels," Van Helsing informs him, raising his voice and his bushy eyebrows. "But these are mere necromancers. Do you believe they are capable of miracles, as Jesus was?"

There is some muttering, and the young priest turns pale. "Of course not," says the Cardinal. "Only God, to whom all things are possible, can raise the dead...but ignorant savages can not be expected to know this. They might be fooled by some trickery, perhaps some poisons, as you suggest. However, we can scarcely convert everyone in the world, nor save every soul, and there are other people in need of—"

"And if it is said, on other islands, that these ignorant savages can do what the Church can not? That they can raise the dead—and not only to work, but to fight, to rebel as the Haitians did?" There is a moment's silence as the Pope's advisors consider this. "This abominable superstition must be stamped out," Van Helsing insists. "The Church must return to Haiti and teach the people— and more than that. It must destroy the hounfors, the filthy temples of this so-called religion, and if there is any truth to the tales and zombis do exist, they *must* be returned to the ground where they belong, even if it means filling their mouths with salt and sewing their lips shut as the voodoos believe. The Un-Dead should not walk; they *must* not walk. The Dead must remain Dead until *God* Himself chooses to raise them."

Ruth Van Helsing stands no more than five feet tall; her features are delicate, her fingers nimble, and her voice deceptively soft. Her sons have never seen her angry, because she always waits until she is sure they are asleep before she takes her husband to pieces. "He should be studying, not wasting his time with the nonsense you give him. Ghosts, and grave-robbers, and now this!" She waves the offending volume of Poe's tales. "Have you read them, or heard him reading them to Isaac? Do you wonder that Isaac wakes nearly every night, dreaming that he's been buried alive!" "They're the stories he wants to hear," says David, keeping his voice low for fear of disturbing his sons. "And he's always had nightmares, because he can't breathe. Stopping Bram reading to him isn't going to change that; it might even make it worse." He knows this will frighten his wife; Isaac is prone to sleepwalking, and they live only two streets from the canal. "And they already know that the world is a frightening place. They know that Isaac is unlikely ever to be well, and that eventually he will die. And if Bram is to be a doctor, he'll have to be prepared for worse horrors than these. Do you know *why* they robbed graves, Burke and Hare and the others? Because medical students couldn't get the bodies they needed any—"

"Don't forget the teeth," Ruth snaps, then softens. "I know that, Duv. But even with all they've learned, no doctor we've seen has been able to help Isaac. I want him to remember happy times, as well as pain and fear. Sunshine and laughter, the free air of Heaven, not just the walking dead and other monsters. Do you understand?"

"All Indians must dance, everywhere, keep on dancing. Pretty soon in next spring Great Spirit come. He bring back all game of every kind. The game be thick everywhere. All dead Indians come back and live again. They all be strong just like young men, be young again."

—Wovoka, "The Paiute Messiah," creator of the Ghost Dance

Abraham reads 'The Facts of M. Valdemar's Case' to his brother. Like the narrator, they are both fascinated by Mesmerism, a skill which Abraham will later use on Mina Harker. They regard it as somehow magical, supernatural, and their plans are boyish: persuading pretty girls to undress, convincing shopkeepers that scraps of paper are banknotes, and so on. Abraham is now ten years old, while Isaac is seven, and will never be eight. Both shudder at Poe's suggestion of mesmerizing a person on the brink of death and seeing "'to what extent, and for how long a period, the encroachments of Death might be arrested by the process'" but it also makes Abraham wonder. He has listened to the parents and to the doctors, and he knows that Isaac is not expected to survive this bitter winter. He has also heard his father talk about what a great doctor he expects Abraham to become, and he believes him...but he knows that this will happen much too late to save his brother.

"'There were other points to be ascertained,'" he

reads, "'but these most excited my curiosity—the last in especial, from the immensely important character of its consequences.'"

"Bram!"

He turns, and sees his mother standing in the doorway. "I need some flour," she says. "Run to Kompff's and get me a pound."

He puts the book down on the bed, reluctantly, and accepts the coins she hands him. She follows him into the hallway as he grabs his coat, gloves, scarf, cap and boots. "Have you done your Latin grammar?" she asks, before he has completely shrouded himself in wool. His expression is answer enough. "Do it as soon as you get back," she says.

"Yes, Mama." He covers his mouth and nose with his scarf and runs outside into the snowy street, Poe's words still echoing in his mind. *For how long a period, the encroachments of Death might be arrested....*

burke, v.t. Smother; hush up, suppress. (*Burke,* executed 1829 for smothering people to sell bodies for dissection.)

—*Concise Oxford Dictionary*

Lieutenant Morris is three years younger than his cousin Quincey, and seems smaller and quieter, but he is obviously strong and, Van Helsing is sure, just as brave. He listens in reverent silence as Van Helsing tells him how Quincey, himself mortally wounded, had stabbed Count Dracula through the heart.

When he has finished the story, the Professor asks him what he knows of the Ghost Dance. Morris scratches his head. "I don't reckon it's nothing to worry about," he opines. "The Colonel says they done it before in Californy and thereabouts, maybe twenty years ago, and it didn't do nothing then. Just a whole bunch a Indians dancing about and chanting, wearing these shirts they say can stop bullets." He snorts at this idea. He shares his cousin's faith in Colt revolvers and Bowie knives; whether in uniform or at home, the last item he removes before going to bed is his gun-belt, which he buckles on again before drinking his first cup of coffee. Like Van Helsing, he also carries a derringer in his pocket, much as a Transylvanian peasant might wear a cross. (Unlike Van Helsing, he has not had the bullets blessed by a priest, ready to be fired into a vampire's grave.) "Guv'mint's banned it, but I don't reckon it does nobody no harm."

"I have heard they are necromancers," says the Professor. The soldier looks blank. "That they wish to raise their dead," Van Helsing explains.

"Can't say's I blame 'em for wantin' that," Morris replies. "Most of 'em's dead, now. I won't say that's not the best kind of Indian, but I ain't scared of the ones who ain't. All the big chiefs are dead, and as long as all they do is dance and all they got is a few old rifles...waal, like I said, they don't worry me none. Have you seen the Hotchkiss guns we got now? They could kill every Indian that's camped outside in less time than it takes to brew a pot of coffee."

"Some things can not be killed with bullets," the Professor tells him, offering him a cigarette from a silver case with a mirror inside the lid. "If these necromancers can raise their dead, your guns will not save you. I've fought the Un-Dead, yes, with your brave young cousin Quincey at my side, and they are foul things, without conscience, but strong, very very strong. It is a terrible task we undertake, but it must be done, for their sake as well as our own, for to the Un-Dead are the gates of Heaven forever shut."

Morris shivers, and not only because it's cold outside and he's used to Texas, not the South Dakota winter. He's a good poker player and spinner of tall tales, and can usually spot a liar, but the Professor seems utterly sincere. "Don't know as some of the Indians I met 'd rightly get into Heaven, less'n they snuck in," he says, uncertainly, "nor as I'd want to meet 'em there. But I reckon I can take you to Colonel Forsyth. He'll listen, but I don't know as there's much he can do."

It is Sunday night, and Abraham waits until he knows his parents are sleeping—his father's snore is of almost Wagnerian power—before rising from his bed and creeping over to Isaac's. A slight shake is enough to wake his brother; the younger boy blinks a few times in alarm, then recognizes the shape looming over him. "I want to try to mesmerize you," Abraham murmurs.

Isaac is silent for so long that his brother wonders whether he's really awake. "Why?" he finally asks, then bursts out coughing. He trusts Abraham, but there is something strange about his intensity, and the need for secrecy.

Abraham waits until he is silent again. "Do you want to be well again?" he asks, his voice as soft as old cobwebs. "Do you want to be strong?"

Isaac hesitates, then nods. He doesn't dare speak again for fear of triggering another paroxysm of coughing and possibly waking his mother. Abraham stares into his eyes and strokes his forehead, making 'mystic passes' as he has read of mesmerists doing, and murmurs reassuringly. When he sees Isaac's eyelids begin to flutter, he is convinced that his brother is entranced, and climbs onto his bed and pins his arms down with his knees. He then holds his own pillow down over

Isaac's face.

His younger brother is so weakened by phthisis that he barely struggles at all, and soon Abraham is sure that he has, like the narrator of Poe's 'The Facts of M. Valdemar's Case' succeeded in mesmerizing a person on the brink of death. He climbs off the bed, places his pillow back on his own bed, and stares for a moment at the motionless body, amazed at what he has done.

Only then does it strike him that his mother might not understand or believe what has happened, and he knows that the family doctor is little more than a dolt with barely as much imagination as a cow. To save Isaac from a premature burial, he decides he must hide the body.

He knows of an empty trunk in the school's cellar, where he has hidden from bullies in the past. The cellar has a window he can open from the outside, and the trunk is more than large enough to hold his brother. He wraps Isaac in a blanket and sneaks down into the street.

He looks at the body every day. Isaac is pale, but seems peaceful, and Abraham is delighted to see that by Tuesday he is growing fatter. He wishes he could reassure his mother, who is obviously distraught, but still doubts that he could make her understand. Better to wait until he can revive him.

By Thursday, Isaac's normally skinny truck has swollen until it is almost bloated, his veins are visible in his pale flesh, and there is a turquoise tint to his neck. Despite the cold, he is also beginning to smell. Abraham tries asking him questions, but there is no response.

He looks for the copy of Poe's *Tales*. His father says his mother has it. His mother refuses to give it to him, saying that it will only upset him further. He searches the house when she goes shopping, and soon finds the book. For the first time, he reads the second half of 'The Facts of M. Valdemar's Case.'

That night, the dreams begin.

The following Monday, the janitor traces the smell, expecting to find nothing more than a dead rat. Despite his obvious horror at discovering a young boy's corpse, he soon becomes one of the suspects; he was drunk enough on the night Isaac disappeared to have only vague memories of staggering home from the tavern. Detective officers interview Abraham, asking whether he remembers his brother leaving the room, or anyone else breaking in. His parents confirm that he was a sound sleeper, at least until recently.

Isaac is buried, and the police watch the crowd carefully. They begin investigating other suspects. An impoverished medical student known to be fond of pranks. The baker's widow, whose own son drowned in the canal earlier that year. A street-sweeper previously convicted of burglary and petty thefts. The sweeper is arrested and Abraham sees his father drunk for the first time. At the dinner table, he hears him express the opinion that no death imaginable would be a sufficiently severe punishment for his younger son's murderer, and he is unable to eat anything more.

Abraham's nightmares become even more vivid. He feels that everyone is watching him, and not because they admire him. He no longer walks through the cemetery on his way home from school; he takes a long detour around it, though he is always careful to be inside by nightfall. When he hears rumours that the sweeper may be released because there is insufficient evidence to convince the magistrate, and the man was too large to have crawled through the cellar window, Abraham begins to make plans to run away—until one night, he wakes from a nightmare of Frankenstein's monster strangling Frankenstein's young brother. Unable to return to sleep, he suddenly remembers how the monster framed Justine, the maid, for the murder.

The next morning, Abraham steals his mother's cameo brooch, and plants it in the medical student's lodgings.

After Colonel Forsyth gives the order that the Indians are to be disarmed, the soldiers go around the tents looking for weapons. The Sioux hand over many rifles, but Morris and the other officers suspect that they have more hidden away. Blankets, baskets and medicine bundles are searched, and not gently. The soldiers had worked hard the previous day, placing another two Hotchkiss guns on the rise overlooking the camp, then celebrated with a cask of whiskey; Forsyth and Van Helsing may be the only two white men present who aren't nursing hangovers. And this is the Seventh Cavalry, Custer's old regiment, and though most of the Indians who have been forcibly brought here to Wounded Knee Creek are women and children, some of the men fought at the Little Big Horn.

Axes, knives, even tent stakes are soon piled up beside the rifles, but the soldiers are still suspicious, and give the order that the warriors are to remove their blankets and submit to being searched. It is cold, that morning, but only Yellow Bird, the medicine man, protests. He begins dancing the Ghost Dance and chanting one of the magical songs. Van Helsing watches him, and waits.

The medical student denies the murder and the theft, but unlike the street-sweeper, he is thin enough to be the burglar. He has no alibi, having spent the night reading. Abraham feels some kinship with him, even some shame, when he hears this—but he does not confess. Instead, he swears that after he becomes a doctor, he will also teach medicine, and always remain a friend to his students.

People are angered by the crime, and agree that someone must be punished. David Van Helsing is called as a witness, and says that if the dead could speak, his son would name his murderer and call out for vengeance.

Abraham becomes silent and spends more time reading and studying, but notices that this only causes people to watch him more closely. This makes him nervous, very dreadfully nervous, and very pale, and he begins to wonder if they suspect…so he makes a deliberate effort to talk, more fluently and with a heightened voice. After the student is hanged, he becomes more confident, and talks even more, more quickly, more vehemently, as though trying to fill the silence in his home. He argues about trifles and often lectures for minutes at a time, rambling from subject to subject, mentioning 'friends' who are rarely more than casual acquaintances and often much less. To avoid sleep, and the dreams that always come with it, he reads more and more…not Poe and other fiction, but science. He crams his memory with facts and maybe-facts, and continues to study long after he has received his medical degree. Law, philosophy, natural history, even theology. When money runs low, he sells the teeth from the corpses he is given to dissect. He is offered a professorship, and teaches medical students how to save lives—because, as he frequently tells them, even the best medicine can not save the dead.

Black Coyote, a young Minneconjou, has a new Winchester hidden under his blanket. When Morris discovers it and asks him to give it up, the Indian raises it above his head and shouts that he has paid much money for the rifle and it belongs to him. Yellow Bird continues to dance, chanting a Ghost Dance song. Van Helsing watches, and realizes that Black Coyote is deaf. He reaches for the derringer in his pocket and cocks it. It holds only one low-powered round, but that will be enough.

From Dr Seward's Diary
Van Helsing examines, he tells me, her teeth very carefully, whilst she is in the hypnotic condition, for he says that so long as they do not begin to sharpen there is no active danger of a change in her. If this change should come, it would be necessary to take steps!…. We both know what those steps would have to be, though we do not mention our thoughts to each other. We should neither of us shrink from the task—awful though it be to contemplate. 'Euthanasia' is an excellent and a comforting word! I am grateful to whoever invented it.

He watches a young man digging up a body and knows he is dreaming, but this is no consolation—nor is the fact that he knows how the dream will end. The man lifts the corpse from the grave, then turns to look at Van Helsing. The Professor can see the skull beneath the skin, but he recognizes the man as the young medical student he framed. Tonight, the carcass is Lucy Westenra's, but as soon as it is decapitated, the hair darkens from red to black, and the pretty face rots away to reveal a familiar boyish visage.

For the love of God
"You're dead!" Van Helsing screams.
Yet the sound increased

"The dead cannot rise!"
louder! louder! louder! louder!—
"The dead cannot talk! *The dead cannot talk!*"

Soldiers grab Black Coyote and spin him around. The Winchester is still held high, not pointed at anyone, but a soldier snatches at it, and Van Helsing fires his derringer into the ground. The sound of the gunshot is enough to startle the soldiers into shooting: there is a thunderous crash like the sky being torn apart as they fire their carbines until the magazines are empty. This is followed by relative quiet as some of the soldiers re-load, while the Indians scramble for any weapons they can use to defend themselves. Unable to reach the pile of rifles, knives and axes, most flee. Once they are a safe distance from the soldiers, the gunners on the cliffs began cranking the five-barreled Hotchkiss guns.

louder! louder! louder! louder! —

Yellow Bird continues to sing and dance amid the hail of cannon-fire, but is soon cut down. Within minutes, twenty-five soldiers and nearly two hundred Indians have been killed by the guns.

It is the end of the Ghost Dance, and none of them rises from the dead. Van Helsing stays at the camp at Wounded Knee for another day, just to make sure, then returns to New York. Confined in the narrow bunk of a Pullman carriage, he still sees the faces, and can only pray that no-one else hears the voices.

> By the dismal tarns and pools
> Where dwell the Ghouls,—
> By each spot the most unholy—
> In each nook most melancholy—
> There the traveller meets aghast
> Sheeted Memories of the Past—
> Shrouded forms that start and sigh
> As they pass the wanderer by—
> White-robed forms of friends long given,
> In agony, to the worms—and Heaven.
> —Edgar Allan Poe, *Dream-Land*

Soap

Tiny mouths of the world, how you dread
The floating bars in a mother's hand as they
Are offered before the cleansing water, and foam
Without a hint of the ash and lye they're made from.

We think the milky white bubbles signify some great purity
Just shy of perfection against a lab-coat's chuckling scales.
That faint whiff of perfume left on the skin
Means we have journeyed to some higher state,

And the resentful tongue will be thankful when reflective
In some long-boned future
As it is washed into nothing like a vanishing moon
Devoured by a malachite frog hungry for the heavens.

Scrubbing and scouring, my Hera, your predacious eyes
Never did find those four-letter words the boy muttered.

Sitting by your righteous hearth in your splendor,
I regret to inform you
His malady has spread with age, despite your remedies.

And in the news today, they say antibacterial soap
May in fact promote the birth of wily superbacteria
Whose monstrous nature will thrust us into the sterile arms

Of titanic pharmaceutical companies
Who specialize in slaying such tiny hydras,
For a price our children may be unable to afford.

—Brian Thao Worra

T. Bilgen memorably enters our pages with this bracing story.

Turning

by T. Bilgen

Someone's at the door, leaning hard on that bell. Charity asks if I'm expecting anybody this late; I'm not.

I open up and there he is, Cleve, that punk, a bucket of KFC under one arm and that harebrained grin on his face. Holy hell, it's been years. We're already laughing when I let him in, but there's a tug in my brain and in my gut; he wants to see me, sure, but I bet he's really here to see the monster.

When I was thirteen and it first started, I thought it was a recurring dream, warm and tender like heaven, and I figured everybody could do the same as me. Then my folks found out and that changed my mind.

They stood there in my room that morning, surrounded by my model airplanes, Mom covering her mouth with her hands and Dad glaring like he might shoot lightning from his eyes. I sat in bed asking what I'd done wrong. They didn't answer.

In the end it was Cleve that gave it to me straight. He was nine, and found the situation hilarious. (I was in trouble, and the school bus had come and gone and no one cared.) "Barry, first Mom screamed, then me and Dad ran in, and there was a big pile of spaghetti, in your bed, and it was gross and slimy, and then it turned into *you*! You're *gross*!" Then he giggled, a chimp in Transformers pajamas.

After that, Mom wouldn't look me in the eye. It was months later, that summer, when she said anything to me about it. I remember her leaning in the kitchen doorway, a cigarette hanging on her lower lip, and she said, "You keep doing that, like what you're doing, and God'll make sure you're alone for the rest of your whole life." Then she blew smoke and nodded. She cleaned houses for a living, so she might've known what God wanted.

Dad was an electrician and a drunk, not always in that order. He'd get to shouting sometimes, and that's usually as far as it went, but when he wanted to use them his fists could bury you like an avalanche.

After that first morning, he lost interest in me. He didn't say a word to me until the day he died, and that was four years off.

Whenever he felt paternal (rare) he focused on Cleve, watching football with him, teaching him about cars, like that. It made Cleve happy; we were always competitive when it came to Dad.

Cleve was more than okay with my turning—he loved it. He buddied up to me a lot more, and wanted to know everything about turning into a monster. He wanted to be ready when he got to be my age.

I said turning felt better than anything else in the world; better than summertime and birthdays and pizza from Paizzano's. You had no worries, no problems. You left your body behind and went floating in a peaceful bath. You couldn't see, but you knew the colors were like a perfect sunset going on forever, orange and pink.

I shouldn't have told him any of that stuff.

I spent so much time turned. I did it whenever I could: at night, all night, and sometimes all the next day. Turning became the only thing I looked forward to.

My hair grew long and greasy, my face broke out fierce, toenails snarled. I didn't care. And forget school, friends, and model-building. Who needed any of that?

Once, I turned for a week straight, just to see what it'd be like. I snuck down to the basement, worked my way into the crawlspace and curled up there, tangled in cobwebs and crammed in between the cardboard boxes, and spent a week without feeling tired or bored or hungry or empty, just perfect. Coming out of it was hell, like I'd climbed a mountain and run a marathon and got hit by a train all at once. And I was so hungry I thought my stomach was chewing through my guts.

Cleve brought me bologna and ketchup and Wonder bread, and while I stuffed everything into my mouth he asked questions. He wanted to know how to be a monster.

The years smudged into each other after that.

It was November, I think, when Cleve stomped into my trainwreck of a room, swearing, loud and ferocious. (Normally he'd watch his mouth, but Mom was at work and Dad was snoring under a table.) Cleve was fourteen now, but he still couldn't turn.

It's not fair, he said and kicked my bookshelf. My old Peacemaker and the F-16 Triple Nickel went nose-diving. Plastic clattered, propellers went everywhere. I didn't mind the planes, it was just more crap on the floor, but I felt bad for Cleve. So bad that I flopped down onto my bed and turned, swam into the sunset, to escape from him and his grief. That's what I thought.

I found a sore spot in the perfection, like a weeping ulcer. So I worked on it. I didn't have hands but I smoothed it over, made it fit into my sunset—I healed it.

I came out of it around two in the morning. My window rattled with the wind and rain. Cleve was still with me; I switched on the light and he lay on the floor with the airplane pieces, looking like he'd just had a slice-and-a-half of heaven.

We were in the kitchen the rest of the night, eating anything we could find: Pringles and tunafish and green grapes. We talked and we figured it out.

Cleve couldn't turn but he could ride the waves I broadcasted, even from another room (we tried it). If someone was in range, and if I could find them in the sunset, I could bring them with me.

And we did a lot of turning together that winter. Cleve said it was the best Christmas ever.

He went mystical, reading Castaneda and Watts and Gloughden, looking for explanations and changing his story all the time: we were tensegrity shamans, we were Buddhas, we were all kinds of hippy-dippy stuff. I told him I didn't care what he called it and he smiled and said, "Barry, you've got no imagination."

That spring we found Dad in the living room, slumped in his easy chair, a bottle of Jack tipped in the crook of his arm. A fly crawled over his lips. It was morning. Cleve called 911 and Mom made a face like she was about to cry but she just shivered and didn't make a sound.

When I was a kid, and Cleve was still a baby, people were over at our house a lot. Men and women laughed and played cards and smoked, talking about stuff a kid couldn't understand except maybe it was funny or sad or unfair. But that was all before Dad's drinking. Nobody came to our house anymore, not for ages.

Now I stood there thinking, here's the old man, the bastard, there could have been so much more to him, there *was* more, but it doesn't matter now he's all done, alone in a room with a stink like sweat and peanut butter. And for nothing.

It made me mad, the waste of it, and I realized I was feeling something for the first time in ages, sharp and cold like a spike in my gut. I was seventeen.

Getting back into school was hell, back into those crooked desks and hallways, with kids I couldn't understand anymore. Remedial classes, night classes, summer classes—I worked like a slave.

I tried, but just couldn't go cold turkey on the turning. My mind would slip down a drain until all I could think of was disappearing into the perfect. Cleve didn't like it either: "Barry, what about my daily bliss, man?"

The airplanes helped. I remember working on a Silver Dragon and before I knew it a weekend went by and I hadn't thought of turning, not once. The gray plastic pieces, the paint and the glue and the newspaper crinkling on my desk, they made a place I wanted to stay in.

I used turning as a reward, for getting through another day of school, for finishing my homework, for not turning the rest of the time. I weaned myself off, using my own zillion-step program.

And whenever I was getting ready to turn, even when I had it down to short weekend trips, Cleve'd be right there, ready to hitch a ride. He'd take any scrap of sunset.

He was pissed that we weren't taking as many trips like we used to. I told him soon I wouldn't be doing it anymore at all and he pitched a fit, like a little kid (so much for that brand new Silver Dragon.) "I know exactly what I want," he said, "but I know I can't have it."

That was the end of his buddying-up days.

There were other ways for Cleve to keep his Buddha-shaman on, and there were enough shitheads in that high school to supply him. He was following my example, only he needed a crowbar to open up the sunset. He stayed home a lot, and stayed away from home, and got brought home by the cops at four in the morning.

I figured I knew where he was at and tried to help him out (and tried not to think I'd put him there in the first place). When I talked to him he wouldn't listen, or he'd lie, and next thing I know he's running down the street in the rain in his underwear with me chasing after, or I'm washing blood off his face in the bathroom sink because he'd said something stupid to someone twice his size.

One night I got him to bed more or less okay. His room was a dump and had a cheddar-smell. He sneered and said, "You're denying me, Barry. You're denying you, too."

Whenever he talked like that the old hunger would hit; it was an animal in a cage, and keeping it locked up was hard enough without watching Cleve sink so deep. It was a vicious year.

Come September I moved into a boardinghouse downtown and started at Seattle Community College. I figured I'd do technical design, maybe work on airplanes, help people fly.

Cleve ran away a few months later.

The punk sent us postcards—from Portland, then Frisco then San Diego—saying he was okay, finding odd jobs and 'chasing realities.' It didn't help; Mom was just this side of nuts. Cleve would turn eighteen in January, then the cops would have to drop the case and we'd just have to deal with it.

I was barely hanging on in school, and I had cravings every day, like angels and devils promising and threatening and offering. I second-guessed everything I'd ever done. Guilt.

Now, three years later, here he is and I can't stop smiling. He's lanky and tanned and taller than me, his hair cut short and his beard scruffy. We're sitting in the living room, me and him and Charity, the air filled with talk and the smell of fried chicken. I guess Cleve doesn't know Charity's vegetarian, but she's a good sport, serving up chips and Coke with ice.

He's been staying with Mom for the past few days, so he knows I dropped out of college ages back and I'm working at Engine Air Services now, buying and selling airplane components (helping people fly.) And he knows about Charity, how we met at school (true love), how she works for the City in Family Services, how we've been renting our little house for a year now, and that our garage is full of model airplanes.

After moving all up and down the coast, doing construction and landscaping, Cleve is back in Seattle. Between bites of chicken he tells stories about his travels and keeps us laughing.

When Charity goes into the kitchen his voice drops low, and he tells me he's tried lots of stuff over the past few years (drugs). I notice his shirtsleeves; they're rolled down, maybe hiding his arms on purpose.

"I've been trying to get back into that sunset zone, Barr," he whispers, "but I'm always left empty." He checks over his shoulder. "Nothing's close to those trips we used to make, you know?"

I take a sip of Coke. "I haven't turned in almost four years," I say. "I walk a tightrope every day, Cleve. Every single day. If I ever do it again, I don't think I could come back. I wouldn't be strong enough." Just saying it starts the hunger.

He nods and sinks back into the couch, cupping his glass in his beat-up hands. "That Charity's really nice," he says. "She know all that stuff about you?"

"What stuff?" she says, back from the kitchen, carrying a tray with three bowls of vanilla ice-cream.

First I look at Charity, then at Cleve—the last person I want in my house. "That I used to be hooked?" I say. "Yeah. And she knows I'm clear now."

"Sure, but do you know what he was hooked *on*?" Cleve says to her, raising his voice, spilling his drink.

Here it is, here we go; either Cleve hurts someone or Charity finds out the truth about me. I see a balance I've worked hard for, I see it tipping.

He gets to his feet and I do too and Charity backs away. He's shouting now, It's not fair, you're denying me, you're hogging it all for yourself.

Then he runs out, slamming the front door and making a clock jump off the wall. My knees are rubber and Charity looks like she's seen a monster and I hope it's not me.

I call Mom, tell her Cleve might be headed home mad, that she should watch herself, and all she can say is, "What did you do to him, Barry?"

I hang up and we clean the mess: the Coke, the ice, the broken clock. I tell Charity I'm sorry and she says, "You don't have to say that, you're not responsible." I want to believe her.

It's midnight when Mom phones, screaming about Cleve and half an hour later we're all at Harborview (hospital).

GLD is a designer drug, the doctor says, and she tells me its chemical name, gamma-something-*eene*. It mimics the brain's chemicals, neurotransmitters, and it stimulates pleasure. It's easy to make in a lab, she says, but the impurities can stick to brain cells and never let go. "The side-effects can be disturbing. Hallucinations, severe pain." She wants us to know this for when we go in to see him.

She wasn't kidding. There's Cleve in a bed, writhing against leather straps, eyes bulging, teeth flashing. He growls and whimpers—and this is with sedation. He's sweaty and he's messed the bed. He doesn't recognize any of us, doesn't know his own name; he's been whittled down to a nub of agony.

Mom found him like this in my old room at home. Now in the hospital she sags and leans on Charity, who holds her hand.

Back in the hallway the doctor says she's seen cases like this before; they're touch-and-go. I ask what she means and she says, "The symptoms intensify, then the basic autonomic functions fail." She lowers her voice. "Functions like heartbeat and breathing. Usually within forty-eight hours."

She's saying sorry and I'm thinking about the waste of it all. But I can help.

When I tell Charity I'm staying with him, she gives me that look; she knows me, she knows something's up. I say it's one-thirty and my mom needs a ride home (true), and so far as Cleve goes, there's nothing anyone can do (false).

We hug and kiss and I have to act like we'll be seeing each other tomorrow. It's pure hell but I can't show it. Then she's gone and I'm alone here and I'll never see her or Mom or anybody again.

Walking through these shiny green corridors, I feel like I'm climbing up a hill, each step getting harder and heavier. I think about Cleve and Charity, about how much of this is my fault and I feel sick. In my heart I feel sick.

I'll have to find a place in here, a closet or a corner in the basement.

Then tomorrow the doctors'll find Cleve lying in his bed so relaxed with a faraway look in his eyes, as if he's remembering something happy. They'll wonder why his last few hours were so comfortable. Then they'll notice other patients have the same dreamy look, the people with the worst pain, cancer patients, burn victims. They'll wonder where all that pain's gone to.

Who knows how long I can keep it up—I might be a guy that turns into muck, but it might be the other way around. Until somebody steps on something pale and slimy in a dark corner, I'll just keep at it and everyone can keep wondering and who knows? Maybe we'll all of us get a little peace.

Patricia Russo's first TOTU story (in #10) was a sharp-edged look at the politics of Snow White. Since then she's appeared here in many flavors and taken us to many locales; here she once again shows us the Realm of Faerie in a glass, darkly.

The Ogre's Wife
by Patricia Russo

She does try to save them, both the boys and the girls, all the lost, sad, wandering children, those who are running from something, or toward something they cannot even vaguely describe. Many are so afraid that dragging a single word from their mouths is sweatier work than carding straw; the majority are so desperate that her only possible offer, that of hiding them in the tiny room behind the pantry, inside the chest, beneath the winter blankets, sounds good. Sounds like salvation. They barely flinch when—if—they recognize the meat turning on the spit, for the pantry is behind the kitchen, and to get to the small storeroom, the kitchen must be traversed. Most of them have traversed worse, or think they have.

She even tries to save the thieves, the sly boys and girls who come sidling along with their fresh rags and new-minted tales of woe, drawn by the stories of gold, of treasure, of hoarded jewels and coins and magic this and enchanted that. She knows these children wish only to steal, she can tell as soon as she sees their eyes, but it makes no matter. She hides them, she helps them, she feeds them what she eats herself, and she loads them with all the advice they will bear. Most of it they shrug off. She knows this, too, that no one will heed, that they will be guided by nothing but their own greed (the thieves) or their fear (the silent ones) or their desperation (the ones who have run the soles of their feet bloody.) So it was with her; she was one of them, once.

Not like the one hiding in the chest now, obediently quiet, compliantly still, his scent disguised by the fresh rushes she has strewn on the floors of every room and the soap she is boiling in the foreyard. The wind is blowing the right way; the distracting smells she has created will certainly be enough to fool her children, and quite possibly enough to fool her husband as well.

The boy now curled in the chest is nearly a man grown, and has been fed well through most of his growth, even if not recently; his bones are strong, though his flesh is scant, and his teeth are as white as new snow. He has come to steal, believing the gaudy stories told around inn fires, told during the long summer nights up in the high pastures, told in the shade when the reapers rest from their labors. Gold, gems, a magic drum that beats out a prince's fortune at every blow, a cape of shadows that renders the wearer as imperceptible as a shadow himself, charmed boots that can carry a person across every mountain and every sea, a white flower whose petals turn to diamonds at each sunrise. Treasure upon treasure piled up in the ogre's house. He has heard all these tales, and he believes them. He wants these riches; he aches for them. He is risking his life, and she, the ogre's wife, wishes him well. Desperation drives him, as it drives the others, the lost, the silent, the runaways. Each of them has a tale, and each is different, and all of them are the same.

Her own father was desperate, when he sold her to the ogre. Not this one, not this husband, but her first, the one with the strength of twenty men and the appetite of a hundred, with a beard down to his knees and shoulders as broad across as a herring boat's keel, with a sword as heavy as a hundred-year oak belted at his waist and one golden hair on his bald head, with a nose like a flattened hand and teeth like gnarled black roots, with silver clinking in his purse and a penis that tore her so badly she bled for weeks and weeks. Though that came later. Her mother, she remembers, cursed her father, cursed him in her soft, powerless voice, and threw her apron over her head. Her curses came louder then, with her face hidden. Her father simply nodded, his eyes down, not looking at the ogre, nor at his wife, nor at the daughter he was selling, nor at his other children, gathered in wonder and fear, silent, shaking, watching, their terror more for themselves than for their sister, for that is the way of human beings, and there was nothing they could have done for her, anyway. She screamed when her father held out his palm and let the ogre drop the coins into them; when her father closed his hand and nodded again, she cursed him as her mother was cursing him, and worse; just before the ogre touched her for the first time, she spat into her father's face. But the ogre picked her up and carried her off, and that was that.

She was twelve, or perhaps thirteen, then. It's strange, she thinks, as she sits and listens to the soap boil (for the soap-pot is enchanted and needs no stirring or tending; she can sit in the front room and embroider headdresses for her daughters, or knit stockings for her sons, or simply sit and watch the clouds float across the sky, and the soap will make itself) what one can remember and what one cannot. She can remember her mother's voice, but not her face; she can remember her father's face, but not the touch of his hand; she can remember her first husband's penis and his one golden hair, but not the color of his eyes. Her little brothers and sisters she remembers hardly at all. She hopes they have not been among the desperate ones who have come to the ogre's house; or, if they have, that they have been among the few who have escaped detection. She doesn't remember how many brothers and sisters she had before her father sold her; she assumes her mother bore several more after the last time she saw her.

It was ten years before the boy came, the boy who wanted to rescue her, the boy who wanted to be a hero. That she remembers; ten years with her first husband.

She was wise already, after ten years. The boy was beautiful, with sparkling black eyes and skin as soft as flour, but that made no matter. You're not strong enough, she said. He'll snap you like a quill. Go home, marry a girl from your village, be happy.

Tell me the ogre's secret, the boy said. You must know it. How can he be defeated, how can he be destroyed?

Of course I know it, she said. The ogre can be killed only by his own sword, the sword of bronze as heavy as a barn, that hangs on the wall above my spinning wheel when it is not hanging from his belt. You will never be able to lift it, not you even with the help of twenty like you; you will never be able to swing it, not you even with the help of thirty like you. You must cut off the ogre's head with one stroke, and as it is still rolling and bleeding, you must shear the single golden hair from his head. This you cannot do, not you, not even with the help of forty like you. Go home. Live. The gold is not worth your life.

It is not gold I come for, the beautiful boy said, but you. I love you.

You love me? This seemed so unlikely she almost burst into laughter, which would have been an unkindness, for the boy was solemn, almost trembling in his earnestness.

I love you, he said, and I shall slay the ogre and rescue you.

He went away then, and she watched him go, slim hips, swinging arms, rough-cut brown hair, until he disappeared around a turn in the road, and she did not see him again for a year.

When he returned, he came boldly, beating at the front door with a hard fist, for he had been to a wise woman, or a woman who said she was wise, and had taken twelve drinks of a potent potion, one each month, to make him strong enough to lift the ogre's sword. When she opened the door, he rushed in past her, to snatch the sword off the wall. But he was not strong enough yet, the wise woman's potion had not done its full work, and after a moment, arms quivering, he dropped the sword. The ogre looked up from his dinner, grease ringing his mouth, and belched laughter. The boy, whom she scarcely recognized, ran.

It is strange what one remembers and what one cannot remember. The second time the boy came, the first time he had tried to fight the ogre, he was taller than the first time she'd seen him, when he spoke to her as she stood on one side of the threshold and he stood on the other, when she had watched him striding away with pity and longing in her heart. His shoulders were broader, too, and his thighs. His hips were no longer slim. She could not be sure, now, if his nose had flattened like an open hand, or if his teeth had begun to twist like old roots, that first time he had returned.

Who was that, her first husband asked, slow and sated after his meal, and she had answered, I don't know, and it had almost been the truth.

The boy came back after another twelve months, and that time he had held the sword well, and swung it once, but the ogre, grinning, had blocked the blow with a careless, almost languid, motion of one arm. Then he plucked the sword from the boy's hand, tossed it into the air, caught it—by which time the boy had fled again. This time the ogre chased him for a mile or two, before losing interest. Fortunate for the boy that this time, too, he had come after the ogre had already stuffed his belly full ten times over.

But not boy, not any longer....she could not call him that, could not think of him that way any more. I love you, he cried, just before he ran, and that earned her a beating from her husband when he came home, out of breath and with an ache in his bowels and sweat pouring from his bald head, but the boy was not the beautiful youth who had spoken to her across the threshold. He looked like the ogre's younger brother.

She was very wise then, twelve years an ogre's wife, and if her first husband did not know what the future held, she did. She lay awake at night and tears pooled in her eyes, but she did not let them fall, for then the ogre would question her, and the less they spoke, the easier it was for her not to take a knife, one of the many sharp kitchen knives, and open her veins.

The next time the boy who was no longer a boy returned, she saw at once that he must have downed a vat of the potion concocted by the wise woman, or the woman who said she was wise. He was as tall as the ogre, as broad as the ogre, as strong as the ogre, as hungry as the ogre, as ugly as the ogre, as terrible as the ogre. He took the sword off the ogre's belt, tore it free through the scabbard with no more effort than a child would spend tearing a leaf, and cut off the ogre's head with a single blow, and sheared off the one golden hair before the head had bounced across the floor three times. Then he turned to her and grinned, and it was the same grin she had seen when her first husband had dropped three or four coins into her father's open hand.

I love you, he said, and she swallowed her own spit and bowed her head.

She and her first husband had not had any children. With the second, they came one after the next. At the birth of each, boy or girl, the ogre was gleeful, and celebrated with barrels of ale and the flesh of twenty men, roasted, boiled, fried.... It made no matter.

The children took after their father. The ogre who had once been a beautiful brave boy roared with pride. She kept silent, and polished the kitchen knives. The children grew quickly, and were the terror of the countryside, and each year or two a new one fought his or her way out into the light from between her legs. She smothered one or two, starved a couple, but still they came, one after another, like their father, all like their father, and she could not stop her eyes filling with tears, but she never let one drop fall.

And still the other children come, the desperate ones, the ones running from something more terrible than any ogre's house, the ones hiding from someone more terrible than any ogre, the ones seeking for riches that would free them from a life more terrible than they imagined the life of an ogre's wife could be.

She cannot remember how many children she has. She knows they will all be home soon, hungry, roaring, wanting food, eager for dinner. Dinner is cooking. She can smell it, despite the rushes and the boiling soap.

She cannot smell the young thief hidden in the chest beneath the winter blankets. She hopes he will remain unfound, that he has heard at least a few words of the advice she has given him, that he will snatch one object, the blue-feathered fowl which craps rubies, perhaps, and escape with it, and be satisfied. She does not want to be turning the kitchen spit tomorrow, with the young thief's body on it, roasting slowly over the fire.

But she will turn the kitchen spit tomorrow, with the young thief's body on it, or another's body, hunted and brought back alive by her children or her second husband. There will be many bodies to roast tomorrow. Or boil, or fry, or stew. It made no matter. One way or the other, the family must be fed.

She would save them all if she could.

She does what she can, and she knows herself as terrible as her husband, as both her husbands, though she has never once tasted human flesh, as terrible as her children, though she has not chosen this, did not choose this, would never have chosen this.

She has bowed her head and kept silent.

She bows her head and keeps silent.

In the chest, the boy, the thief, is silent. He believes the stories of riches, of wealth unimaginable, of magic, and why should he not? They are all true.

She has saved a few. Thirteen years with her first husband, more than twenty with her second, she has saved a few of the young and lost, the young and adventurous, the young and dreadfully hurt. She sits in the front room, dinner almost ready, the soap almost solid, the rushes fresh and fragrant, and hates herself ten times more than she hates her father.

The children will come home first, and then her husband.

The boy, the thief, lies in the chest, as still as a live boy can lie.

She sits, the ogre's wife, listening for footsteps.

Palimpsest Fugue

A rainy night in Tokyo breaks through
this pallid Russian sunlight, & he knows
down to the phantom aching in his bones
it's happening again.
      The glass he holds
for dear life (—lives—) implodes within his grip
to bloody shards of some kaleidoscope
turned maelstrom murder done…& done, & done,
till all the faces run to one bright point
extinguished as he blinks another self
away in sleep.
      To dream is to awake:
abraded mind a crazing mirror held
too long before too many lies played out
along reflexes honed in actions lost
between the news & truth.
      He takes that word
between his teeth like sugar—tries to sip
the tea now bleeding through his hands until
those subtle men in suits who always come
are back again, the spray-hype & the scent
of black seat leather riding into night
he prays he might not waken from this time.
                         —Ann K. Schwader

*Robert P. Switzer, whose first published fiction was the funny "Chief of the Sexy and Cool Committee (*TOTU #26) *returns with this heart-breaking tale.*

With Your Blood I Wash My Hands
by Robert P. Switzer

I've been fantasizing about you again.

It's a habit I should soon try to break. Another such habit is watching a particular documentary, one that I've already seen dozens of times; I can't seem to turn it off whenever I come across it.

The first time I saw it, it was on the Friendly Demon Channel. I remember being mildly disgusted.

"Our demon friends drain blood from their skulls on a nightly basis," said the program's host, "not because some incomprehensible ritual dictates such behavior, but simply because it is physiologically necessary. Every night, it is vital that excess blood produced during the day be let out. At one point in the history of the purperson race, this bloodletting was achieved naturally. When primitive purpeople sat down to sleep for the night, their heads would roll onto one of their three pairs of shoulder spikes, and spare blood would flow from forehead punctures."

Computer graphics illustrated the entire process, and the announcer continued, "The ancestors of our demon friends decided that this was an uncivilized and unseemly way of fulfilling their needs. Waking up every morning encrusted in blood was deemed unacceptable. So they designed a blood tap that could be twisted into the back of the purperson head each night, sanitarily releasing all excess blood. An entire realm became clean and civilized. Now the shoulder spikes of baby purpeople are ground down into dull, useless nubs, and all purpeople use blood taps."

A real purperson demonstrated. She held the blood tap against the back of her own head, then screwed clockwise. It went in without much effort. She attached a blood bag to the tap, flipped the valve, and blood trickled out.

Like I said, I was mildly disgusted. But that was before I met you.

I chose a seat in the back row of the classroom, pulled out some paper and a pen, tucked my knapsack beneath my chair, and out of the corner of my eye I saw purple. It was you.

You walked past me, heading for a seat near the front. I remember staring foolishly, watching your hips twist around, one way and then the other, as you incorporated all three of your legs into the smooth motion. I noticed how your ankles twisted to keep your feet pointing forward, and how your shoulders turned and your three arms swung in the opposite direction of your hips. Such grace, such beauty, such flexibility.

I wanted to get to know you. I wanted to find out who you were. What I didn't particularly want was to listen to the prof's introductory remarks about Shakespeare, and so I didn't.

After class, I lingered outside the doorway until you strolled through. And I asked, "Is Shakespeare a popular playwright where you're from?"

"You'd be surprised," you told me.

With that, I'd exhausted my list of clever things to say, so I said, "I guess I'll see you next week."

"Take care," you replied.

As I watched you walk away, a hundred ways to keep a conversation going came to mind, but I refrained from shouting any of them out.

A brief and awkward encounter—I remember it with nothing but fondness.

Three days later I admitted the truth to my best friend Phil. "I've been fantasizing about her."

"The Shakespeare-loving demon?" he said.

I nodded.

He laughed. I think he knew that I was serious, but he couldn't help but laugh. "Are there no eligible humans in the class?" he asked.

I thought about his question for a moment, especially its irrelevance. "She really is amazing," I told him.

"Are humans and purpeople even compatible?" Phil went on. "I mean, have you thought about what sex with her would be like? Extra limbs flying around all over the place."

"One extra arm. One extra leg. So what?"

"So where's that extra leg going to go?" he asked.

I shook my head. "I've hardly even spoken with her. I don't think I need to start worrying about where the extra leg is going to go yet."

"You haven't talked to her?" he said.

"Just briefly and awkwardly," I replied.

Phil nodded. "That sounds like your style."

I stared at him, unable to deny it.

He laughed again, then put on a serious expression and schemed for a moment. "Okay, here's what you do. You sit beside her next week. At the end of class, you suggest that the two of you get together sometime to study. She comes over to your apartment, and suddenly your five-legged fantasy's halfway to becoming reality."

Phil has never prided himself on being consistent, but I needed a moment to absorb his switch from admonishment to encouragement. Afterward, I decided that I actually liked his idea.

"Our first test's in two weeks," I pointed out at the end of the next class.

"Yes it is," you said.

"Maybe we should get together to study."

"Would you like to come over to my place on Saturday?"

Your invitation threw me off, because I was supposed to be inviting you over to my place. "Your place?"

"I have an apartment in the city," you told me.

My arm didn't need any more twisting. "Sure. Okay. That sounds great."

Saturday arrived quickly, and with an armload of Shakespeare I made my first visit to your apartment. You invited me inside and gave me a brief tour, during which I was once again mesmerized by your beautiful, graceful walk. It made me doubt that you'd ever want anything to do with a clumsy, unrefined human, and yet I clung to the possibility that you would.

Glancing around, I decided that your apartment didn't have the demonic feel to it that I'd been expecting. The one thing that I did notice right away was that there were no chairs.

"My people don't normally sit so high above the floor," you explained. "Will you be comfortable on one of my comfort mats?"

"That'll be perfect," I said.

You pulled two mats together and we sat and discussed *All's Well That Ends Well*.

"What kind of questions do you suppose our prof will give us?" I asked.

"She'll probably want to know whether or not we feel the play ends well," you said.

"And ironically, it doesn't."

"Doesn't it?"

"Well, Helena apparently thinks it does—she gets her man. But come on. Bertram certainly isn't much of a prize."

"You don't care for Bertram?"

I shook my head in reply, and I tried to pinpoint what I most disliked about the character. "Maybe his biggest fault is that he's just too human."

"I think a lot of humans are like that," you suggested.

Later we ordered a pizza. I thought there was going to be leftovers, but you continued to eat even after I'd finished, until it was gone. "Were you hungry?" I asked.

"I'm eating for three," you told me.

"Three?"

"Twins," you said, gently placing a hand over your stomach.

"Oh. Well. I didn't think—I mean, I never would've guessed. You're so thin. Pregnant. Wow. Does this mean that you're married?"

"I do not have a life partner, no," you replied. "My pregnancy is the result of a brief relationship."

"A fling," I suggested.

Perhaps you didn't care for that term. "A brief relationship," you repeated.

Sometimes I tell my best friend Phil things that I should probably keep to myself.

"She's pregnant and you're still fantasizing about her?" he cried.

"Don't judge me," I told him.

But he couldn't not judge me. And he couldn't not laugh.

We studied other plays—*Hamlet, A Winter's Tale, Othello*—remember *Othello*? You argued that Iago was simply misunderstood, that he wasn't the evil creature that everybody imagined. I'm afraid that I never did come around to your point of view on that one.

Our Shakespeare course ended, but we remained good friends. I was there when your babies were born. For another six and a half months, I watched them grow.

"You are familiar with our phlebotomical practices?" you asked me one evening.

"The blood thing?" I said. "Sure, I'm familiar. I watched a documentary on it."

You fetched the bloodletting paraphernalia. "It's time for me to drain my children's blood."

"Oh," I said. "Would you like me to leave?"

"No," you replied. "I would like you to participate."

"Ah," I said.

"Unless it would make you uncomfortable," you added.

"Uncomfortable? Me? Good heavens, no. I've never been uncomfortable in my life," I stammered.

Your children were asleep on their comfort mats. As we approached them, you handed me one of the blood taps. "Just do what I do," you told me.

You held the tap against the back of your daughter's head and gently but firmly twisted. When it was all the way in, you turned toward me. I swallowed. Carefully, I placed the tap against your son's head. I took a deep breath, and screwed it in. No problem. We connected the blood bags, tripped the valves, and watched the blood drip out. Your children, obviously accustomed to this kind of treatment, slept through the whole operation.

"You do this every night?" I said.

"It must be done," you replied.

Ten minutes later, we removed the taps from your

children's skulls. "Very little blood," you commented. "But it is crucial that it be allowed out."

"I understand," I said.

"Then I will ask you a favor," you said. "Next Friday I'll be going on an overnight field trip. Could you take care of my children?"

"I'd be happy to."

"It would be much appreciated, if you could."

"I don't anticipate a problem," I said.

The phone rang.

"Hello?"

"Listen," Phil began with his usual enthusiasm. "A little party is starting to brew at my place. You've got to come over. Wendy's here, and her sister's visiting from out of town. Juliana, I think she said her name was. Anyhow, you've got to come meet her. She's perfect for you. What do you say?"

"I don't think so," is what I said.

"Huh?" said Phil. "What's the trouble? You still saving yourself for your purple friend?"

"As a matter of fact, I'm babysitting her children tonight."

Phil was silent for a moment. "Well," he finally said, "if you can break away for a minute, we'd love to see you here. If you can't, then you can't."

"Thanks anyway," I told him.

As I hung up the phone, I thought about how Phil tended to have a way of making me want to be where he was. His little parties were always fun; I rarely missed one.

The phone rang again and I answered, "Okay, maybe for just a minute."

"A minute of what?" you asked.

"Oh," I said. "Nothing. I mean, I thought you were my buddy Phil. He just called and invited me to a small gathering at his place, but I told him I couldn't make it. Crazy Phil—I think I've told you about him, haven't I?"

"You should go," you said.

"What? No, I don't need to go."

"If you want to go, that's fine. Young purpeople don't require the constant supervision that baby humans do. They just need someone to release their excess blood for them."

"But I couldn't just leave them alone," I said.

"They would be perfectly all right," you insisted. "They only need you for that one task."

"I'm not going to go," I said with finality, and then I asked you why you'd called.

You told me it was just to say hi.

After I'd set down the phone again, I went to check on the children who didn't require supervision. I'd placed their comfort mats in my bedroom; I peeked in and saw two young demons sleeping soundly.

It was early; I still had a few hours before it would be time to drain their blood. I could pop over to Phil's for one drink and be back in plenty of time. There'd be no harm in making an appearance.

The thought came and I acted on it. In an instant I was at the party, laughing with Phil and meeting Wendy's sister Juliana, hardly noticing as Phil brought out his pill bottles and started shaking them over our drinks. Something made a splash in my glass.

"Hey!" I said, probably startling Phil, since I usually let him give me whatever he had. "What was that? If it was a forgetter, I don't want it. There are things I need to remember tonight."

"It wasn't a forgetter," said Phil.

"What was it?" I asked again, watching the last of whatever it was dissolve in my beverage.

"It was a calmer," he said, laughing at my sudden seriousness.

"Are you sure?"

"I'm sure, I'm sure," he said, and he wandered off to mingle with people who were less sober.

Phil only bought the high-grade stuff—his calmers and forgetters always did what they were supposed to do. A forgetter was the last thing I wanted right then, but maybe a calmer would hit the spot.

I believed Phil.

I finished my drink.

I'd like to say that the rest of the night is just a haze but in fact I remember it clearly—a forgetter makes you forget the past, not the present. So I remember thinking there was no reason not to stay for a few more drinks, I remember thinking I ought to get to know Juliana better, I remember getting to know her better in Phil's spare bedroom, and I remember that she was so—

She was so.

It was noon the next day when I finally returned to my apartment. I didn't remember your children until I saw them. They sat on their comfort mats with their heads slumped far too low, and their skin looking much less purple than before.

They'd fallen asleep, confident that someone was watching over them, looking after their needs. I wasn't. I didn't. In the middle of the night, blood vessels had exploded in their brains.

You didn't get angry. I killed your children, and you didn't get angry. Anger simply isn't a part of a purperson's repository of emotions. I wished that it was, and I begged you to strike me, to hurt me, to hate me.

You should have been utterly disgusted with me. How could you not be disgusted?

Instead you told me you realized that it was an accident. Accidents happen. But we both knew the truth. Accidents happen because ignorance happens.

One moment of ignorance. I wanted to blame Phil, but I couldn't; he had lied to me, but he hadn't known what was at stake. The only person I could blame, and hate, was myself.

The hatred festered inside me. I never expected you to understand my unbearable self-hatred, just as I could never know the pain that grew inside you. But I could see that it was growing. It grew until you could think of only one way to release it.

The police let me into your apartment. They let me touch your beautiful purple hair. I tried my best to explain to them your terrible need to experience exactly what your children had experienced.

It's been months now since you've been gone and what I feel inside is a jumble of emotions, sadness of course and bitterness and other feelings that I can't define, and lately I've been thinking about you the same way that I used to and—

And I've been fantasizing about you again.

The fantasies are all the same. I fantasize that we're still taking that Shakespeare course together. I come over to your apartment to study. We sit on comfort mats facing each other, and we argue about which characters are good and which are evil.

Afterward, I stand and move toward you. I briefly run my fingers through your hair, then lower my hands to massage your shoulders. I work one shoulder at a time, kneading the flesh surrounding each pair of shoulder nubs. The flexibility of your neck lets you face each shoulder as I rub it, but you close your eyes and sway your head to the rhythms of my massage.

Around your body I move, working lower and deeper, until you offer me one of your gorgeous purperson smiles, and you stand and step out of your gown. I am quickly similarly unclothed.

Despite the presence of extra limbs, our lovemaking is never awkward. It is gentle and rejuvenating, inspiriting and tender.

We rest for a while and then I resume my massage. We both hum softly, because everything is right in this world.

You remind me that it's time to drain your excess blood, and I offer to do it for you. You hand me the blood tap, and turn your head away. The tap goes in smoothly, I flip the valve, and I hear you sigh. Blood flows out.

And with your blood I wash my hands.

Tales of the Unanticipated was founded in 1986 by the Minnesota Science Fiction Society, who served as publisher of its first 23 issues.

The TOTU staff wish to thank SF Minnesota for a Donor Organization Grant that helped defray expenses for Tales of the Unanticipated #27.

HYDROTAXIC PERSONALS: BETWEEN THE LINES

Relaxing in the pool, the chemist thinks about
the wet honeymoon of oxygen and hydrogen.

Physicists alone in the dark touch themselves
and savor the sexiness of hydraulics.

Divorcing engineers feel positively electric
about their marriage's hydrolysis.

The radio astronomer in his lonely outpost
is comforted by the 21-centimeter glow.

The fancy-pants new-age rain-dancer
seeks a like-minded hydromancer.

The canine acting coach can teach
you to simulate hydrophobia.

Each of these couplets, cut off,
could reproduce like a hydra.

—JOHN CALVIN REZMERSKI

If you enjoyed William Laughlin's "The Story of Winnie-the-Poe" (TOTU #25), you just might like this offspring of another twisted muse. Let's have a big, bloody hand for Jason D. Wittman....

The Tale of Roderick Rabbit, by Beatrix Stoker

by Jason D. Wittman

Once upon a time there were four little rabbits, and their names were Lenore, Morella, Madeleine, and Roderick.

They lived with their mother near an old iron fence underneath the root of a very big yew tree.

"Now children," their mother said one evening, "you may go to church or stay here and do your homework, but don't go into Carfax Abbey. Your father had a bit of a mishap there; Count Dracula got hold of him and he was never seen again. Now be off with you and stay out of trouble. I have errands to run."

Then old Mother Rabbit took her crucifix, a wristlet of garlic, and another wristlet of wolfsbane, and went through the iron fence to Frau Von Tiggenwinkel's, the old hedgehog who told fortunes alongside of her bustling laundry business. Mother Rabbit had had a dream of an apple that fell from a yew tree into an open grave. It troubled her, so she wanted to ask Frau Von Tiggenwinkel's opinion of it.

Lenore, Morella, and Madeleine, who were sensible rabbits, all stayed home and did their homework.

But Roderick, who was not very bright, ran straight to Carfax Abbey, and squeezed through a hole in the stone wall.

First he ate some daisies and some wild thistles, and then, feeling a stomachache coming on, decided to go home to ask Mother Rabbit for some medicine.

But round the corner of the stone building, who should he meet but Count Dracula!

Count Dracula was on his hands and knees drawing unholy symbols in the dirt, but then he looked up at Roderick and said: "Welcome to my house. Come freely. Go safely; and leave something of the happiness you bring!"

Roderick was very scared. He turned and ran all over Carfax Abbey, having forgotten how to get back to the hole in the wall.

He lost one of his shoes in a thornbush, and the other shoe in the root of an oak tree.

When he lost the shoes, he ran on all fours and made better speed. He might have got clean away had he not tried to run through another thornbush and got caught by the big buttons on his jacket. It was a red jacket with silver buttons. Mother Rabbit had bought it for sixpence at the corner store.

Roderick thought he was done for, and he cried big wet tears, but his cries were overheard by a nearby raven, who flew to him very quickly, telling him not to be frightened and that everything would be all right. But Roderick saw what he was trying to do, and dodged just in time to avoid the beak that was darting for his eye.

Then Count Dracula came up and, grabbing Roderick, planted his fangs firmly in his neck. But Roderick thought quickly, plucked a silver button from his jacket and poked Count Dracula in the eye with it. Count

Dracula shrieked and dropped Roderick, who ran away as fast as he could, never looking back until he reached his home under the yew tree.

He was so tired from exertion and blood loss that he collapsed on the dirt floor of the rabbit hole.

Mother Rabbit did not even look up from the wooden stake she was carving. Frau Von Tiggenwinkel had given her a very clear interpretation of her dream, and very clear instructions. But just to be sure, she checked Roderick's teeth as he lay on the ground. They had grown longer and sharper. Roderick was turning into a vampire-rabbit.

So Mother Rabbit hammered the wooden stake through his chest, then burned his body on the pyre she had set up outside. Then she mixed the ashes with holy water she had borrowed from the church, put them in a silver urn, and buried it in the back yard next to Roderick's father.

Then Mother Rabbit went back into her rabbit hole and had a supper of baby carrots and strawberries with Lenore, Morella, and Madeleine.

An Archaeology of Snow Forts

There's not much left to be said
That some well-washed stone hasn't heard before.
History is composed of broken walls and bad neighbors,
Just ask these chips from Berlin, the Parthenon and Cathay
Or these cool magma hands of Pompeii, dark and grey.

If you listen carefully in the right place
On University Avenue, you will learn
There is a minor wall near the Yalu River
Dancing on the hills of Qin for the moon,
Who knows exactly what I mean
In every tongue worth mention.
She's moonlighting as a curved garden serpent
Coiling around old Laocoon,
The Suspicious One with his astute eye,
Crooning with a sly wink,
"Come, touch true history."

And how the moon must laugh when she spies
The tiniest hill in Minnetonka,
Where the small hands of the earth have erected

A magnificent white wall,
A snowy miniature Maginot
Raised some scant hours before,
Already melting into a hungry, roiling river
Who is not yet finished eating Louisiana for brunch.

—Brian Thao Worra

"I'll let you have Cleveland, if you give me Detroit."

Anticipations

Coming in *Tales of the Unanticipated* #28, March or April 2007—our "Heroes" Issue. S.N. Arly returns to our pages with the tale of a young woman offered a chance for heroism by an unusual mentor. Terry Black makes his *TOTU* debut with the rip-snorting yarn of that legend of the cosmos, Johnny Quantum. A. Christopher Drown's first *TOTU* story explores the ups and downs of being a superhero sidekick. Martha A. Hood shows us a man on another world willing to do hard time to help his people. Judy Klass serves up the quietly moving tale of a human trying to get back to the time where she belongs. Jeff Kouba makes his first *TOTU* appearance with a sensitive story of a troubled father/son relationship, in and out of Counterpane. Mary Soon Lee offers a tale of alien artisanship and its effect on two humans. Paul E. Martens returns to ask what would happen if a special ability suddenly descends on an ordinary person and just as suddenly goes away. Barbara Rosen makes a powerful *TOTU* debut writing about an elderly woman offered the opportunity to remake humanity for the better and having to decide if that's a good idea. Fred Schepartz returns with what is either a "Monster" or "Hero" story, depending on how one views the magical being at its center. Ka Vang enters the *TOTU* ranks with the story of an officer in wartime who risks everything to see his new-born son. In #28 or #29 William Mingin presents the predicament of a man who, while clinging to a mountainside, discovers something strange.

Coming in *Tales of the Unanticipated* #29, late 2007 or early 2008: reporter Terry Faust gives the inside scoop on a terrified teen whose santum sanctorum is violated by four beings with plans of their own. Joyce Finn enters our pages with the tale of a little kingdom who climbed a hill and what they found there. Sue Isle shows us the grim efforts of a few friends to survive with dignity in a future city. Michael A. Pignatella makes his *TOTU* debut with the riddle of the dead fist that changed three lives. And Katherine Woodbury climbs in the *TOTU* window with the story of a man with a deadly talent who finally meets his match. And there'll be lots of other cool fiction, poetry, artwork, and perhaps nonfiction—perhaps including something submitted by you.

We're 20 years old and counting. What's past is prologue.